EARLY'S FALL

A JAMES EARLY MYSTERY

EARLY'S FALL

JERRY PETERSON

FIVE STAR

A part of Gale, Cengage Learning

GALE
CENGAGE Learning™

Detroit • New York • San Francisco • New Haven, Conn • Waterville, Maine • London

GALE
CENGAGE Learning˜

LIBRARY OF CONGRESS CATALOGING-IN-PUBLICATION DATA

Peterson, Jerry A.
  Early's fall : a James Early mystery / Jerry Peterson. — 1st ed.
    p. cm.
  ISBN-13: 978-1-59414-678-7 (alk. paper)
  ISBN-10: 1-59414-678-0 (alk. paper)
    1. Sheriffs—Fiction. 2. Murder—Investigation—Fiction. 3. Kansas—History—20th century—Fiction. I. Title.
  PS3616.E84286E26 2009
  813'.6—dc22   2008043357

Published in 2009 in conjunction with Tekno Books and Ed Gorman.

Printed in the United States of America
2 3 4 5 6 7 12 13 11 10 09

ACKNOWLEDGMENTS

There is the old saw that every newspaperman has a novel in the bottom drawer of his desk. I did not.

But I did collect stories that intrigued me during my reporting days in Kansas, Colorado, West Virginia, Virginia, and Tennessee, stories that I felt might one day provide grist for a book. I fashioned the first of those into a series of short stories for novelists and University of Tennessee creative writing professors Wilma Dykeman and Allen Wier while I was a graduate student at UT/Knoxville.

Several years later, Boston crime writer Jeremiah Healy and University of Wisconsin writing coach Marshall Cook critiqued portions of a crime novel I set in Tennessee and in the process became supporters of my work.

It was a short story competition that fostered the birth of the character of Kansas Sheriff James Early who is at the center of the novel you are about to read. The Great Manhattan Mystery Conclave sponsored the competition, and the judges selected both Early stories I submitted for inclusion in the Conclave's anthology, *Manhattan Mysteries: Deadly Tales from The Little Apple* (KS Publishing, 2005). Encouragement came from and continues to come from Conclave organizer Marolyn Caldwell. And Manhattan historian Lowell Jack provided a wealth of material to me that was important in the writing of those stories and this novel. It is one of those curiosities that Lowell and I knew each other decades before our collaboration, when he ran

Manhattan's K-MAN radio station and I ran Kansas Farm Bureau's communications department.

The best characters we writers create take on lives of their own. Early is one of those and thus *Early's Fall*. Chicago crime writer Tom Keevers read a twenty-page section when he and I were at Love is Murder, a mystery writers conference in Chicago. Tom went to John Helfers of Tekno/Five Star—his publisher—and said you have to read this book. John did, or rather a panel of readers working for Tekno did and said buy this book. Chicago and now West Virginia crime writer Rob Walker became a booster for the book after he read the manuscript, as did Minnesota crime writer William Kent Krueger and Arizona crime writers Jim Mitchell and J.M. "Mike" Hayes. Here's another one of those curiosities. Mike writes a crime novel series that features a Kansas sheriff.

Now to the good people at Tekno and Five Star to whom I am indebted for their assistance in getting this novel from manuscript into print and onto library and bookstore shelves: acquiring editor John Helfers, book editor Bill Crider, acquisitions editor Tiffany Schofield, project editor Alja Collar, cover designer Deirdre Wait / ENC Graphic Services, and copy editor Janet Patterson. I am a sharp copy editor, but Janet is better than me. Her work on my manuscript has proved to be of exceedingly great value and for that I thank her.

And here comes the list you would expect if this were Oscar night. I wish to thank my mother who asked time and again why is it taking so long to get this book out—she's ninety-two; John Armstrong and his wife Ula—John is a former president of Kansas Farm Bureau and I was at one time his speech writer; a fellow writer from my newspaper days who wishes not to be named; my first wife Sallie who always supported me in my desire to write—she passed away before I got a book contract and then it was for a book I wrote after her death; my current wife Marge who is my confidante, my proofreader, and a resource on medical matters; freelance editor Rose Kennedy; Pam Harris, a writer and colleague from graduate school days; Bonnie Hufford, a journalism professor at the University of Tennessee and an editor; and fellow writers Gary Anderson and Ned Ricks—Gary critiques everything I write, and Ned is a regular resource on weapons and the soldier's life.

Also I thank with sincerity *Tuesdays with Story,* my writers group in Madison, Wisconsin. We *Tuesdays* writers are one another's first-line critics, line editors, copy editors, and boosters. If you would like to know more about this superior writers group and read the weekly e-letter I write for them, please go to our Web site: http://www.tuesdayswithstory.org/.

CHAPTER 1

August 15—Monday Afternoon
The Jayhawk

"Is that someone on a horse?"

Jim Early twisted around in time to see a paint and rider slow-walk past the Jayhawk Bank's front window. "Yup, what's unusual about that?"

Rance Dalby, the owner of the smallest bank in Kansas, nudged at Early's arm with the notary seal he'd been playing with. "Come on, Cactus, when's the last time you saw anyone ride into Randolph on a horse?"

"Before Roosevelt marched us off to war," Early said—Early, the sheriff of Riley County and a leathery cowboy in his own right.

"That's what I mean. That's ten years ago."

"Rance, we got ranches up on the high ground, and they got cowboys."

"But, dammit, they drive pickups today."

"So now you know, the Old West ain't dead."

The cowboy who had ridden past reappeared at the door of the one-teller bank, his hat pulled low, his spurs jingling as he came in. Dalby, the sleeves of his white shirt rolled to his elbows, ignored him other than to toss a perfunctory glance his way. He picked up a loan paper and fanned himself. "I tell you, I'm going out to the Blue and put my big bare feet in the water, maybe fish a little after Mavis and I close up. Get myself cool."

An explosion brought Dalby and Early out of their chairs. Early, still suffering from shell shock four years after the war, dove for the floor. When he came up, there stood the cowboy, a nylon over his face, a vapor of acrid smoke curling up from the barrel of a Forty-Five he held high.

"Excuse me," the cowboy said, his voice not much above a whisper. "Now that I got your 'tention, I'm here for your money."

He tossed a duffle bag to Dalby. It slapped down on the banker's desk and slid across, dislodging a stack of financials.

Dalby attempted to work his mouth, but nothing came out. The cowboy waved his pistol at him. "Pick it up. I want everything from your teller's cash drawer, then your vault."

Early pushed himself to his knees. He brushed the front of his shirt. "Now, son," he said, "you don't want to be doing this."

"Why not? I got the gun."

"Well, you could get yourself a nice long prison term, and I'm told Leavenworth's not the most pleasant place to be."

The cowboy brought his pistol down. He leveled it at Early, lowered it just a bit and jerked the trigger. The bullet threw up splinters as it tore into the plank floor by the sheriff's knee.

"You're serious," Early said, his eyes like saucers. He twisted around. "Rance, better do what he wants. As for me, I'm gonna just sit down here and wait."

"Good idea," the cowboy said.

"Yeah, I think you're right." Early settled on his rump and crossed his legs in what his father had called Indian-style. Dalby hustled past. He held open the bag to his teller, Mavis Anderson, her face blanched white. She fumbled with her cash drawer as she dumped its contents in, and half a dozen coins missed the bag. They fell to the floor, bouncing, rolling, several to ring flat at the bandit's feet.

"If you don't mind," Early said, tapping his shirt pocket, "I'd like a chew." He slipped two fingers in and drew out a package of gum. Early shook a stick out to the cowboy. "Teaberry. Got a flavor that relaxes you."

He waved it away as Dalby dashed by and into the vault.

"Throw the mortgages in that sack too," the cowboy called after him.

Early, with great deliberation, unwrapped a stick of gum. He folded it and put it into his mouth. "Do I know you?" he asked.

"Doubt it."

In the instant that the cowboy glanced at Early, the banker slammed the vault door shut, locking himself inside.

The bandit ran to the vault door, cursing. He banged the butt of his pistol on the steel and rattled the handle. When the lock refused to give, the bandit whirled on Early. "You did this," he said, his voice a spitting snarl.

He swung his gun hard at Early's head, and the crack of metal on bone sent the sheriff sprawling.

The bandit whipped around to the teller. "Open the gawd-damn vault."

Mavis Anderson, built to hold her own with any man, stepped back from her counter, her jowls trembling. "It's on a time lock. Won't open 'til eight in the morning."

"Shit. Then I hope he croaks in there." The cowboy turned away. He ran, not for the street door, but for the window in the back wall of the bank. He dove through it, glass and wood shattering.

Mavis Anderson peered after the cowboy before she hurried away from her counter, first to the vault, then to Early. She reached down for the sheriff's arm. "You all right, Jim?"

"Phheww, Lordy, he clipped me good." Early felt at his head with his free hand while Mavis hauled at his other arm. "Think I'm gonna hear telephones ringing for days."

"I thought he'd killed you."

Early got a foot under himself. "Mave, I got myself movin' when I saw it coming. Where's my hat?"

"Over there."

He made a swipe at it as he came up, and a second swipe before he got hold of the crown. Early slapped his cattleman's hat on, wincing at the pain of it.

"What we going to do, Jim?"

"I guess go after him. Which way did he go?"

Mavis hurried to the window. She leaned out. "There he is. He's riding up the alley, past the old hotel."

Early forced his legs to work for him, to carry him out the front door to his war-surplus Jeep. He twisted the ignition key, and the Ford V-Eight he'd dropped under the hood roared to life. Early slammed the shifter into first. He mashed the gas pedal, and his spinning tires threw up a spray of dirt that showered Everett Morgan running up from his grocery store.

Early glanced down a side alley as he rammed the shifter into second—nothing. He turned back and blanched. A pickup came motoring down the middle of the street, toward him. Early jerked his Jeep to the side, jammed the shifter into third, and glanced over as he shot past the next alley.

Another block and the town ran out with the Jeep rocketing up through sixty. That's when Early saw the cowboy, off on the Olsburg Road, the paint churning dirt, galloping east toward the rise that would take him and his rider out of the Big Blue Valley. Early tromped on the brakes, downshifting, spinning the steering wheel. He whipsawed the Jeep onto the Olsburg and again floored it, the war machine whistling across the tracks of the K&N and into the open, eating into the cowboy's lead.

Ahead the road bent.

But the cowboy and his horse didn't.

The rider rammed his spurs into the paint's flanks and the

beast took to the air in a leap that carried him and his rider across the borrow ditch and over a woven wire fence. They came down on the far side and disappeared into a field of August-tall corn.

Early slowed. He steered the Jeep around the bend—looking, looking—and floored it one more time, speeding off toward a farm lane. Early grabbed up his microphone.

"Alice, you there?" he bellowed over the whine of the Jeep's engine.

"Yes," came back a voice over the Motorola.

"Robbery at the Jayhawk Bank. Guy on horseback. Lost him going east on the Olsburg."

"Robbery at the Jayhawk. Got it."

"Call the Pott sheriff, state police, and get Hutch up here."

"On it."

Early threw the mic aside as he tromped hard on the brake pedal. He skidded the Jeep into a drive that led onto the Bert Torben farmstead, dust billowing, his whip antenna whacking from side to side. Again Early floored it. He shot through the yard, Em Torben's chickens flying off in a claque of squawking and loose feathers. Early slurried the Jeep around the buildings, slowing when he saw Torben belting up his silo filler. The sheriff slid the Jeep to a stop near the elderly farmer, and dust rolled up over them. Early tried to wave it away, hacking at the taste.

"You got a horse I can have, Bert?"

Torben, gape mouthed, flapped at the billowing dust too. "Gawd, I haven't had a horse since I bought my Farmall in 'Thirty-Nine. What you need one for?"

The sheriff sprang from his Jeep, gesturing across the way, toward a far pasture and the cowboy and his horse racing away across it. "To catch that sumbitch."

Early, angry, reached back for the Winchester in its scabbard in front of the windshield. He yanked the rifle out and sighted down the barrel at the retreating figure, adjusting for windage. Early squeezed the trigger.

"Hell, you'll never hit him at this distance, sheriff."

"I know that, but he doesn't." Early levered a new shell into the chamber. He fired, levered again, and fired a third time. Then and only then did he step back. Early brought the rifle up and rested the stock against his hip.

Torben pulled off his straw hat. He wiped a hand back over his nearly hairless dome. "Guess I'm lucky I didn't have no cows out there, wouldn't ya say? You know, yer bleedin' from the ear."

"Huh?"

Torben touched his own ear. "Bleedin'. Up here. Yer not hearing too good?"

Early put his hand to his ear. When he brought his hand away, his fingertips were wet and red. "Got clipped."

The sheriff wiped his fingers on his tans, then levered a fresh round into his rifle's firing chamber. The gun again ready, he slipped it back into its scabbard.

Early took a bandana from his back pocket. He dabbed at his ear as he and Torben stood watching the horse and rider, now no larger than their thumbs, clear a fence at the end of the pasture and disappear into a distant woods.

"Shoot," Early said, "he can go any direction now."

"So what's this all about?"

"Robbery at the Jayhawk."

"He got the community's money?"

"No. Your money's still in the vault. Locked in with Rance. I guess I better get back. Sorry for the disturbance."

"You know," Torben said, "if you was to go up the Olsburg, you can cut over through Jessie Smith's land—he don't have it fenced. That'd bring you around to the back side of that woods. You might see him."

"Worth a try. Tell Em I'm sorry about her chickens. I probably scared a week's worth of eggs out of them."

Before Torben could answer, Early wheeled his Jeep around. He motored at a leisurely pace past the buildings and through the yard, but once in the farm lane, Early drove like a man possessed, skidding his Jeep onto the Olsburg Road. He raced away only to downshift at the end of Torben's fence line. There he bucked off through the borrow ditch into a hay field and tore across the newly mown hay, waving to a kid barreling down a slope in a doodlebug with a mower attached, laying more of the bluestem prairie hay flat.

Early clung to the steering wheel with one hand while he held tight to his hat with the other, the ride across the hay field and into a distant pasture like that of a bucking horse in a rodeo ring.

He topped the high ground and stopped, the end of the woods a couple hundred yards below. Early leaned on the steering wheel as he scanned the open fields to the north of the woods. No horse and rider. No horse without a rider. Not even a man on foot.

Early could see a mile across the valley and, to his right, almost four miles, up toward where the waters of the Black Vermillion mixed with the Big Blue and flowed this way. Cattle country up here on the bluffs, some of the richest soil for farming in the valley below. Memories of his grandfather flowed back to Early. The old man loved the bottoms, called it the garden lands of the state. He had one of the finest peach orchards and grew melons the size of bushel baskets there, down by Bigelow, closer to Manhattan, the county seat town, the college town, home to Silo Tech, as the kids over in Lawrence called Kansas State.

Early stepped out to stretch. He rarely went armed, preferring talk to weapons. Yet there were those times. So he had the

Winchester in the scabbard and his pistol, a military Forty-Five he'd taken off a dead lieutenant in Tunisia's Kasserine Pass and had carried through the war. That pistol usually laid in a holster belt beneath his seat. Early could not have said why, but he took out the holstered gun and strapped it on.

That done, he got back in his Jeep. Early let out the clutch and guided the machine on a meandering journey back down into the valley. As he approached the Kansas & Nebraska's tracks, a steamer sounded its whistle. Early glanced toward Randolph and a ten-car freight rumbling up the tracks, bound for Maryville in the next county north. He stopped.

He waited.

He liked trains.

In the Dirty 'Thirties, he'd hoboed some, ridden the rails under, in, and on top of boxcars, had crossed the country a couple times before Pearl Harbor. He was in Georgia when the Japanese sank half the Navy. Word traveled through the hobo jungles with the speed of a prairie fire. The next day, Early made his way to Minnville. There he enlisted in the Army along with a hundred sixty-three others, eighteen men, like himself, from the camp under the trestle.

Early rode the rails some more, this time in troop trains, home after basic training and to New York to board a troop ship bound for North Africa. Desert country. He'd never had much use for sand, even less once he got there.

Early waved to the engineer as the Baldwin I-One-S "hippo" rolled by. He gazed at the engine and the cars with no particular interest until a movement caught his eye, someone waving a hat from the open doorway of a boxcar.

The cowboy.

The bank bandit.

"Sumbitch!"

Early seethed, waiting for the last cars and the caboose to

trundle by. When they did, he bucked his Jeep across the tracks and raced up through the gears, slowing to slide onto State One-Seventy-Seven. Early let out the string. The Jeep's speedometer needle topped seventy-five on the dirt road as he raced after the freight.

The sheriff paralleled it in three miles. When the fireman and engineer did nothing more than wave in response to his frantic wig-wagging, Early sped on by. Two miles on, where the tracks crossed the road, Early skidded his Jeep to a stop. He grabbed a flare from beneath his seat, lit the flare, and dashed to the tracks. He waved the blazing, spark-showering thing in great arcs, an arm's length over his head.

This time the engineer responded. Early was sure of it, for the train began to play off speed as it neared the crossing. And then he heard it, the screech of steel on steel, the engine's drive wheels locked up.

Early jumped to the side as the hippo slid through the crossing, the engineer bellowing, "What the hell's the matter with you, Cactus?"

"Sorry, Lukey. You got a bandit back in the second boxcar."

"The hell you say."

But Early didn't hear that. He had his Forty-Five out as he galloped back along the train. When he came to the second boxcar, he stopped. He poked his pistol ahead of him as he eased around the open door. He leaned in.

"Damn."

Empty, except for bags of sugary-sweet-smelling dried beet pulp stacked in a far corner.

He hunkered down. Early scanned beneath the car, and the cars behind, and the one ahead.

More of nothing, other than a winged grasshopper that took to the air, green against blue.

He scrambled up the boxcar's ladder to the roof, but there

was nothing on top of the train for the length of it other than a meadow lark that had flown down to the roof of the next boxcar. The bird puffed his speckled chest out and sang of the glories of the day.

Early holstered his pistol. With disappointment showing in his face and his frame, he slid down the ladder to the gravel of the rail bed.

There stood a giant of a man, the engineer, smelling of coal dust and lubricating oil, Luke Blackwell. He'd driven the hippo on this run for almost as many years as Early was old.

"Well?" Blackwell asked.

Early pulled off his hat. He slapped it against the leg of his tans. "Back there at the crossing outside of Randolph, this guy who tried to stick up the bank, he was sitting in the door of this railcar. The damn yahoo waves at me."

"Maybe he made his way back to another car."

"It's possible."

"Tell you what," Blackwell said, helping himself to a club wedged behind the ladder of the boxcar, "you go down this side and I'll go down the other. If he's here, we'll catch him."

The engineer hefted himself over the coupling between the boxcar and the car ahead of it.

Early hunkered down again. When he saw the striped legs of the engineer's railroad britches opposite him, he moved out and down the length of the train, peering under and into boxcars. When he came to the two hopper cars, he climbed up their ladders and gandered in to see whether the cowboy might have tried to bury himself in the cargo of grain. The surface would be disturbed. It would show.

Nothing.

Just a lot of nothing.

Blackwell came around the end of the caboose. "He gave you the slip, huh?"

18

"Looks like it."

The engineer put his meaty arm around Early's shoulders as they walked back toward the head of the train. "I won't tell nobody if you won't tell nobody."

"Why's that?" Early asked.

"We railroad men are supposed to catch the bums who hop our trains."

"This was no bum, Lukey. Damn, he's familiar. . . . Must of jumped off somewhere in the last five miles."

Gravel crunched beneath the men's boots as they ambled on.

"Well," the engineer said, "he'd get beat up some if he did because I was doing a good clip. If he didn't break himself a leg though, he's gone."

"Yeah, probably."

"Cactus, if I were you, I'd call it a day an' go home to that wonderful wife of yours."

"Just might do that after I write up the paperwork."

"As for me, I got to get this here train up to Maryville an' bring the Nineteen back to the big little city of Manhattan. I won't be done until after ten o'clock."

At the cab, Blackwell's fireman leaned out, Oscar Miller, as burly a man as the engineer. He spat a gob of chewed tobacco to the side. "Didn't find nobody, huh?"

Blackwell grabbed hold of the ladder. He pulled himself up. "False alarm. What say you and I git?"

"Fine by me."

The two railroaders disappeared inside the cab of the hippo. Moments later, the engine snorted as Blackwell put the power to the drive wheels. The knuckles of the couplers banged hard against one another along the length of the train as the freight hauler started to move. Then it became quiet, except for the rumbling of the trucks and an occasional squeal when a wheel flange rubbed against a rail.

And the train rolled on, disappearing around a bend as it made its way to the northeast.

Early kicked at the gravel as he shuffled across the tracks to his Jeep. There he stooped to pull his flare from the dirt where he had jammed it to extinguish the flame. He tossed the flare under the seat, figuring he might use it another time.

The sheriff did not hurry back to Randolph. He drove slowly, gandering across the way to the railroad tracks, scanning the gravel and the weeds beyond for a crumpled body in case the cowboy killed himself when he bailed out of the boxcar. Early picked up his microphone. "Hutch, you on?"

"Go ahead, chief," a voice came over the Motorola.

"Where you?"

"Coming up on Randolph from the south."

"I'm north, coming in. Meet you at the bank in a couple minutes."

"Roger that."

Early leaned his windshield forward as his Jeep rambled along. He kicked his right foot up over the glass and rode at ease the last three miles. When he rolled up in front of the bank, there stood Hutch Tolliver, Early's chief deputy, leaning against the back end of his own Jeep, holding the reins of a saddled horse. A paint.

"Found him out in the field beyond the depot," Hutch said, nodding at the beast.

Early came alongside. He ran his hand over the paint's haunch, his fingers stopping on the brand burned into the hide. "Sumbitch. I know who the bandit is."

CHAPTER 2

August 15—Monday Afternoon Late
The Rocking Horse

Early slapped the paint's haunch, and the horse hunched up. "See that brand? The Rocking Horse E."

"Yeah, Walter Estes's place over by Leonardville," Tolliver said. "Not the old man."

"No, his boy, Sonny. Wiry little guy. Does that Audie Murphy bit with that whispering voice."

"You're sure?"

"Hutch, it all fits. If it weren't for that stocking over his face, I'd of known him right off."

Rance Dalby came roaring out the door of the bank, Mavis Anderson half a stride behind. "Well, you catch him?"

Early let off with a weak laugh. "No. . . . How'd you get out of the vault?"

"Mavis let me out."

The sheriff turned to Dalby's teller. "I thought you told the bandit the vault was on a time lock."

"I lied."

Early leaned an arm on Dalby's shoulder. "You wouldn't happen to be holding a mortgage on the Estes place?"

"Yeah, I got the paper."

"There isn't anything about it I should know, is there?"

"Well, old Walter's two years in arrears. Called on him the other day and said we had to work something out or I was going to have to foreclose."

Early winked at Tolliver.

"What's this got to do with anything?" the banker asked.

"The bandit's Sonny."

Dalby's jaw went slack.

"Uh-huh, Hutchy's got his horse. Look, if Walter's got troubles, they've just doubled. How about you find it in that shriveled-up, old cold heart of yours to let him skate awhile?"

Dalby swung around, nose to nose with Early. "After his boy tried to rob me?"

"Come on, Rance."

"I don't like this."

"There's a lot of things you don't like."

"I s'pose," Dalby said, shrugging.

"Good enough. You got your horse trailer parked around back?"

"Yeah, why?"

"We gotta haul Sonny's beast home to the Rocking Horse."

Early sent Tolliver west on Sixteen, then south while he hauled Dalby's trailer and the bandit's paint toward the southern climes, then west on County Nine. The lawmen drove the perimeter of a block of farm and ranch land five miles square on the off chance Sonny Estes might try to thumb his way home. Over their radios they filled the air with idle talk as they rolled along, hardly anyone other than themselves out on the county roads as the sun dipped to the west, forming itself into a fireball that grew in size the closer the sun came to the horizon, shimmering the evening air.

A quarter of the sun had slipped below before Early drove into the lane that led to the Rocking Horse E, Tolliver's Jeep parked beside a gate twenty yards up.

Early keyed his microphone. "Been here long?"

"Couple minutes. I'll get the gate."

Tolliver killed his Jeep's motor and hopped out. After he opened the ranch gate, he held it while Early drove his Jeep and the horse trailer through, then hitched the gate closed and slid his long frame into Early's passenger seat. "How you want to handle this with old Walter?" Hutch asked.

Early got the Jeep and trailer rolling while he thought about that. "Oh, I guess I'll dance a little," he said, clawing at his mustache.

The lane dipped through a dry wash that ran full in the spring, during the snow melt, and at other times when a stray thunderstorm parked itself close by and dumped a load of water. On the far side of the rise laid a corral and a rough collection of outbuildings. In a grove of cottonwoods beyond stood a low-slung house, its roof swayed from age.

Early followed the track around the buildings and the corral smelling of dust and dried cow flop. On the back side, the biggest, blackest Newfoundland dog the sheriff had ever seen loped out as a greeting committee of one. He turned parallel to the Jeep and continued along, just beyond Early's reach. When the sheriff stopped in front of the house, the dog parked himself, and his tail stirred the dust.

"The boss home?" Early asked the dog, his hand out. The dog sworped it with his raspy tongue.

"Just what I need, a handful of dog spit." Early rubbed the dog's ears, then went on toward the house. "Walter? Nadine? You home?"

The screen door squalled open. Out stepped a slightly stooped man and behind him a woman who, from her heft, appeared to enjoy her own cooking. While worry tended to cloud Walter Estes's face, smile lines marked his wife's. She wiped her hands on her apron as she came on down the porch, her arms coming out to embrace the world. "Jimmy, so good to see you," she said, and hugged him hard.

Early, struggling for breath, forced a smile. "Nadine, before you say it, I know I should come by more than I do."

"But you got your work." She turned back to her husband. "Don't he look good, Walter? I tell you, him gettin' married to that little Thelma Nelson was the best thing that ever happened to him."

Walter nodded his agreement, his gnarled hand coming out to shake with his company.

"So you going to have a mess of children now?" Nadine asked.

Early blushed through his tan. "Got one on the way."

"Oh, Walter, you hear that? Jimmy and Thelma got a baby coming. . . . When's it due, Jimmy?"

"A little after Thanksgiving. . . . Sonny around?" Early asked, shifting the subject.

Nadine's face shifted too. Her smile fled. "Oh, you don't know, do you? I'm afraid he's left us."

"When this happen?"

"This morning. Said he was going to go some south in the Flint Hills, get on with a bigger ranch. Said he'd send his pay home, his way of helping out after that barn fire last year." Nadine put a hand on Early's arm. She looked up in his face. "Why you askin' about Sonny?"

Early motioned to Tolliver.

The deputy opened the gate on the back of the trailer. He squeezed in past the horse, then pushed him back out.

"That's Sonny's," Nadine said.

"Kinda thought so." Early glanced at Walter, the worry lines visibly deepening in the old rancher's sun-crisped face. "Can we set here on the edge of the porch?"

Tolliver led the horse away toward the corral while Nadine sat down, Walter beside her. It took him longer. He hung onto a porch post and eased himself down, grimacing as his knees and hips bent.

When Early sat down, the Newfoundland plopped himself in front of the sheriff's boots. He put his head on Early's knees, his tongue lolling from the side of his mouth.

Early stroked the big dog's muzzle. "Walter, Nadine, Sonny didn't go south."

"How do you know?" Nadine asked.

"We found his horse in Randolph. Sonny stuck up the bank."

What joy remained in the old couple's souls fled. They turned to one another, Nadine reaching for her husband's hand. She squeezed it hard. "Where's our boy?" she asked, a quiver in her voice.

"He got away."

"Anybody hurt?"

"No. No, not really. . . . If Sonny's smart, he won't come home. Now I know you don't have a telephone out here, but if he does come home, I want you two to promise you'll get word to me. Sonny's got that Forty-Five pistol and, if someone else was to try to catch him, it could go all wrong."

Early sat in his Jeep for the longest time when he got home that night—home, a little shotgun house on the edge of Keats. The yard backed up against Wildcat Creek, and the neighbors had warned him away from the house. "You'll get flooded out in the spring," they said. "Happens about every year."

But that made the place cheap, all he could afford when he lost his own small ranch after two bad years.

It hadn't flooded this year, and Early and his wife counted themselves lucky, but luck wasn't what kept him from going inside. He watched the lightning bug show around the mulberry bushes and the trumpet vines, the air sweet with the smell of the flowers' nectar. Some fireflies even rose up with their wink-ing lights to the lower reaches of a catalpa tree.

A hand reached out. It tipped his hat forward. " 'Scuse me, big boy," a husky female voice said.

Without even looking, Early reached over for Thelma's hand. "Didn't hear you come out."

"Hon, I gave up on you coming in. It's been twenty minutes."

"I didn't know."

"You and clocks don't have a sympathy for one another, do you?"

Early went silent. His wife of a year joined in that silence. She was a sprite of a person, the way Early imagined Nadine Estes must have been when she was young. They both had a joy for living that he found remarkable. Nadine had dragooned Early into going to the picnic at the Leonardville Christian Church. He wouldn't have gone on his own for he'd grown up a Baptist over on Troublesome Creek. But there at the picnic he met Thelma—Thelma Nelson, one of the new teachers at the Leonardville school, fresh out of K-State and more than a decade younger than he.

She massaged his hand. "What are you thinking about, hand-some?"

"The baby . . . Thel, I don't know nothing about taking care of babies. Worse, I don't know how you grow 'em to keep them out of trouble."

"We just do the best we can." She leaned in to Early, kissed him on the ear, her warm breath melting his heart.

Thelma came forward and turned quarter to look into his face, though his gaze was still somewhere off on the purple-black bluffs on the other side of the creek. "Where's this com-ing from?" she asked.

"Remember Sonny?"

"Sonny Estes?"

26

"The damn fool did a poor job of robbing a bank today. I got to run him down and put him in jail."

CHAPTER 3

August 16—Tuesday Noon
The Killing

"How much?" Early asked the girl at The Brass Nickel's cash register.

She, a gum-chewing brunette, soon to be a freshman at the college, squinted as she glanced up toward the tin ceiling.

Early glanced up too, wondering what might be of interest there. "That where Nels keeps the answers?"

"No, running the numbers. He doesn't let us use order pads like they do over at The Chef. That'll be seventy-five cents."

The sheriff pulled out a handful of change. From it he pushed a fifty-cent piece onto the counter, then three dimes.

The waitress pointed to another coin. "Give me that one, the quarter. You keep the dimes."

"Your mother raise you to be this bossy? Did it ever occur to you I might want a nickel change?"

"Why?"

"Maybe to leave for a tip if I were in a good mood."

A silent *oh* formed on the girl's lips. She rang up the lunch sale and gave Early his nickel.

He placed it on the counter, then slid it to her.

She slid it back.

He slid the coin to her again.

She slid it back, this time giggling.

Early raised an eyebrow as he pushed the coin one more time.

Beefy Nels Arneson, the owner and short-order cook, leaned in, hitching his grease-stained apron up under his armpits. "If you two can't decide whose money that is, it's mine."

He slapped a hand over the nickel, and two hands slapped down on his.

"All right, all right," Arneson said, taking his paw away.

Early took his hand away too, only to see the waitress again push the coin back to him.

This time he picked it up. Early nodded military-smart and turned on his heel. At the screen door, he turned back. "Sue!"

The waitress looked up. Early tossed the coin to her and ran out.

On the street, he shambled back toward Poyntz Avenue and the courthouse. As Early came along the front of the Manhattan Mercury, Chronicle & Commercial Printing Building, a voice from above called down, "Hey, Cactus."

He glanced up to see Red Vullmer, K-MAN Radio's newsman, playing out a line with a microphone at the end. "How about a little chin time, a little man-on-the-street?"

"What do you want to talk about?" Early asked.

"We'll find something. I'm desperate to fill air."

"Heck, then spin another one of those big records you got."

"No, come on, talk to me." Vullmer, his face flushed and almost as red as his hair, parked his butt on the windowsill. He threw a hand signal to some unseen soul inside the station's second-floor studio, then gazed down at Early. Vullmer held a microphone. "Ladies and gentlemen in the audience of K-MAN's Noontime Merry-Go-Round, I have for you live on the street, Sheriff James 'Cactus' Early. . . . So, sheriff, what's going on around the county?"

Early moved to the microphone dangling in front of him.

"It's summer, Red, kinda hot. I could give you a garden report. I got tomatas comin' on that are the size of—"

"No no no no," Vullmer said, "my audience is interested in *crime*, and you're the sheriff."

Early glanced up at his interviewer. "Crime, huh?"

"Yes."

"Well, it's summer. It's hot, almost so hot a dog won't drag himself across the street to get to better shade. I'd say a whole lot of nothing."

"That's not what I hear from up Randolph way."

"What, you mean that bank thing?"

"Indeed. . . . Ladies and gentlemen, yesterday afternoon, our super sheriff was up in the Jayhawk Bank when this robber walks in and sticks up the joint. What'd you do, Cactus?"

"Kinda kept my head down. He had a gun, I didn't."

"How much he get away with?"

"Nothing but a little change. Banker locked himself in the vault with the real money."

"So, you catch him?"

"The banker?"

"No, the bandit."

"Um, no, he got away."

"But you got that souped-up Jeep. He must have had one of those big old Packards to outrun you."

"He was on horseback."

"Horseback?" Vullmer roared with laughter, grabbing at the window frame to keep from falling out. After he steadied himself, he made a cut signal to whoever was inside. "Oh Lordy, Cactus, you are an entertainment."

"Yeah, well, I seem to be, don't I?"

"We got to do this again," Vullmer said, snickering and snorting as he reeled his street microphone back up.

"I'm thinking of taking lunch at The Chef so I don't have to

30

walk by here anymore."

"Aww, Cactus, you'll never quit The Nickel. Best food in town and you know it."

A Jeep rounded the corner from Poytz and barreled in the direction of Early, Hutch Tolliver at the wheel. He skidded the Jeep up to the curb. "Chief, we got us a bad one."

"A bad one?" Vullmer called out, reversing directions and reeling the street mic back down.

Early ignored it. He jumped in the shotgun seat, and, as he and Tolliver sped away, he turned back. Early grinned at Vullmer and waved his cattleman's hat.

"What was that all about?" the deputy asked as he shot the Jeep through the Bluemont intersection and onto US Twenty-Four going north.

Early held tight to his hat. "Ease up, man. We're in town."

"Well, people can get out of the way." At that, Tolliver laid on the horn button and swung around a grocery truck. "Killing up at Leonardville. Judith Smitts. Constable called it in."

"You call the state police?"

"Figured I better find you first." Tolliver slowed for the curve that took Twenty-Four up a hill and out of the Big Blue River Valley.

Early grabbed up the radio microphone. He squeezed the transmit button. "Alice, you there?"

"Go ahead, Jim."

"Hutch and I are headed for Leonardville. Call the coroner. Get him moving."

"Done. Doc's finishing surgery. Be ten minutes behind you."

"State police?"

"I called."

"You tell 'em I want Trooper Dan?"

"They can't raise him."

"Shoot, most of the time Dan'l's too far from their transmitter. If we had his frequency, we could raise him."

"Jim, we can buy the crystals for our radios."

"We can?"

"It's right in the Motorola manual. It's just that state law won't let us have any other frequency than our own."

"Hell with the state law. You call Motorola and tell them I want those crystals, and I want them installed no later than Monday."

"You're gonna get in troouble . . ."

"Won't be the fiiiiirst time."

To say Leonardville wasn't much of a town would be about on the dime. When horses were the only transport, it thrived. But with the coming of cars and trucks, those who lived there and on the surrounding ranches and farms traveled to Manhattan for most of their needs. Leonardville still had a small grocery, hardware store, clothing store, a gas station, a café, a three-room school, and a dozen or so houses, including one on the edge of town built after the war when lumber and cement again became available for civilian use.

Early pointed off to the side, to the lane that led to that house. It stood on a slight rise and gave the Smittses a view of the surrounding prairie that was ambrosia to Westerners. There parked across the drive, twenty yards short of the house, was a 'Thirty-Two Chevy coupe, its black paint sun bleached. A man sat on the running board, cradling a shotgun.

He rose and came over, moving with a limp, when Tolliver stopped the Jeep. "Hi-dee, Hutch, Jimmy."

"Hi-dee, Mose," Early said. Tolliver touched the dip in the brim of his Big-brim Alpine, a modified ten-gallon.

"Yer not going to believe how bad this is."

The county lawmen stepped out of their vehicle, and the trio moved on toward the house, Early massaging his rump.

"You hurt yerself?" Mose Dickerson asked.

"Hutchy took us through some chuckholes as deep as canyons at a terrible speed. I'm lucky to be alive. . . . So how did you find out about this?"

"You know I run a little mail route."

"Uh-huh."

"This is my last stop. I'm puttin' letters in the box down there by the road, and I hear their dog howling something piti-ful. I figured maybe they were away, you know, with school bein' out, and they hadn't fed the dog, so I come up here to check on him, and the screen door was open."

"That would get your attention."

"Sure got mine."

The trio stepped up on the porch.

"Well, I knock and I call out," Dickerson said, pushing on through. "No answer. So just like now, I go on in."

Early and Tolliver gazed around. Furniture in what would be the front room upset, the glass in a hutch in the corner smashed. They went on into the next room, in the plan of houses recently built, the dining room, the heels of their boots clicking on the oak floor.

Early swore. "You'd think a tornada passed through here."

In the kitchen, blood well dried on the counter and cabinet doors. More in a side hallway leading to what Early assumed was one or more bedrooms, the door to the first open. He looked in.

"Oh Jesus . . ."

"You gonna throw up?" Dickerson asked. "I did."

"No. Four years at war, you've seen bodies taken apart in about every way possible."

The constable pushed his sweat-stained Stetson onto the back of his head. "Damage like this, Jimmy, he had to use an axe."

"Damn shame." Early shook his head as he gazed around at the mess of the room, then back at the body, grotesque in the way it lay, arms twisted, one almost hacked off. "She didn't deserve this."

"No one does."

"Find the axe?"

"Didn't look. Went to call you," Dickerson said.

"Use their phone?"

"Jimmy, I know better than to touch stuff."

Gravel crunched under tires outside. A car door slammed, that followed by footsteps coming across the porch.

"Cactus?" a voice called out.

"Back in the bedroom, Doc. Watch where you step."

A moment later, a man who, by his girth, gave testimony to eating well, came around the corner from the kitchen. "Who we got, Cactus?"

Early stepped back out in the hallway. "Judith Smitts. She taught with my wife over at the Leonardville school."

"Know her, did you?"

"Not real well."

Doc Grafton elbowed by and into the bedroom. He went down on his knee next to the body. "My Lord, and I thought I had blood in the operating room."

"What'd you have?"

Grafton examined a gashing wound. "Old cowboy from up by Stockdale. Gored by a bull. I tell those guys they ought to whack those horns off their cattle."

He took a penlight from his pocket and played it over the back of the head. Fragments of bone reflected back the light.

"How ya gonna call it, Doc?"

"I'd say death by an unnatural cause. How's that grab you?" Grafton took a tongue depressor from his shirt pocket. He probed into the head wound. "Damn, it's deep. Axe, you think?"

"Mose thinks so. I have to agree."

"Well, it's certain she couldn't do this to herself, so if you want, I'll call it murder. Now you just got to find out the who and the why." Grafton rolled up on his haunches. "She doesn't smell too ripe, so can't have been dead long. You want an autopsy?"

"Not much point. She's got a little boy about three years old. Do a partial. Find out if she was pregnant."

"Right. Can I use your radio, have Alice call Brownie and get his hearse out here?"

"Have at it."

Grafton pushed up. He shook his head as he gazed at the corpse, then left the room.

Early turned to his deputy. "Why don't you get the fingerprint kit? Dust everything you think might tell us whether anybody untoward has been in the house. Mess like this, could be robbery gone bad."

Tolliver hop-stepped to catch up with Grafton.

"Mose," Early said, "let's you and me poke around outside."

The two went back to the kitchen, then out the front door rather than touch the handle on the back door. "You see any tire marks out of place?" Early asked.

Dickerson rubbed at the stubble on his cheek. "Like what?"

"Like maybe somebody drove across the yard."

"Not in front, but I haven't been around back."

Grafton, at the Jeep, called to Early. "You want me to fingerprint the body to help Hutch with his work?"

"Do that," the sheriff said, and he and Dickerson continued around to the side of the house. "The husband is William, is that right? Know where he is?"

"Travels for his work. Something to do with the Union-Pacific. Gone sometimes three, four, five days at a time."

"Well, we'll have to make some calls to find him. This is going to destroy the man. . . . I didn't see signs of the child. Did you?"

"No. Then some days Etta Gibbs takes the boy, you know, to give Missus Smitts a break. You want me to go check?"

"Yes, and if Etta's got him, see if she'll keep him until we find the husband."

"I take it you don't know him," Dickerson said.

"Met him only once."

"Neither are local. Judith was from over Kansas City way. Mission, I think. Bill out by Wakeeney in Trego County."

Beyond the kitchen, the men found a black mongrel chained to a shelter beneath a hackberry tree, the dog whipping his tail from side to side as they came up. Early stroked the mutt's head. "Lonely out here, huh? Wish you could tell us what happened."

"Would be nice," Dickerson said. "Jimmy, we can't leave him here alone. Why don't I take him home? He and my dog are good buddies."

"Yup, you do that, and you see Etta. I'll do the walk-around by myself."

"You don't mind?"

"No, go ahead."

Dickerson unsnapped the dog from the chain, then scooped him up and carried him around front to where he had left his car.

Early scratched at his head as he looked around. A garden off to one side—sunflowers taller than a man's head, in rich bloom, a rank of delphiniums in front of them. A lawn mower stood idle in a patch of grass grown shaggy. A sandbox near the kitchen door, a blue pail and a small shovel in it. Back a ways a building that may have been a ranch shop in a previous life, a rolling door at the end of the front side, a brick chimney poking above the roof, a couple bricks missing from the top. Two windows looked out toward the garden and the lawn mower. A double track, wide enough for the tires of a car, came around the far side of the house, through the backyard and up to the rolling door.

"Gotta be checked out."

Early sucked at his teeth as he went over to the building. He rolled open the door. Nothing. No vehicle. Early wasn't quite sure what the Smittses drove. Might have been a Mercury, maybe. Dickerson would know.

Four bald tires lay in a corner. Above them, on nails, hung a fan belt and several water hoses. Someone had tacked a license plate from a previous year to the wall near an inside door.

The sheriff opened this door. He stepped through and into a workshop, a wood shop from the shavings on the floor and the tools on the wall. This man's *organized.*

Above a bench that spanned the back wall was a tool storage board where handsaws of different kinds and sizes hung. Someone had painted a red silhouette behind each tool so, just by looking at the shapes, a person knew where to hang what— carpenter's square, a one-foot level and a three-foot level, hammers, mallets, planes, pry bars, wood clamps, a hatchet, a single-bit axe, and a double-bit axe, this one gone. Nothing covered its silhouette.

Early let out a long lungful of air, then went to rummaging in tool drawers and cabinets. He even poked through a trash barrel half filled with wood scraps and sawdust, sneezing when the dust rose. If that was where the axe was . . . well, it had to be somewhere else. Early brushed the sawdust from his hands.

He went back outside, closing first the shop door, then the garage door, taking care not to touch the handles. Could it have been thrown out in the grass? He walked the backyard in three-foot sweeps, scanning, scanning. Early stepped across a gopher hole.

Grafton came around the side of the house. "What you looking for, dog piles?"

The sheriff glanced up. "Found a couple. Pretty well dried out. . . . A double-bitted axe is missing from Smitts's shop."

"Think that's the weapon?"

"Could be. Doc, when you get working on that autopsy, buy a double-bitted axe at Water's Hardware. See if the length of the blade matches the wounds."

"Charge it to your department?"

"Don't you always?"

A highway patrol black-and-white, a Ford still with its new-car shine, rolled in, around the house, and stopped in the backyard. The trooper flicked off his bubble light. He stepped out and reached back inside for his campaign hat.

"Cactus," Daniel Plemmons said as he planted his hat regulation square on his head, "understand you got a murder."

Early continued his walk over the grass, his head down. "Yeah. Body's inside—Judith Smitts. You want to take a look? Hutch is in there."

"Right."

"Go in the front door, if you would."

"Right."

Plemmons, a shade taller than Early, moved with the ease of an Old West gunfighter as he ambled off. The long-barreled Colt Forty-Four revolver he carried in an open holster low on his hip added to the effect.

Early, intent on his search, stopped at the side of the garden, near a raggy stand of weeds. He moved the toe of his boot through pigweed and lambs quarter until it struck something. Early bent down.

A weed hook, a hand scythe. He picked it up and examined it.

Bits of rust on a blade otherwise sharp enough to cleave a

one-by-two.

Bad place to leave this when you got a child around.

Early carried the weed hook with him as he moved out into the garden, to a melon patch rich with vines and leaves the size of serving trays, the melons giving off a musky, ripe aroma. He used the hook to lift leaves back. *Someone sure could grow these big boys.*

He rapped on one, and a black snake near it slithered away.

The movement startled Early. He jumped back.

"Melons biting?" Plemmons called out as he came back around the house.

Early grabbed at his chest, as if his heart pained him. "Snake, and I didn't see him."

"Cool place for him out there under all those leaves, I expect. You wouldn't be thinking of stealing a melon from the dear deceased?"

"Hardly. I was hoping to find an axe." Early held up the weed hook. "So far only this. . . . Got any thoughts based on what you saw?"

Plemmons waited on the sheriff high-stepping across the rows of rutabagas and parsnips. "Probably about the same thoughts as you. Helluva lot of damage, in the house and to the woman, someone with a sorry lot of mean in him. You thinking the husband?"

"Most people murdered are killed by family, but Mose says the husband's off traveling for the U-P."

"So you think that takes him out?"

"I didn't say that. Until we find out where he was this morning, he's in."

"Still, I can't see a husband doing all that," Plemmons said. He grubbed a pouch of Red Man tobacco from his pocket and held it open to Early. The sheriff waved it away. Plemmons took a wad. He shoved it in his mouth. "You consider that one of the soldiers may have slipped off the reservation? They got some real hell-raisers there."

"Fort Riley? It's possible."

"Well, as many drunks as I've had to arrest, driving back to the post from Junction City—some of them real nasty—I got a pipe into the post. You want me to shake the bushes? If one of those mutts did it, he's gonna brag to his buddies."

"Mutts? You talk like a drill sergeant."

"I was."

A smile spread across Early's face. He noodled the turf with his boot toe. "Knew there was a reason I didn't like you."

"Buck private?"

"Two-striper."

"Then why'd you ever pick up a badge?"

The sheriff glanced up sideways. "Same reason you did. It pays the bills."

Plemmons spit a stream of amber juice at a potato vine. The splat sent a potato bug tumbling. "They say the stuff in tobacco makes a terrific insect killer," he said, and turned again to Early. "Supposing it was just a stranger passing through, some ghoul with an itch to kill. We had one of those down in Lyons County, down by Bushong."

"Heard about that. Killed three before you got him."

"Then it was by damn luck."

"I got my deputies and we got the town constables. Hardly a stranger comes through we don't hear about. I'll have Hutch call around."

"One other possibility you've got to check out," Plemmons said, settling in for a contemplative chew.

"What's that?"

"She was seeing someone on the sly." Plemmons handed over an object the size of a dime. "Found it in the toe area, under one of the kitchen cabinets. A uniform button."

40

"Army," Early said as he turned it over.

"Maybe the woman decided not to leave her husband and the whole thing went bad."

CHAPTER 4

August 16—Tuesday Evening
Taking the News Home

Early cut the engine of his Jeep. When he stepped out, he saw his wife in the twilight, sitting on a tree stump down by the creek, her back to him, her hair breeze-blown. Early strolled toward her. He picked up a stick and slapped at milkweed along the path, sending great clouds of gossamer parachutes into the air, to drift on the evening currents.

He tossed the stick aside when he came up behind Thelma. After some hesitation, Early put his hand on her shoulder. "You heard, huh?"

"The Friendly Neighbor—the radio—yes . . . Was it bad?"

How truthful dare he be? Some moments passed before Early said yes.

"Where's Judy's son?" Thelma asked.

"Etta Gibbs has him."

"That's good," she said, staring off into distance. "Be hard on him if strangers had to take him in. Does he know?"

"How do you tell a three-year-old?"

"I suppose."

"So how long you been out here?"

"I don't know. Late afternoon, I guess."

"Mind if I sit a spell?"

She didn't reply, so Early eased himself down on the stubbly grass. He hugged his knees until a hand, so warm, filled with care, touched his shoulder. Early reached for the hand and leaned back, coming to rest against the stump and Thelma's hip.

"It's a hard world to bring a child into, isn't it?" she said.

"Some days seem like."

"You think anybody would ever come after me?"

"No."

"You seem awful sure of that."

This time Early didn't reply.

"Come on, Jimmy, talk to me."

"Look, I'm the sheriff. If people get mad at me, they're going to come after me."

"And leave me a widow."

"That's not going to happen."

"Can you guarantee it?"

"Of course not. You want me to quit?"

"No, but I've been scared, thinking about Judy. Who do you think killed her?"

"Thel, I've got no idea."

"Did you find her diary?"

"I didn't know she kept one."

"Every day at school, at lunch, and sometimes after school, she'd be writing in her diary. I asked her why, and she said it was a way to keep her mind organized, a way she wouldn't forget the things of the day."

"No, there wasn't a diary at the house."

"Strange."

"So it would seem."

"You think someone could have taken it?"

"Thel, you ask questions that don't have answers."

"That's what wives do."

"So I'm coming to learn."

"You hungry?"

43

Lunch at The Brass Nickel was an awfully long time back, yet Early sensed a "yes" would be the wrong answer. "Not particularly," he said.

"I wouldn't mind sitting here, watching the stars come out."

Early felt a tiny sting on the side of his face. He slapped at the sting and, when he brought his hand away, there on his fingers laid a crumpled mosquito and a splash of red.

"They don't bother me," Thelma said.

"Apparently, you don't taste good."

A hand swatted Early's hat forward, over his eyes. "Envious, I know," he said.

"You can be the devil. . . . You think Bill killed Judy?"

"I can't picture that. Besides, he's off traveling for the railroad. We've got calls in, trying to locate him."

"This is going to be hard for him."

"I expect it is."

"If he's away, who's arranging for the . . . you know."

"These things take care of themselves."

"What do you mean?"

"Well, after Doc Grafton does what he has to do—"

"An autopsy, yes."

"—Sherm Brown and his boy get the body. They prepare it for the ground."

She rubbed Early's shoulder. "Well, with Bill away, I'd better go over to the house and pick a dress for Judy to be buried in. You wouldn't think of that."

"The house, it's not pretty."

"I can deal with that. She was my friend."

"And I'll bet you want to go now."

"Cowboy, you said you weren't hungry."

Early turned the steering wheel of his Jeep. He guided the machine off the county road and onto the drive that led up to the Smittses' house, the tires crunching gravel.

"Doesn't look right, the house all dark," Thelma said from the passenger seat.

"Well, nobody's there. Not even the dog. Mose Dickerson took him home rather than leave him here alone."

Early stopped the Jeep near the front door. He recovered his heavy Eveready flashlight, the kind with the long barrel filled with double-D cells, and came around the front of the Jeep to find Thelma waiting for him. "Well," he said, flicking on the light, "I suppose."

He offered his arm to his wife. She took it, and they went on, up the steps to the door and inside. Early flashed his light to where the wall switch should be and turned on the light in the front room.

"Ohmylord."

"We're thinking robbery," he said. "Until we get Bill back here, we don't know what's missing. You have any idea?"

"I can't be sure."

They went on through the dining room to the kitchen, Thelma's shoes lightly touching the floor as they walked, Early's boots coming down with a firmness that suggested there was nothing new here to him.

Early turned on the room's light. He felt Thelma's hand tighten on his arm and, when he turned to her, saw horror in her eyes. "Hon," he said, "there's going to be a whole lot more blood, all of it dried. You don't have to do this."

She whispered, "I have to."

"All right, then." Early led on down the side hallway. At the first bedroom, he reached inside and turned on the light.

Early went on in, his wife close behind. He heard her gag and run from the room, toward the kitchen. "You all right?" he called out as he trotted after her.

The sounds of retching echoing from the sides of a porcelain sink provided the answer.

Thelma gasped for air. "Think I'd be used to throwing up."

Early filled a glass with water, handed it to his wife. While she spat and spat, and spat again, he soaked a towel under the faucet and wrung out the excess. "Come on, let's get you sat down," he said, guiding Thelma to a chair.

"I can't go back in there."

"You don't have to." He gave her the towel. "Here, clean up some. I'll go see what I can find."

Early watched as his wife put the towel to her face, chalk white. "You be all right?"

"Yes."

He backed away. Two steps and he turned and went down the hall to the bedroom. Early pawed through the contents of a closet. He pulled out a couple summer-type dresses on hangers that looked good to him and a dark blue suitdress that struck Early as the woman's Sunday-go-to-meeting outfit. He held them out for Thelma when he walked back into the kitchen.

"The suitdress," she said. "She made that for her college graduation, then wore it at her wedding."

"No white or lace?"

"Said that wasn't the kind of person she was." Thelma wiped the towel down her face and pressed it against the back of her neck. "She was proud she could still fit in that dress. Now you need to find some jewelry."

"And a blouse?" Early asked as he laid the suitdress across the table.

"Hon, didn't your momma teach you anything? A suitdress is a dress with a jacket. It doesn't need a blouse."

Early's face took on the look of a small boy who'd just had his hands slapped by a ruler-wielding teacher. He mumbled a sorry as he went back to the bedroom.

"And shoes," Thelma called out. "Should be blue heels

somewhere that match the dress."

"Jewelry and shoes, jewelry and shoes, jewelry and shoes," Early muttered as he played his flashlight over the floor of the closet. Two pairs of men's shoes—work shoes and polished shoes that appeared to be almost new—then three pairs of women's shoes, one pair of dark blue heels. These he carried over to a mirrored dresser.

"If I were a woman and I had jewelry," Early said, opening drawers, shining his light in . . . men's shorts and socks, women's underthings. One more drawer on the right. There among hair brushes and combs, a velvet box. Early brought the box out. He smiled when he opened it.

A voice came from the kitchen. "Finding everything?"

"Oh yes." Early stuffed the box under his arm. He picked up the shoes and left the room, turning out the light as he went.

"How are these?" he asked, holding out the shoes.

Thelma motioned for them to be placed with the suitdress.

He then slid the velvet box in front of his wife. "I don't know nuthin' about jewelry."

"I can believe that. You gave me a cigar band for an engagement ring."

"Well, I didn't have any money."

Thelma sorted through the contents. "Was Judy wearing her wedding ring when you found her?"

"I don't think so. . . . No. Come to think of it, Doc thought that was odd, he being an old married man."

"Well, it's not here in her jewelry box."

"So?"

"What kind of sheriff are you?"

"Apparently not the best."

"Well, look around the sink. Sometimes we take off our rings when we're washing dishes."

Early found an SOS pad in a dish, but nothing more. He

came back to the table, holding his hands out in an exaggerated shrug.

Thelma again sorted through the velvet box. This time she stopped on what appeared to Early to be a modest piece of costume jewelry, the type one would pin to a blouse or a jacket. He took it and turned it over. "A Star of David?"

"Didn't you know she was Jewish?"

"My God, I'm beginning to think there's a helluva lot of things I don't know."

CHAPTER 5

August 17—Wednesday Morning
David and Bill

Early strolled into Weichselbaum's Clothing Store in Leonardville. When he didn't find anyone tending the stock, he called out, "Granny, you here?"

"Back in the kitchen, Jimmy. You look for yourself a new suit, I'll be with you in a minute."

Herschel Granville Weichselbaum, second generation in Leonardville. His father, a tailor, had come within three years of the founding of the town, and had made and sold men's clothing well into his eighties. Granny had been at it himself for four decades.

This was the second location for Weichselbaum's, a long, narrow store with the standard pressed-tin ceiling. Granny had paneled the walls with chestnut oak after the old man died, an extravagance he would not have approved. Granny had also gone to stocking ready-made suits and shirts, heresy to the old man. Tailoring was going the way of the buggy-whip trade, Granny had told Early when the first shipment arrived.

A short man bustled in from the back, an apron tied up under his arms. He held out a plate. "Jimmy, you gotta try this. Ambrosia. Best candy I've made yet."

Early took a chocolate cup from the plate—one of six on it—the cup filled with a gooey white something. Melted marshmallow?

He bit in, and the cup crumbled. And Early scrambled his hands beneath his chin to catch the pieces and the goo, half smiling as he chewed. "Bit messy."

"Yes, I haven't got the thickness right, but what do you think?"

"Cherry in there."

"Syrup, that's right."

"Marshmallow."

"Yes."

"Really good chocolate."

"Milk chocolate, that's why it's so sweet. With the craze in this country for candy, if I can get this all worked out, I could be the next Mister Hershey. Be a millionaire."

Early licked the last from his fingers. "Would you settle maybe for a thousandaire?"

Granny's jowls drooped. "You wouldn't buy it?"

"I didn't say that. I'm just not much of a candy man. You try this out on the kids."

Granny popped one of the cups into his mouth. He set the plate aside and, while he ate, gave Early a wet rag.

The sheriff worked it around his fingers, then wiped his mouth. "It is good. Got a name for it?"

"How about Weichselbaum's Superior Gooey-Good Chocolate Cups?"

"That's a lot to get on a package."

"Well, maybe," Granny said, taking back the rag. He again held out the plate, but Early refused it. "You find you a new suit?"

"No."

"Then why'd you come by, just because I'm such a sweet fella?" Granny ate another chocolate cup.

"Information."

"And what would that be?"

"You heard about Judith Smitts?"

Granny pushed his glasses up on top of his bald head. "Tragic. Simply tragic."

Early took the Star of David from his pocket. The tailor-cum-candymaker pulled his glasses back down. He examined the jewelry. "Yes, this is Judith's. You didn't know, did you?"

"Apparently not."

"Most of us Jews, we keep our heads down."

Puzzlement crept across Early's face.

"Jimmy, we aren't all that popular amongst you Gentiles. If you've got a name like Weichselbaum, you can't hide. But if you are a Silverberg and you marry a Smitts, and you don't have a hooked nose, you can pass. Mm-hmm."

"Smitts, I assumed Catholic or Lutheran."

"Lutheran, when you could get Bill to church. So Judith mostly attended temple with me in Manhattan."

"When you aren't at the Christian church down by Keats."

A smile brought new life to Granny's face. "Yes, I'm the spy amongst you. Maybe you should come to temple with me, find out what drove Judith to be the person she was. And I won't even make you wear a yarmulke. . . . You find Bill, yet?"

The telephone rang, a jarring ring that demanded attention.

Granny turned away, to the counter where his cash register resided. He went around the counter, to the wall, to his crank telephone, and took down the receiver. "Granny, here," he said into the mouthpiece. "Yes, just a minute."

The tailor held out the receiver. "Jimmy, your office."

Early took the receiver and pressed it to his ear. "Yeah."

"Jim, we've tracked down Mister Smitts. He's at the Central Elevator in Salina. I've got him on the other line, but I haven't told him why you want to talk to him."

"Can you patch him through?"

"Just a minute."

Early took out his notepad and felt his pockets for a pencil.

51

When he repeated the patting exercise, a pencil came into view. Early took it from Granny's hand, and gave a self-conscious smile.

A click came across the line. "This is Bill Smitts, sheriff. You want to talk to me?"

"Bill, you sitting down?"

"Oh Lord, this got something to do with Judy?"

Early drummed his pencil on the pad. "When did you leave home on this trip, Bill?"

"Monday. Why? Has this got something to do with Judy?"

" 'Fraid so. . . . There's no easy way to put it. We found her dead."

A clattering came over the line, as if a receiver had been dropped on a desk or the floor. A hollow and distant "Oh Lord, oh Lord" followed.

A new voice came on the line. "This is George Watson, manager out here at the Central. What'd you just tell Bill?"

Early pushed his hat onto the back of his head. "Mister Watson, this is the sheriff over in Riley County. Bill lives out here by Leonardville."

"I know."

"His wife's dead. Yesterday. . . . Mister Watson, you still there?"

"Yeah. . . . Yeah, I am."

"Can you get Bill home?"

"Sure. I'll get him on the next train to Manhattan. Fact, I'll come with him because he looks to be a wreck."

"Can I ask you a question, Mister Watson?"

"Sure."

"When did Bill get into your place?"

"Couple hours ago, from Abilene. . . . How'd his wife die?"

"Murdered."

"I can't tell him that."

"You get him back here, I'll tell him."

Early and his deputy, Hutch Tolliver, sat on a bench on the Union-Pacific station's platform, flipping pocketknives, playing mublety-peg.

Hutch balanced his knife on its point on the tip of his index finger, then flipped the knife high. He watched it thunk down into the pine-plank platform. "Think you'd be better at this game, boss," he said as he recovered the two knives. He handed one to Early.

"Guess who's got too much time on his hands. You a candy fiend?"

"Oh, I buy a Clark bar now and then."

"Next time you're over in Leonardville, go into Granny's and ask him if you can try one of his new candies. Chocolate and marshmallow thing. Not half bad."

A shadow came over the two, interrupting the game. Early glanced up. "Hey, Trooper Dan."

"Hey, Cactus," Patrolman Daniel Plemmons said. He removed his silvered aviator sunglasses. "Gladys said I'd find you here."

"We can't keep secrets from you at all, can we?"

"So you got the husband coming in on the train."

"Couple minutes, yup."

"Where's he been?"

"Abilene, then Salina," Early said. "That's all I know so far."

"Huh."

"You know something, super trooper?"

"Not really."

A steam engine's whistle moaned somewhere to the west. Early and Tolliver leaned out to see the One-Seventeen rounding the base of Sunset Hill, chuffing, slowing, the engine's bell clanging as the train glided toward the station. The men rose to stand with Plemmons.

"So he's been out since Monday," the trooper said.

"According to his boss in Topeka." Early folded his knife into its handle and slipped it in his pocket.

"Convenient."

"You're one suspicious soul. . . . According to his boss, Bill was working his way out to Wakeeney. He was to spend the weekend there, then next week work on out to Goodland, calling on shippers, talking freight rates, scheduling rail cars, that sort of thing."

"Uh-huh."

The Baldwin A-Five, steam hissing from its drive cylinders, slipped by those waiting on the platform and stopped so the express car and four passenger cars faced them. Ajax Reynolds, from the post office, rolled out a handcar. He pitched sacks of eastbound mail aboard the express.

A conductor stepped off, waving for the passengers of the first car to come down the stairs.

Early and his partners watched.

Half a dozen came off and a couple handfuls from the other cars, one man helping another.

"Come on," Early said and pushed his way along the platform. He waved as the two men stopped, one reaching back up the steps for a suitcase.

Early shook hands with the man who looked the most unsteady. "Bill, I'm sorry for all that's happened. Missus Gibbs is looking out for your boy."

"What did . . . what did happen?" Bill Smitts asked, slump shouldered. In his better days he could have played tackle on a football team, and did at Fort Hays Normal School.

"Why don't we go over where we can sit a spell?" Early asked. He guided him to a bench, and Smitts sat down.

"Was it a heart attack? Judy's had heart problems."

"I'm sorry. You're not going to find any comfort in this, but someone killed her."

His face went slack. What little color it had drained away.

"Before you ask, we don't know who and we don't know why."

Smitts tried to make his mouth work, but no words came out.

Early looked up at the man with the suitcase, the man about the same age and build as Smitts, but with sandy hair showing beneath his western straw hat. "You're George Watson?"

"Yes."

"It was good of you to come."

"Well, Bill and I have been friends for a couple years. No one should be alone at a time like this. I know I wouldn't want to be."

"You gonna stay awhile?"

"I can. It's up to Bill."

Smitts drew a hand down his face. Words came this time but in little more than a whisper. "No, you got a business to run."

"You sure?" Watson asked.

"I'm not sure of anything."

"Then I'm staying." He moved toward the door to the station. "If there's a pay phone inside, I'll call my office. They can get along without me for a couple days."

After Watson disappeared, Early turned to Smitts. "Quite a friend there."

"My dad said you're entitled to one good one in a lifetime. I guess G.A. is it for me."

"G.A.?"

"George Albert. He's not in love with either name."

"Bill, where's your car?"

"Junction City. That's where I leave it when I catch the train going west."

Plemmons brushed the tip of his nose in a subdued effort to get Early's attention. He shook his head.

Early gazed from Plemmons to Smitts. "You ever meet Trooper Plemmons?"

Smitts twisted around toward the state policeman.

Plemmons took out a small notebook and opened it. "Mister Smitts, you have a Mercury, current model, isn't that right? Kansas license R-I-eight-five-four?"

"Yes."

"It's not in the parking lot at the Junction City station. I checked."

"You don't mean somebody stole it?"

"Been known to happen. Half-drunk soldiers from Fort Riley have been known to help themselves to cars that don't belong to them."

"Oh damn."

"Mister Smitts, I'll tool around the post. It'll probably turn up."

"I appreciate that, but I better . . . I guess I better tell my insurance man."

"Yes, there's always paperwork."

Watson came hustling out from the station. "Got through all right. Told them they can reach me at the Wareham Hotel."

"That's a good place to bunk," Early said. "Bill's got another problem."

"What's that?"

"It appears his car's been stolen. I can have my deputy take you over to the Ford dealership. Ed McCarter will loan you a car so the two of you can get around."

"That'd be good," Watson said.

Early turned back to Smitts. "I expect you'll want to go by the funeral parlor first. I asked Sherm Brown to handle everything. He'll help you with the funeral, get a preacher, whatever you need."

Smitts, glazed, didn't respond.

Early put a hand on the man's arm. "Bill, I hate to ask, but we think it may have been a robbery that started it all. We need for you to meet us out at the house, see what's missing."

Watson interrupted. "You really need to do this?"

"Yes. The more time passes, the less chance of figuring out who did this and catching the man. We're already a day behind."

"So when?" Watson asked.

"Say after supper. About seven." Early nodded to Tolliver, and the deputy helped Smitts up and took him and Watson to the near end of the platform where he had left his Jeep.

Early and Plemmons drifted out among the last passengers hurrying to board the eastbound, the engine's bell clanging, the conductor bellowing out, "All aboard! Topeka, Lawrence, and Kansas City!"

"Do you believe that," Plemmons asked, "his car being stolen?"

"Happens. The man seems genuinely shook to the soles of his shoes."

"Yeah, maybe."

The Baldwin A-Five belched. It jerked its string of cars into motion, the lawmen walking along with them, then falling behind as the train gathered speed.

"You be out at the house this evening, when we walk through it with Bill?" Early asked.

"Naw, yours isn't the only case I'm working on. I got to be down in Council Grove tonight."

A voice called out from the train. "Hey, sheriff?"

Early turned and, as he did, a hand slapped away his hat.

"Sumbitch!" The sheriff wheeled and pounded away after the last car of the train, a cowboy on the back platform, laughing, waving joyously his own hat.

CHAPTER 6

August 17—Wednesday Afternoon
The Diary
Early gave up the chase when it became apparent he couldn't catch the train.

Plemmons trotted up beside him, clutching the sheriff's hat, Early bent forward, wheezing.

"What was that all about?" the trooper asked.

" 'At's our damn bank robber."

"We can call ahead. Get the train stopped."

"A waste. He'll jump off long before anybody can look for him. Gotta be hiding out around here somewhere. Dammit, I hoped he'd run away."

"Why?"

"I wanted him to be somebody else's problem."

Early and Mose Dickerson stood gassing in the dusty grass next to their vehicles, the sun lowering in the west, when Hutch Tolliver drove in and, a couple minutes later, a new Ford Woody with dealer plates on it. The two-door station wagon stopped behind Dickerson's old Chevrolet coupe, and two men got out, George Watson from the driver's side and Bill Smitts.

"This take long?" Watson asked after Early introduced him to the Riley constable.

"Tell you where we'd like to start," Early said. "We found lots of fingerprints in the house. That's no surprise. We've got to know which ones are Bill's so we can eliminate them and see if we got any strangers in the collection."

"You want to fingerprint Bill?"

"Hutch has got the kit."

Watson motioned for Smitts to go with Tolliver. When he turned back, he asked, "What about his wife? There got to be lots of her fingerprints in there."

"And you're right. We fingerprinted the body, so we know which ones are hers."

"So if you find some fingerprints that don't match Bill or his wife or his little boy, you might have something?"

"That's what we figure."

"You got any leads?"

"Well, we think we got a couple. Nothing real promising yet."

"So you really are banking on fingerprints."

"If we come up with one or two unexpected and, say, in the right place, could be a plus."

"Well, here's hoping," Watson said.

Early moved off into the yard, leading Watson and Dickerson away. "You say you've known Bill for a couple years?"

"Ever since the U-P put him out here."

"You have occasion to meet his wife?"

"Once. Bill and she were going out to Wakeeney, to see his parents. He telegraphed me to meet him at the station for the couple minutes the train would be stopped, wanted to tell me about a new rate schedule that would be coming out."

"So you and Missus Smitts didn't get to talk."

"Just to say hello."

"And Bill?"

"What about Bill?"

Early took off his hat. He scratched at the back of his head. "Might as well be direct. These traveling types have been known to have women in other towns. He ever mention any?"

· Watson's eyes narrowed, a hint of steel showing. "I'm not even going to dignify that with an answer."

"Look, I'm sorry, but we've got to consider everything."

"Maybe you do, but I don't."

Smitts came over, scrubbing ink from his fingers onto a handkerchief. "Guess this stuff will come off."

"What doesn't," Early said, "a little bleach will get it if it concerns you. You ready to go inside?"

"No, but let's get it done."

Early and Smitts chatted as they ambled across the dry lawn—the last rain three weeks ago and then not much. They sidestepped a Mason jar with holes punched in the lid, dead bugs inside—a child's experiment. That disturbed Early, and he forced the image of the Smitts' boy playing here out of his mind as they stepped up onto the porch. "We didn't straighten up a thing or clean up," Early said as he opened the screen, then the storm door. "It's a mess inside."

Smitts stepped in and, at the sight of the front room, sucked in a breath. "Who could have . . ."

"As we said, we don't know. Take your time. Tell us what might be missing."

Early switched on the room light, to supplement the dwindling light from outside.

Smitts moved around, pain, increasing pain, showing about his eyes with each step he took. He stopped in front of one corner. "The radio. We had a big Crosley sitting right here."

Tolliver and Dickerson took out notepads and wrote.

"Mahogany cabinet," Smitts said. "Bought it two years ago from Fletcher's in Manhattan. They can probably get the model number for you, maybe even the serial number."

He moved on to a glass-front cabinet, the glass broken out. "Judy kept the things that were important to her here."

"Like what?" Early asked.

"A couple Hummel figurines I got her, some pieces of her mother's china—soup tureen, I think—and a pot, teapot I guess, some cups. She'd started a collection of spoons, from states we visited."

"You traveled some, as a family then?"

"Advantage of working for a railroad. Free passes. You can go anywhere." Smitts turned. "On the wall there, that's where we hung our wedding picture. Who'd want to take that?"

"You keep any guns in the house? We didn't find any."

"No. Judy was deathly afraid of guns."

Dickerson scribbled a note and handed it to Early. He looked at it, then slipped it in his shirt pocket.

"Suppose we go on to the kitchen," Early said.

Smitts and Watson went first, the lawmen following, the hard heels of their boots clicking on the floor, sounding hollow in the barren hallway. Early switched on the kitchen light when he came in.

"This blood?" Smitts asked, motioning at some red-tinged splotches on the floor and the cabinet faces.

"Yes."

He blanched and his knees buckled as he stepped back. Watson grabbed him to keep him from falling.

"Sorry," Smitts said, "it's just that . . ."

"You need to sit?" Early asked.

"No. I'll . . . I'll . . . she die here?"

"The bedroom, but we're not going in there unless you kept valuables there. It's pretty bad."

"Just, um . . . um . . . Judy's jewelry box, I think."

"We found it."

Smitts steadied himself. He gazed about, turning. "Um . . . Can't think of anything . . . uh . . . anything anybody'd want from a kitchen, you know. The stove's here. The refrigerator. They're the only things of any value."

He opened a cupboard. "Oh Lord."

"We wondered about that," Early said.

"Who'd go and break our dishes?"

"Yes, and they kept all the pieces in the cupboard. Didn't let anything fall out."

Smitts's hand went to his face. "I don't understand any of this."

"Come on, Bill, let's get you out of here," Watson said. He put his arm around Smitts's shoulders and pushed the man along, out through the dining room and the front room.

Early leaned against the counter near where Smitts had stood. He jacked his hat onto the back of his head. "So what do you think?"

"He sure seemed shook," Tolliver said as he scanned down his notes.

"I'd say."

"As to theft, whoever did it didn't take much of value."

"That's what's got me curious."

"Pardon?"

"Hutch, guns would be worth something, but according to Bill, there weren't any. That leaves just the radio worth, what, a hundred bucks?"

"Only if it was a top model, and who'd pay that much if it might be hot?"

"So he's got to discount it. Try to get maybe forty, fifty dollars? A new officer at the post, at Fort Riley, might pay that."

Tolliver scratched at his sideburn. "So you're thinking some soldier."

"One of us has got to check it out."

Dickerson cleared his throat loudly. All eyes turned to him.

"Jimmy, how about my note?" he asked.

"Why don't the three of us talk about that after we get these fellas on the road."

Early led the way out, his hands stuffed in his back pockets, Dickerson next, Tolliver last, the deputy turning out lights and closing doors. They found Watson pacing beside the new Ford and Smitts slumped in the passenger seat, the door open.

"Sheriff, if it's all right with you," Watson said, thumbing at Smitts, "I'm going to get Bill back to the hotel. This day's been awful on him."

"You do that. He set the funeral?"

"Day after tomorrow. Friday."

Early went to the passenger door. After he closed it, he leaned down to the open window. "Bill, I'm sorry for all this. You been a fine help. All of us, we'll be at the funeral. You can count on it."

He stepped back as Watson started the car. The lawmen watched the Woody back away, turn, and drive out.

The three lawmen sighed and exchanged glances that could only be described as professional. Then Early took Dickerson's note from his pocket. He handed it to his deputy.

Tolliver read it, and his eyes widened. "The sonuvabitch lied?"

"Would appear so."

"Jimmy," Dickerson said, "she asked me to teach her to shoot. You know, we get rattlesnakes up in our yards sometimes. Had this little silver Thirty-Eight."

"She get any good?"

"Floored me. She was dead-on with the first bullet, could knock tin cans over at twenty yards. Never missed."

"My. Is it possible he couldn't have known?"

"What wife's going to keep this from her husband?"

Light streamed from the kitchen window when Early drove in. He parked under a hackberry tree and turned off the motor. Early pulled the keys, tossed them in the air, juggling them as he walked to the house, to the back porch and on in. There

63

before him, with her back to the door, sat his wife, hunched over a Formica-topped table, the radio playing in the background. Was it Billy Eckstein singing? Sounded like him. Bluesy.

"Reading the paper?" Early asked as he hung his keys and hat on a peg beside the door.

Thelma held up a brown, tape-bound notebook. "Judy's diary."

He swiveled around, catching his boot toe on the rag rug, stumbling.

"Careful there, cowboy," she said turning to him.

Early straightened himself up. He raked his fingers through his hair in an attempt to appear casual. "Where'd you get that?"

"At school, the first under half a dozen other notebooks in her desk drawer. A box full of them in the back of her coat closet."

"Not exactly out in the open."

"No, I had to look some. I hid my diary under the mattress."

"You keep a diary?"

"No. Not since I was sixteen, hon."

She turned back, and he looked over her shoulder. "Anything interesting?"

"Oh yes."

"Can it wait while you get me some supper?"

She twisted around and kissed Early on the cheek. "You need a shave, stubbleface. Your supper's in the refrigerator."

He wandered over to the Kelvinator while Thelma returned to her reading. Early opened the door and spied a sandwich on a plate and a bowl of potato salad. He took both, and a jar of pickles, to the table. "You want any of this?"

"I'll have a pickle."

"This got anything to do with the baby?"

"No, I just like pickles."

"Uh-huh. Coffee?"

"Pot's on the back of the stove."

"Fresh?" he asked, going for a china mug and the metal pot he had brought to his marriage from his bachelor days on the ranch.

"Three days old, the way you like it."

"Mmm, range coffee."

Early filled the mug to the rim, then threw a leg over a chair. He sucked in a mouthful of the brew and contemplated its texture and taste. "Chewy," he said after he swallowed it. "What's the matter, you not going to laugh?"

"There's not much here to laugh about." She turned a page.

He opened the pickle jar. He helped himself to a dill stick before he pushed the jar to her. Thelma reached for it, fished a stick out, and ate it while she read.

Early sampled the sandwich. "This from the pork roast?"

"Yes. I shredded it and mixed it with that barbecue sauce you make. I thought it was rather good."

"Do love the smell of barbecue, and you can't beat the taste." Early swabbed some of the errant sauce up from his plate with his finger. He sucked it off. "Well?"

"Well, what?"

"The diary."

Thelma straightened up, flexing her shoulders. She took another bite from her pickle. "This is volume twenty-eight or so of I don't know how many. The box is there on the floor."

Early chuckled. "So many. Serious writer, huh?"

"The first dozen are when she was a child up through high school. Next ten are college. I just glanced at some pages in all those, didn't really read them."

"And then?" Early asked as he shoveled potato salad from a bowl onto his plate.

"Like this one, from when she started teaching to a week ago. There are stretches she'd write every day, and times when she'd skip a week or more."

"Thel, I got the feeling you're about to tell me something."

She turned forward a fistful of pages, scanning, then stopped and tapped at a paragraph. " 'I've been seeing him for three weeks now. He's a colonel, sinfully handsome in his uniform. Just to think of him makes me perspire.' And she's drawn something here."

Early glanced over. "Crossed cannons. Insignia of the artillery. What's the date?"

Thelma's finger moved up the page. "August third, last year."

"Trooper Dan thought she might be cattin' around."

"That's not a nice thing to say."

"Well, what do you want to call it?"

"I don't know. I was just amazed when I found it."

"I thought you girls were supposed to gossip about everything."

"James Early." She leveled a look at him intended to freeze him down to his boot heels. He threw up his hands in surrender.

"Can I at least ask how many times she mentions this 'seeing' business?" he asked.

"Half a dozen near as I can tell. I haven't read it all."

"She mention a name?"

"Never."

"You think it was serious?"

Thelma leaned back. She massaged her face, pulling her fingertips down to her jaw line, then below. "We don't write things in our diaries unless they're serious, or at least serious to us."

"So this might not have been serious for the artillery man from Fort Riley?"

"You can assume, but there's no way of knowing, at least not from what I've read."

Early took another monstrous bite of his sandwich. He chewed to the big-band music of Arty Shaw coming from the radio, the Eckstein song gone now. Early slurped his coffee. "A man on the side, that sure complicates a marriage."

"What are you thinking?"

"In most murders, the killer is someone who knew the victim." Up came the counting fingers, Early ticking them off. "Usually the husband. Sometimes the wife. Sometimes a jealous lover."

"You think it was Bill?"

"He was out of town, as they say."

"The officer?"

"You got a better candidate?"

CHAPTER 7

August 19—Friday Noon
Late for the Funeral

Early motioned to the waitress. When he had her attention, he pointed at his cup. This had been a day he was glad no one asked to go to lunch with him. The morning meeting with the county commissioners had left Early with a headache and a desire to divorce himself from office.

"You look like you got the grumps," Sue said as she filled his cup.

"Had my corns tromped on."

"You want to talk about it with someone who doesn't care?"

Early glanced up at the young woman. Young woman—eighteen—he remembered her from four years previous, when he had met her mother bawling after a ruckus over what Early had not fully understood, except that Sue had sassed her mother, then run off. He caught up with the girl on US Twenty-Four, thumb out, trying for a ride to Kansas City. Early paddled her and took her home.

He grinned. "You are good at sticking it to me."

"Learned from the best."

"Pardon?"

"You," she said and swept away to another table.

Hutch Tolliver shambled in, his hand on the collar of a morose fellow a good forty years his senior and, by the wear and grime on the man's clothes, a hobo. "Boss, he says he knows you."

Early arched an eyebrow.

"Found him howling around up by Randolph, roaring drunk."

The sheriff studied the bearded specimen of the poorer side of humanity, hair gray and thinning, a calico bedroll slung over his shoulder. "Pop Irv?" he asked.

The man swatted at Tolliver. "See? I tol' yah he knew me."

"Pop, what's it been, ten, twelve years?"

"Since before yah went off to fight Hitler, least tell that's what I heard yah did. Looks like yah come out all right, and a sheriff now, huh?"

"When you eat last?"

"Yesterday. Caught me a rabbit and, with a few vegetables I 'borrowed' from somebody's garden, cooked him into a good stew."

Early pointed to the bench across from himself. "Park it. I'll stake you to lunch."

Lester Irving dropped his bedroll beside the booth. He pulled off his tattered railroad cap and stuffed it in his back pocket as he sat down. With both hands Irving mopped his hair forward into some semblance of order.

"Tell Sue," Early said to Tolliver, "a blue-plate special for Pop. . . . Pop, coffee with that?"

"Could I get milk?"

Early motioned Tolliver away. "Still riding the rails, huh?" he asked Irving.

"Fer the last time. I've come home."

"That I find hard to believe."

Irving clawed at an itch in his beard. "It's true. Got in a helluva knife fight out in Pueblo, you know, Colorado? Doctor who sewed me up found some awful stuff in me. Wouldn't tell me what. Just said I'd be damn lucky to see fall."

Early's cheeks puffed out as he exhaled.

Sue came by from the kitchen. She leaned down and slid a plate of meatloaf and mashed potatoes in front of Irving, then a glass of milk. She took silverware and a napkin from her apron pocket and placed them on the table too. The waitress, puzzled, glanced at Early.

He silently mouthed the words *On my bill.*

She shrugged and moved away to the cash register to ring up a waiting customer.

Irving made a business of stuffing the corner of the napkin into his collar. He smoothed the rest over his shirtfront. "Jimmy, cain't tell yah how long since I been in a sit-down restaurant."

"When we were hoboing together back a bit, wasn't anybody'd let us in a restaurant."

"We didn't have a sheriff for a friend who's got money in his pocket." Irving packed his mouth with well-catsupped meatloaf and chewed.

Early sipped at his coffee. "Ella know you're back?"

"I ain't had the courage to go by," he said, some of the loaf dribbling from the corner of his mouth. Irving swallowed, then shoveled in the potatoes and gravy.

"See your kids?"

"Not since 'Thirty-Three."

"You're a grandpaw twice over, old man."

Irving stopped in midchew. He wiped at a rheumy eye.

"Betts married," Early said. "Lives over in the next county. Got two children, both girls. Real nice family."

"And my boy?"

"Ronnie? Sophomore at K-State come September."

"How can Ella afford that?"

"We got him a scholarship and a couple part-time jobs. I expect he looks a lot like you did when you were a young sport."

"Damn, so they turned out all right without me." Irving

swilled the milk down. That done, he attacked the meatloaf again.

Early stopped Sue on her way back to the kitchen. "Apple pie with ice cream for my friend."

She leaned in. "He needs a bath."

"He doesn't believe in it."

"Well, at least spritz him with some Old Spice," she said and moved on.

Irving sopped up the last of the gravy with a slice of bread. "Always like to leave a shine on my plate. . . . Jimmy, you and me, we sure saw a lot of country, didn't we?"

"Two years of it for me." Early sipped at his coffee.

"Then you went off an' joined the Army. I was too damn old."

"You should have got a job in one of the war industries."

"I just wasn't dependable. . . . Thankee," he said to Sue when she set the dessert and a clean fork in front of him. Like a hog at a trough, he gobbled up the pie and ice cream.

Early watched him, wondering at how little separated him from the old man other than years and a job on the county payroll. Irving had run off when the Depression destroyed his employment as a drummer of men's shoes.

Early glanced under the table. "See you're still wearing fancy footwear."

"These got some age on 'em. Yeah, wingtips. Nunn-Busch, nothing but the best. One thing I know, Jimmy, it's quality."

"Must cost you."

"First time maybe. Resole them every six months, I can get five, six years out of a pair of shoes."

When the dessert plate had the same shine as Irving's main-course plate, Early tossed his coffee back, and spit up a coin into his hand. "Sue!"

She turned away from the cash register. "Your tip," she said

71

when she saw him hold up the nickel.

Early exchanged it for a quarter from his pocket. He slapped the larger coin on the table as he pushed himself off the bench. "Come on, Pop," he said, motioning for Irving to get up, "time for you to make peace with the family."

"I told you I ain't got the courage."

"Then why'd you come back?"

"To buy me a grave. I got a little money put back," he said, patting his bedroll as he slipped its tied-up ends over his shoulder.

"Who'd you steal it from?"

"Jimmy, I've had me some honest employment. Worked at a store out in Denver, repairing bicycles. Always been good with my hands. When I had enough five-dollar bills put by, I caught me a freight for home."

"Well, now you're gonna catch a ride in my Jeep, and we're going out to see Ella."

"Aww, Jimmy—"

"Don't go awwing me. Let's git."

Early counted out a dollar forty-five at the front counter. "That right?" he asked the waitress.

She looked at it as she raked the coins into her hand and from there into the correct boxes in the cash register's drawer. "To the nickel. Do I get a tip today?"

"Hell no."

Early stopped his Jeep in front of a shabby two-story on Fifteenth Street. Boarders and laundry supported Ella Irving and her two children after her husband disappeared. There had never been money enough for paint and precious little for repairs.

"The place'd look some better if you'd been here," Early said. "Come on, Pop, let's go in."

Irving froze in the passenger seat. "I cain't do it, Jimmy."

"Well, I can." From the sidewalk, he turned back. "If you run while I'm in the house, I'll come after you."

Early went on. He glanced back and saw Irving fidgeting. "Pop, keep your hands off my radio."

At the door, Early shaded his eyes while he peered through the screen. "Aunt Ella, you home?"

A voice came from somewhere in the depths of the house, then much rustling. After some moments, a woman appeared on the other side of the screen door.

"Jimmy? Jimmy Early?"

"The only one. How you doing, Aunt Ella?"

"Oh, you shouldn't 'Aunt Ella' me," she said as she bustled out onto the porch. She, squat and powerfully built, hard muscled from years of scrubbing clothes on a washboard, hugged Early only to stop when she saw the profile of the man sitting in the Jeep at the end of her walk. Missus Irving pulled back. She looked up hard into Early's eyes. "That who I think it is?"

"Could be."

"Damned old fool. I told my children he was dead and I wished he was."

"Ella, Pop's come home to make peace. He's dying."

"He can go to his grave with a troubled soul for all I care. He can go to hell."

"Won't you at least—"

But she slammed the screen shut. It bounced and shook on its hinges with the same anger as its owner.

Early stood there, his mouth open and no one to talk to. "Aunt Ella?"

"No!"

The main door slammed, rattling the window glass.

Early shrugged. With nothing better to do, he wandered off

the porch and back to his Jeep.

"She a mite upset?" Irving asked, his face still straight ahead.

"And I caught the load." Early climbed behind the steering wheel. He started the Jeep and got it rolling, cranking the wheel hard to U-turn in the street. He headed the machine back to Poyntz Avenue, Manhattan's main business street. "Look, I got a funeral I got to attend. I'm going to take you to the jail. You get a bath there. Get yourself cleaned up, and we'll talk when I get back."

Early came hustling away from his Jeep to find Mose Dickerson sitting on the liars' bench near the steps that led down to the sheriff's basement office in the courthouse, Dickerson bobbing his foot, his face clouded.

"You're gonna catch it when you go in there, Jimmy," the constable said. "Yer sweet wife's waitin', an' yer late."

"Thanks for bringing her in."

"Brought your suit too. That's what friends are for."

Early tiptoed down the three steps. He eased the door open. When he didn't see Thelma—only Alice at the dispatch radio and Gladys, the secretary he had inherited from his predecessor—he stepped inside, a finger to his lips. He made silent strides across the lobby area of the office, the dispatcher, her ear near the radio monitor, doing her best to ignore him. But the secretary rubbed one index finger over the other in a shame-shame manner.

"That you, Jimmy?" came Thelma's voice from Early's side office.

He cringed. Early gave up all pretense at stealth and stepped out, speaking to the blue-haired secretary as he went by, "I'll remember this come the time you want a day off."

He went on into his office. "Thel, I'm sorry, but Lester Irving came back to town. I was trying to patch things up between

74

him and his wife."

"You're always thinking of somebody else." She took his blue-serge trousers off a hanger. "Come on, get out of those tans."

"Change in front of God and Gladys?" Early asked as he sat on his desk. He stripped off a boot.

"I can close the door, Mister Modest."

"No, they've all seen my hairy legs."

Laughter burst from the women in the outer office. "Right," Alice said, snorting, a hand over her microphone. "Jimmy's chasing this drunk along Thirteenth Street for the police chief and they cut through this yard—"

"No, let me tell it," Gladys said, slapping her desk. "Jimmy said the owner's dog went for the drunk, missed him, and turned on your husband, Missus E, got a mouthful of pant leg and ripped his pants off."

"Oh, yuck, yuck, yuck. Close the door." Early kicked his boots aside as Thelma passed by. He dropped his tans and pulled on the blue serge. Early hauled his shirt off over his head rather than go through the business of unbuttoning, then thrust his arms into the white shirt Thelma held for him. She stuffed the back in his pants while he got the front . . . buckled his belt, buttons, necktie. Early got one boot and hopped about the office as he pulled it on, then the other.

"I'll put the coat on at the church," he said, grabbing for it and his hat.

"Your hair."

"Hats are so we old boys don't have to do hair."

He whisked through the door, Thelma after him.

"Halfway presentable," Gladys said to her associate.

Alice waved him on. "We know where you'll be."

Early, on the run, threw the door open. As he burst outside, with Thelma working hard to keep up, Dickerson rose. "Take my car?" he asked.

"My Jeep," Early said as he bent around the corner for the back parking lot. "I got a siren."

They packed in, Dickerson scrambling over the passenger seat to the back, then Thelma, Early at the wheel. He slammed the Jeep into reverse, threw gravel as he whipped around, and more gravel when he found first gear.

Early bolted the vehicle onto the side street. He headed north toward Bluemont, snapping on the siren and weaving around cars pulling to the side of the street.

"Jimmy, do you have to?" Thelma asked as she clung to the seat to keep from being thrown out.

"You said we're late."

Four blocks on and Early skidded the Jeep around a corner onto Bluemont Street and raced away toward Aggieville and the grand limestone edifice beyond that was Saint Mark's Lutheran. He slowed for the S turn, then stepped down on the accelerator, whipping around a hardware truck. At Twenty-First Street, Early snapped the siren off. He scanned ahead for a free parking place in front of the church.

Nothing.

Early swerved the Jeep up onto the sidewalk. He nipped the vehicle between two maple trees and slid the Jeep to a stop near the steps that rose up to the church's great oak and brass doors.

"How's this?" he asked as he hopped out.

"You don't mind," Dickerson said, bug-eyed in the backseat, "next time I'll drive."

Early helped his wife down, then the constable. And the trio trotted up the steps, Early pulling on his suitcoat.

A somber man in black—Sherm Brown, the undertaker—opened the door for them. "Sheriff," he whispered, "they're about finished in there."

"Sorry about being late."

Brown handed each a folded paper. "Little information about

the deceased."

The three moved on inside. As Early came abreast of the back row, a man seated on the right beckoned to him. He patted the pew.

Early motioned Thelma in, then followed. He reached across to shake hands as he sat down. "Granny," he whispered.

The man in the yarmulke nodded. "I lobbied for the temple, but I lost."

"One place is as good as the other for a funeral, I expect."

Granny Weichselbaum gave a quick turn of his hand as if to say, "Ehh."

Thelma pointed up to Early's hat.

He raked it off and parked it on his knee.

At the front, in the pulpit, Saint Mark's pastor—known as the great bear of the Flint Hills—glanced up from his Bible. "Tragic," he said to the sea of faces before him, "a death for one so young. But that's the way we see it, we small beings limited in our view of things. But in God's view, it's merely a coming home, a coming home to Him, a coming home to Heaven. That we should celebrate."

He turned away, toward his organist. She struck the first chord for "In the Sweet By and By." People throughout the sanctuary shuffled to their feet. Many opened hymnals, but the Baptists among them, like Early, sang the words from memory.

Far to the front, the pallbearers moved up to the bronze casket. They lifted it to their shoulders and began the long, stately walk to the back of the church, the husband of the dead teacher and his friend stepping in behind, the husband carrying a child—his son. Next came an elderly couple Early did not recognize, then the great bear, Reverend Ellsworth, a dominating presence.

After the four verses and the four-part harmony amen, the organist continued playing but at a subdued volume. Brown and his son, Randy, came in from the outside, to the back row. They motioned for the people there to process out. Dickerson stepped into the aisle, then Early and Thelma, and Weichselbaum and others from the Leonardville area. They went out into the midafternoon sun and down the steps.

"Your hair," Thelma said.

Early ran a hand back over his spiky thatch. When it refused to cooperate with his finger combing, he slapped his cattleman's hat over it.

At the Jeep, Weichselbaum tugged at Early's sleeve. "Parking on the sidewalk, are we?"

"What can I tell you?"

"You were late, I know, but it doesn't show you in the best light, you the county's chief law-and-order man."

Early gestured toward the old couple getting into the second car behind the hearse. "You know who they are?"

"Judith's parents."

"Bill's family get in?"

"Haven't seen them."

A man in city-police blues, graying at the temples, pushed through the stream flowing from the church. "Cactus," he said, "I could arrest you for parking where you have."

"Guess you could, chief." Early held out his hands. "Want to cuff me?"

"Tell you what, I'll let you earn forgiveness."

"How's that?"

"I got my squad car up front. I'll lead the procession to the cemetery. Why don't you fall in at the end, complete the honor guard?"

Early touched the brim of his hat in salute. He turned to Weichselbaum as the police chief pushed back into what was now a flood. "Want to ride with us?"

"Can't think of better friends," Granny said.

Early motioned for Weichselbaum and Dickerson to take the backseats. He then settled Thelma in the front. When Early came around to his side of the Jeep, he went to fishing under his seat. From somewhere beneath it he recovered a bubble light and planted it in the middle of his Jeep's hood, a wire trailing back and over the windshield. Early plugged the wire into the cigarette lighter. That brought the bubble light to life, the motor that turned it grinding away.

He backed the Jeep up the sidewalk and off into the intersection. Early stopped catawampus in the middle and flipped on his four-ways before he strolled around to direct the traffic coming up from Aggieville.

Hutch Tolliver made a show when he pulled that duty. He would roll his hands to get drivers to speed up, then throw both to the side to get them to turn where he wanted. When Tolliver wanted them to stop, he would leap in the air with one hand out. Early, in contrast, leaned against the back of his Jeep, the heel of one boot hooked on the bumper. He gave a small "come here" with one index finger and, with the other, would casually point off to the side street.

"Granny," he said over his shoulder, "no luck negotiating the rabbi into the service?"

"You don't win much with the great bear. 'Tis his church after all." He brought a Star of David from his inside pocket, the star made of pot metal and mounted on a stake of the same material. "I'll put this at the head of the grave. It's enough."

"How'd her parents take it?"

"Badly. They haven't been able to pry more than three words out of Bill."

"He's pretty bad hurt himself."

A pickup, a pre-war Dodge, brakes squalling, stopped in front of Early. The driver leaned out. "Sheriff?"

"Yeah."

"Kin I go up that way?" he asked, waving off to the south. "I got groceries to deliver."

Early thumbed in that direction. When the pickup cleared the intersection, he beckoned the next car and pointed off north. "They staying at the hotel?"

"Seemed awful cold, alone there among strangers," Weichsel-baum said. "So I have them at my place. That way, we can hold our own service. Cry together."

"Granny, you got a good heart."

Dickerson twisted around. "Jimmy, the funeral procession's starting to move."

Early gave a Hutch hand-roll to the final car and sent it onto the side street. By the time he slipped in behind the steering wheel, the last vehicle coming out of the church lot turned toward town, not away in the direction of the procession. Early let out the clutch and rolled on.

He followed the procession to the end of the church block, then left and left again as the long line of cars and pickups made its way back toward Eighteenth Street, a cross street that would take the procession south to where Poyntz became Sunset and led up to the cemetery. Early gave a small wave to several kids he knew biking along the sidewalk.

At Sunset, the procession wound its way up Sunset Hill, toward the city cemetery, the cemetery on one of the few promontories around Manhattan that had soil deep enough for graves to be dug without the workmen having to bring out the dynamite to blast rock.

Drivers turned their vehicles off onto the grass that bordered the cemetery's boulevard and the side lane that led to Judith Smitts's grave. Early, last in the procession, parked the farthest out, something that didn't bother him for he didn't mind walk-ing, although his rancher father was of the opinion that if God had meant man to walk, He would have given him four legs.

Thelma curled her hand around Early's arm as they strolled along. "You know, husband mine, someday we're going to be buried here."

"I hope you're not in a hurry."

"Hardly. But it is nice up here, isn't it? No trees. You can see for miles."

"Nice if the prairie wind doesn't blow you away."

"There isn't any today."

The quartet cut across lots, stepping around graves of the long dead in the older section of the cemetery to get to where the more recently dead rested, to where an open grave waited for its occupant.

"You thought where you want to be buried?" Thelma asked.

"Gawd no."

"Why not?"

"I came through a war darn lucky to be alive. I'd like to enjoy my time some."

"But we have to plan."

"For something forty years, fifty years away?"

"I love you, James Early."

"Well, that's a comfort."

"Still and all, we have to plan."

They slowed as they came up on those clustered around the funeral party. The great bear raised a hand. "Brothers and sisters in Jesus," he said, "the time has come to place the body of our sister in Christ, Judith Smitts, in the ground for its final rest, knowing full well that her spirit, her soul, has already been swept up to heaven, to be with the Father. Please pray with me."

Early and Dickerson pulled off their hats as those around them bowed.

Ellsworth's voice rang above the assembly. "Dear God, we came from dust and we return to dust, our time here but a moment. For most of that moment for Judith Smitts it was good and we praise You for that. Now comfort Bill. Care for their child and keep him safe from the hurt of these days. Comfort Judith's parents, Lord, comfort us all for none of us likes to give up a wife, a daughter, a friend. Yet we must, but we have her memory to hold dear until such time as we see her again when You call us all home. Amen."

A number in the crowd murmured amen. Then some began to shift about, most queuing up to pass by the grave, to shake hands with Bill Smitts, to say what words they could muster to Judith's parents. Before Early's group could move, another man stepped in.

"Trooper Dan," Early said in greeting. "You look tolerable in a suit."

"You too, Cactus. Didn't see you at the church."

"We got there for the last hymn. Before you ask, it's a long story."

Plemmons pointed across the way to a man in a black suit holding back from the crowd, keeping to himself. "What do you think?"

"Regulation haircut. You don't suppose?"

"Maybe we should ask."

Early turned to his wife. "Thel, looks like we've got to do us some work. Why don't you go with Granny through the receiving line. We'll catch up."

She squeezed his hand. "Do you really have to?"

"We better." Early backed away, turning. He strolled off flanked by Plemmons and Dickerson, Dickerson doing his hop-step limp. The man in their sights—tall, straight, but less than square shouldered, as if he were tired—did not appear to notice them, for he stared off to the west.

Plemmons slipped Early a scrap of paper as they walked. "The colonels on the post, last year to present. Four of them have moved on."

"Helpful. . . . Excuse me, colonel?" Early asked as he came up behind the man.

He turned slightly. "Pardon?"

"Colonel Taggert, isn't it? Out at the post?"

"Do I know you?"

"Jim Early, sheriff of Riley County. Mind if I ask why you're at this funeral, colonel?"

"Missus Smitts taught at the post school for a year. My boy was in her class. My wife had died, and she helped him work through it. I came to pay my respects."

Early glanced around. "Your boy here?"

"No. He's with my parents for the summer, in Texas. He doesn't know."

"Be hard to tell him."

"Yes, it will be."

"Was there something more between you and Missus Smitts than just parent and teacher?"

"Pardon?"

Plemmons brought his hand out of his pocket. He held up a button. "Colonel, this yours?"

The man took the button. He examined it and handed it back. "It's regulation, but I doubt it's mine."

"You sure?"

"I had to get all my uniforms ready for inspection last week. All the buttons, all the ribbons were there. What's this about?"

Early glanced down at the toes of his boots, then up into the man's eyes. "Colonel, you're mentioned in Judith Smitts' diary."

The tan on the man's face faded. "You'll have to excuse me, this conversation has ended," he said and pushed around the trio of lawmen. He moved away toward a black Ford.

"Ooo, touched a nerve," Plemmons said. "How'd you know

he was Taggert?"

"I didn't and I don't. That's just one of the names on your list."

"Clever."

"Now don't get excited. He didn't acknowledge the name, but he didn't say he wasn't Taggert. Want to go out to the post in the morning?"

CHAPTER 8

August 19—Friday Evening
Comfort

Early yelped and grabbed for the railing, Thelma scrabbling, reaching for him.

"You all right?" she asked.

"Damn step just went through." Early spit over the side of the stairway as he hauled himself upright.

A light came on overhead, and a door opened. Granny Weichselbaum leaned out. "Somebody out there?"

"Just your company, Gran," Early said as he massaged his shin. "One of your steps busted."

"Oh Lord, Esther's been after me to fix that."

"I can understand why."

Weichselbaum hustled out onto the landing. He reached down and caught Early's hand. "I'm sorry about this. We never use the outside stairs, just the stairs in the store."

"I'll remember that the next time we come calling." Early stepped across the void where a stair tread had been. When clear, he reached back for Thelma. "Can you make it, girl?"

"Better than you." She pulled against his hand and made a hop that carried her up two steps to safety.

"Let's get you inside," Granny said. He held the door for his guests, and Early limped by, Thelma after him.

"You sure you're all right?" she asked, the concern etched in her face apparent in the stronger light from the clothier's apartment.

"Aw, just barked my shin."

Thelma stopped Early and turned him back. "Your pants are ripped."

"So they are," he said as he glanced down.

She pulled his pant leg up. "And you're bleeding."

"Hon, it's nothing."

Granny hauled his glasses down from where they rested on his dome. He studied the wound. "That's no nothing. You come in the kitchen, and I'll get some iodine and a bandage on that."

A woman came up, as short and as round as Granny, and for the first time Early became aware that he had limped into a room filled with people. He sensed the gaze of a dozen pairs of eyes. "Are we interrupting something?"

"Just some of the temple congregation," Granny said. He waved a hand around the apartment's main room cluttered with overstuffed chairs, a couch, and half a dozen hard chairs. On every seat a person. "We were sitting 'shiva' for Judith."

"We can come another time."

"Oh no no no no, you should be here. Just let me get you patched up." Granny turned to the woman, his wife. "Esther, Jimmy's gotta have new pants. Would you run downstairs to the Levis counter and get a pair of jeans, what, Jimmy, thirty-two, twenty-nine?"

"That's not necessary. Thel can patch these."

"Jimmy, who owns a clothing store here?"

The answer took all the fight out of Early's resistance. He instead followed Granny, mumbling "excuse me" and "howdy" to several people he stepped around—limped around—in his journey to the kitchen midway between the sitting room over the front of the store and the bedrooms over the back.

Everything gleamed white in the kitchen including the gas

stove Granny had bought for his wife. He patted the stove as he went past it and took a first-aid kit from a drawer.

"The Four-H club was selling these. This is the first time I get to use it." Granny touched the counter. "Hike your leg up here, Jimmy."

While Early did, with Thelma steadying him, Granny opened the iodine bottle. He splashed a portion of the contents onto a gauze pad and slapped the pad over the sheriff's torn and bleeding skin.

Early grimaced.

"Stings some, huh?"

"Worse than that powder the Army medics poured on wounds."

"This stuff's supposed to be better at preventing infection." To Thelma, Granny said, "Hold that there."

He ripped the paper covering from a fresh gauze bandage and laid it over the wound when, at his nod, Thelma took the iodined pad away. Then he pulled off strips of adhesive tape from a roll and padded the strips across the bandage and onto Early's skin. "Jimmy, time to skinny out of those pants."

"No no no no," Early said as he brought his leg down. He stepped on his foot, testing the flex of his leg's muscles.

"Out of those pants."

Thelma turned her husband toward her. She pointed at the floor. "Strip."

"Good Lord." Early frowned as he leaned against the counter. He pulled off one boot, then the other.

"I tell you, Granny," Thelma said, "he's as stubborn as some of the little boys I had in my class last year."

Early dropped his pants at the moment Esther Weichselbaum hustled through the door, holding out a new pair of jeans. "Fresh from the Strauss company," she said.

"Could we maybe invite a few more people in here?" Early muttered.

Granny went to the door. He leaned through it. "Hey, everybody, our sheriff is changing his trousers. Would any of you like to come and watch?"

Early side-armed a boot at the clothier's well-padded rump as "no's" and snickers came from the other room.

Granny hopped around at the hit. He waggled his finger at his guest before he picked up the errant boot and tossed it back.

"Like children, that's what they are," Esther said.

Early pulled on his new pants and recovered his belt from the pair that had suffered the trauma. "Shiva," he said, "what's that?"

Granny leaned back. He put the heels of his hands against the stove. "We Jews have a lot of traditions and rules. You sure you want to know all this?"

"I wouldn't of asked if I didn't." Early pulled on a boot.

"When a family member dies, we're required to mourn them for seven days, what we call shiva—seven. For Judith's parents, they would be home in the evening for the seven days, and the neighbors would come in and they'd reminisce and offer prayers. Well, it wasn't possible for them to get home to Kansas City tonight."

"So you thought you would—"

"It's not in strict adherence to the rules, but I didn't think Jehovah would rain down bolts of lightning upon us."

Esther patted her husband's hand. "My father was a rabbi. Were he alive, he would look askance at this, but my Herschel's heart is in the right place."

Granny smiled at his wife with a warmth that came from sharing forty years of life.

Esther patted his hand again. "Shall we take our guests in

and introduce them to the people who loved Judith? They're all members of our temple in Manhattan."

"Except the Silverbergs," Granny said. He motioned for Early and Thelma to follow him, and led the way back into the front room.

Five couples rose.

"You know the Rennebergs," Granny said, motioning to the old couple at the far end of the room. "Next to them, that's Zack and Myra Durskowitz . . . David and Ruth Jenkowski . . . Bernard and Rebecca Lippman . . . and, of course"—Granny stepped between the last couple and put his arms around them—"these are Judith's parents, Mishka and Ethel Silverberg."

Early snatched his hat off before he shook hands with Mister Silverberg. Thelma clasped Missus Silverberg's hands and whispered something that caused the woman to return an uneasy and tearful smile.

"These good people," Granny said, indicating the Earlys, "are friends. Missus Early—Thelma—taught school with Judith. And Mister Early—James—he's our sheriff. But he's not wearing a badge tonight."

Early glanced around. He nodded to those he knew. And then he saw several things that to him were odd—someone had removed the cushions from the chairs and the sofa, and the men, including Granny, stood about in stockings. Early's eyebrow, like a startled caterpillar, arched.

Granny, with his back to the others, whispered, "Part of the rules of shiva."

Early gestured at his boots.

Granny shook his head. "You're not a Jew." Then he hauled over two hard chairs and put them next to the chairs where the Silverbergs had been sitting.

"Come," Granny said, motioning for Early and Thelma to sit

down, then the others. "I want you to notice the sheriff's new Levis. He buys all his trousers here. So, gentlemen, if you feel you are in need, before you leave. . . ."

Laughter moved about the room, Granny, the affable host, grinning in response. He leaned down to Early and slipped him a note card, whispering, "Read this to the Silverbergs."

Early studied the words, his eyebrows pinching together.

"I'm sorry. That's Yiddish," Granny said. "The other side."

Early turned the card over. He read it aloud, with care. "May the Almighty comfort you among the mourners of Zion and Jerusalem."

Mishka Silverberg, a bespectacled man with thinning hair, squeezed his wife's hand. "Thank you," he said.

Granny whispered to Early, "Traditional greeting at shiva."

The sheriff's lips formed an *o*, and he put the card in his jacket pocket.

The host looked around the room. "Shiva is a time for sharing. Thelma, you taught with Judith. Perhaps there is something from the time you two worked together that you'd like to tell Mishka and Ethel."

Thelma squirmed on the hard chair. She tugged at her skirt.

Missus Silverberg, slim as her daughter had been and wearing wire-framed glasses similar to her husband's, reached for Thelma's hand. "Please. It would mean so much to us."

"Well, I suppose. Let me see." Thelma put her hand to her face as her mind turned back time. "There are so many things, but maybe this one. Last year, one of Judith's students came down with scarlet fever. When you teach three classes, your hands are full, but every afternoon, Judith went by the girl's house with her lessons. They worked together into the evening for almost four months so she wouldn't fall behind and have to repeat the year. Missus Silverberg, Judith loved to teach. She loved children."

"And Isaac—her boy, our grandson?"

"Oh, she was so proud of him. But I can tell you he was all boy. He was a handful."

"Bill won't let us see him, except for the few moments at the funeral," Missus Silverberg, said, a harshness in her tone. "He's our grandson for God's sake."

"Now Mother," Mister Silverberg said.

"Mishka, it's not right. There's something not right."

"Ethel, he's lost his wife. We can't imagine the pain. So what if he makes a wrong decision?"

"I've lost my daughter. What of my pain? I will not let that Gentile stand between me and my daughter's child—Isaac, my grandchild."

"Now Mother—"

"Don't 'now Mother' me." She turned away, the handkerchief in her hand going to her eyes.

"Ethel," Granny said, "there are some things we cannot control. Maybe we should have a little something to eat. Everybody, please, come to the kitchen."

The women rose, except for Missus Silverberg, and moved with dispatch. The men shambled after, most stopping to chat with Early before they moved on. Mister Renneberg, the last, asked, "Have anything that will tell us who did this terrible thing?"

Early put his arm around the old man's shoulders. "Sam, I wish I could say yes."

"Nothing, huh?"

"Now I didn't say that."

"So then you do have something."

"I didn't say that either."

"Well, sheriff, you can't have it both ways."

"Sam, we've got some ideas, and that's all we've got. Until we've got some proof, I can't talk about it."

"So you think it was Bill."

"I didn't say that."

Renneberg looked up at Early, hound-dog sadness filling his face. "Sheriff, it's gonna be hard to vote for you come next election."

He went on, and Granny swung in beside Early. He ushered him along, after Renneberg. "Jimmy, I don't envy you your job."

"There are times I don't have much envy for it either."

As they passed through the doorway, one of the women handed Early a plate on which resided a hard-boiled egg shucked from its shell, a handful of chickpeas, and something that looked like a doughnut only it didn't have any sugar on it.

Granny saw the quizzical look. "That's a bagel. It's a kind of boiled bread."

Early salted the egg, then took a bite from it. From across the kitchen, Thelma pushed through with her own plate and two cups of coffee, one she handed to her husband.

"Isn't this wonderful?" she asked.

"I guess." Early tore a bite from the bagel and chewed. "Bread's kinda tough."

"No no no, Jimmy," Thelma said, "everything on your plate, it's round."

"So?"

"Husband mine, there's symbolism here. Ethel was telling me the egg is fertility, the renewal of life in the face of death. The chickpeas and the bagel, they're circular—the never-ending cycle of life and death and life again."

Early forked up a mouthful of chickpeas. "Least these aren't bad."

"Jimmy—"

"Hey, if it's food, I eat it."

"It's not just food." Thelma pulled on Early's sleeve. He

leaned down, and she burred in his ear, "Sometimes you are so dense."

Granny chuckled. "And thus endeth the lesson for today," he said.

The locals made their good-byes. They rattled down the inside stairs and out to the street to their cars, leaving behind three women—Thelma, Esther, and Ethel Silverberg—clustered around the sink, washing and drying dishes, Granny and Mishka Silverberg hunched together in a corner, visiting, and Early alone at the table, salting a fourth egg, wondering how the hell he was going to ask the questions that had been plaguing him.

Granny pushed Mister Silverberg toward a chair next to Early and took another for himself. "Looks like something's working on your mind," he said.

Early dabbed his egg at some stray grains of salt on his plate. "I s'pose."

"What is it?"

He turned to Silverberg. "The more I dig into this, the more I realize how little I know about your daughter. She served in the war?"

"Yes, Judith joined the Army to drive ambulances. Mother and I were opposed to it. We felt it was too dangerous." Silverberg took a Meerschaum from one side pocket and a pouch of Prince Albert from the other. He packed the pipe's bowl with tobacco. "I understand you and your lovely wife are expecting a child."

"Yes."

"You will find, Mister Early, that a time will come when that child does what he or she wants to do despite your desires. You can either argue endlessly or you can give him or her your blessing, then ask God to watch out for your child. That's what we did with Judith. Were you in the war?"

"Infantry."

Silverberg struck a match. He put the flame to the tobacco and sucked on the stem of his pipe. He blew a cloud of cherry-scented smoke toward the ceiling. "You came home all right?"

"Pretty much."

"He has a leg full of shrapnel," Granny said.

"Sorry."

Early turned up the palm of his hand as he shrugged. "Still I was lucky. And after the war for your daughter?"

"She caught the fever."

"What fever?"

"The Zionist fever. Mister Early, we Jews have been wanderers for almost two thousand years, a people with no homeland of our own. The war ended and Judith and friends from Holland—Dutch Jews who had been in hiding—joined the exodus to Palestine. They went to establish the new Israel."

"I expect that was a bit more dangerous than driving an ambulance," Early said.

"More than a bit, but Mother and I know only snatches. Much of what Judith did that year she wouldn't talk about."

Early pulled a bagel apart. He dunked half in his coffee. "Not bad this way," he said. "You think she made enemies who would want to harm her?"

"The Jews who sneaked into Palestine had enemies all around them. But I can't imagine anyone would follow her here, not three years later."

"But wasn't she raising money for Israel here?"

"Yes, and a very persuasive fund-raiser." Silverberg chuckled. "Let me tell you, I would see this very wealthy man write a check to the XYZ fund and Judith would look at it with those great sad eyes of hers, and he'd write another check, and, if she didn't smile, he'd write a third. And then came that rich, warm, genuine smile that would thrill you to the very depths of your heart, that would tell you you had just done what God had wanted."

"Who should I be talking to?"

Silverberg took a long pull on his pipe. "You come to Kansas City, I can introduce you to some people."

Early dunked the second half of his bagel. "Mind if I ask what you do?"

"Like my daughter and your wife, I'm a teacher, only college—Eastern European history, not terribly exciting. My Ethel, she plays first-chair viola for the Kansas City Symphony. I'm afraid the only exciting thing we ever did was get out of Vienna with little Judith before the brown shirts marched in."

"When was that?"

"Nineteen Thirty-Three. Seems like a lifetime ago."

"How old was Judith at the time?"

"Fourteen, I think. Fathers never remember these things."

"I never heard an accent."

"Oh, our Judith was so good at learning to speak American. A couple years and she sounded like every other teenage girl in our neighborhood. Ethel and I joked about it, we would introduce her as our American daughter."

The women, finished with putting dishes away, came to the table, Esther Weichselbaum with a pot of hot water. "Tea, anyone?" she asked. Only Ethel Silverberg raised a hand.

"Mother," Mishka Silverberg said, "Mister Early was asking about Judith's time in Palestine. Well, we can say Israel now. Judith was there when Mister Truman recognized our new nation. Mister Early, we can only wonder if he might not have done it had not his partner in the haberdashery been a Jew."

Ethel Silverberg sniffed. "Not likely. We are not a loved people, but you were asking about Judith in Israel." She reached for her husband's hand. "We know so little. Judith wrote only four letters during that year. In one, she told us of having been taken a prisoner with two others in an ambush."

"How did she escape?"

"She wrote that they did not search her boots. She had a knife, so she killed her guard. A terrible thing, but what more terrible things they might have done to her had she not?"

CHAPTER 9

August 26—Friday Morning
The Post

Trooper Plemmons swerved his cruiser over to the guard post at the east entrance to Fort Riley, the post a wooden structure in the middle of a boulevard flanked by limestone pillars. He touched his badge when the guard, a corporal in a well-pressed uniform, turned to him, a clipboard in hand.

"State trooper to see the commanding general," Plemmons said.

"You expected, sir?"

"No."

"You'll have to wait a moment then, sir." The guard waved an Army deuce-and-a-half through the entrance, then picked up a telephone receiver. While he talked to a distant presence, Plemmons spit a stream of tobacco juice into his empty Coke bottle.

"Hate these damn waits."

"That's the Army way," Early, his passenger, said.

The corporal put the receiver back in the bag of his field telephone. He turned to Plemmons. "The general's not in, sir, but if you'll drive on to HQ, the adjutant says he'll direct you to him. You know where HQ is?"

"Been there a time or two."

"Your name, sir, for my records?"

"Plemmons—P-L-E-M-M-O-N-S—corporal, Kansas State Police."

The guard leaned down. He looked through the window past Plemmons. "And your passenger, sir?"

"Early," Plemmons said, "spelled the normal way. Sheriff, Riley County."

"Thank you, sirs, another moment, please." The guard turned back to a desk in the post. He hand-stamped something and handed it to the trooper. "Put that on your dashboard, sir. That pass will get you around. Return it on your way out, sir."

Plemmons saluted and drove on. "Kid can't be more than nineteen, and we're trusting the safety of our nation to him?"

Early took off his sunglasses. He cleaned them as the cruiser rolled along, past manicured hills, the grass mowed so evenly Early could picture a ground-pounder measuring each blade with a ruler. And no clippings left behind to detract from the appearance of regulation neatness.

"You were probably his age when you went in," Early said.

"No, twenty-four. You?"

"Two years older."

"I'm tempted sometime to blow past him on lights and siren, just to see him mess his pants."

"Dan'l, he'd have the MPs all over you."

"Not before I gave them a merry chase. I got a V-Eight, and all they've got are those dinky four-cylinders in their Jeeps."

The road ahead split. Plemmons slapped his clicker down and bore left. After he and Early passed through a meadow, they topped a rise. Before them laid an expanse of limestone buildings, each one story and long as a football field.

"Horse barns when this was a cavalry post," Plemmons said. "You can almost smell them. I tell you, it had to be something to see a thousand soldiers lead their horses out for morning parade and mount up."

Early hooked the bows of his clean glasses back over his ears. "I did, a couple times before the war."

"The heck you say."

"Dan'l, I grew up not ten miles from here. My dad raised horses for the Army."

"And you went in as infantry?" Plemmons pushed his clicker up and aimed his cruiser toward another cluster of limestone buildings, these two- and three-stories tall. He parked in a slot marked "visitor" in front of the most imposing of the buildings, an American flag and a unit flag for the First Division—the Big Red One—flying from poles at either side of the entrance, the flags limp in the breezeless morning air.

Plemmons and Early left the cruiser. They shambled up the walk, Early in his wrinkled tans, a contrast to the trooper in his pressed uniform and his campaign hat worn regulation square.

A full colonel trotted down the front steps, his hand out. "Daniel, good to see you. If you'd called ahead, you wouldn't have had to wait at the guard shack."

"Not a problem. Steve, this here civilian is James Early, sheriff of Riley County. You know him?"

"Haven't had the pleasure," the colonel said, Davidson on the nameplate over his breast pocket. He shook hands with Early.

Davidson turned back to Plemmons. "The corporal said you want to see the Old Man. Mind if I ask what it's about?"

"You heard about the murder of the schoolteacher up by Leonardville?"

"Read it in the paper."

"We've got reason to think the doer might be here on the post."

"Oh shit."

"We're going to need the general's help."

Davidson, hands on his hips, kicked an imaginary stone away from the edge of the sidewalk. "Daniel, he's in a sour mood. Just got word the division's budget's been cut, that we may be losing one, maybe two companies of men and equipment. He's not going to like this. . . . Well"—the adjutant gestured to a squad of horse cavalry cantering across the parade ground that fronted on the headquarters' buildings—"that's him on the white charger, out there with his boys, shaping them up for a ceremony this weekend."

Early nudged Plemmons. "He's got a saber. You sure you want to do this?"

"I'll take you over," Davidson said. He stepped out at a quick pace that took the trio across the road and onto the parade ground. A quarter of the way out, they stopped and watched the general drill his color guard. "I've got an old sergeant who does this, but when the general's mad at the world, he orders his horse saddled and tells the sergeant to go suck coffee for the morning."

The unit moved with precision, wheeling on command, the four horsemen of the color guard and their mounts moving as one, flowing seamlessly from a walk to a canter to a full gallop and back. The unit rode by the three men on foot. One rider— two stars on his hat—peeled off and trotted his horse up to Davidson.

"They're looking good, general," Davidson said.

"Nothing like being chewed out by the Old Man to shape them up." The rider, ramrod straight, rested his reins hand on the pommel of his saddle. His face, with not a hint of a smile upon it, showed age and a confidence in his authority, yet the man ignored the civilians and continued to watch his color guard. "Custer, if he was alive, would be proud to have these men riding with him. . . . Who ya got here, Steve?"

"Trooper Plemmons and Sheriff Early. There's something pressing they have to talk to you about, the murder of that civilian last week."

The general swiveled toward the intruders. "Spill it. I'm listening."

Plemmons took a scrap of paper from his pocket. He glanced at it, not because he needed to see anything on it, but for effect. "You got an officer on your post, a colonel whose wife died a couple years ago, he's got a little boy?"

"Yes."

"His name Taggert?"

"Seth Taggert, that's right. Commands one of my artillery companies. What's this about?"

Plemmons put the paper back in his pocket. "We need to talk to him."

"Not 'til I get some details."

Early, listening, shifted his weight. "General," he said, "we have reason to believe your Colonel Taggert is involved in the murder."

"Sonuvabitch. All right, let's hear the reasons."

Early sucked in a lungful of air. "He had an affair with the murdered woman."

"That doesn't mean beans. What else you got?"

"It's enough for a start. We'll know more after you order him to talk to us."

"Not gonna happen. You bring me some real proof and I'll have the sonuvabitch up on charges in my own court."

"But this is a civilian matter," Early said.

"Look, the colonel's my boy. You don't like it? Write your congressman." The general rammed his spurs into his horse's flanks and rode off at a full gallop toward his color guard.

Davidson turned to Early and Plemmons. "I told you he was in a sour mood. I could order my inspector general to make a discrete investigation . . . keep it from the general."

"And your inspector'll paper it over," Plemmons said. He squared off in front of the adjutant. "Worse, the general will transfer Taggert to Europe. I'm an old Marine and Cactus is former Army. We know how you guys play the game."

"He won't be transferred."

"The general's authority trumps yours."

"Dan, I can do things here."

"Huh-uh. The only one who can do something here with this matter is the general. You know it, and I know it."

"Dan—"

"No. This was a courtesy call, and I want you to tell the general that. And I want you to tell him the next calls he gets are going to be from the governor, two United States senators, and the biggest damn busload of newspapermen he's ever seen."

CHAPTER 10

August 26—Friday Afternoon
Scrimmage

"You really think you can get the governor in on this?" Early asked as Plemmons backed his cruiser out of the visitor slot.

"Oh yes, he's my uncle." Plemmons grinned, his grin as wide as morning. "First year I was a trooper, I was his driver. Absolutely hates the Army."

"Why?"

"He was a buck private when Patton was the commanding general here. Got his bee-hind kicked by Patton for some minor infraction. But I'll do one better than call Uncle Frank. Want to go for a ride tonight?"

Plemmons, at Early's request, dropped him off in front of Manhattan's Ranchers & Merchants Bank, the biggest bank in the county, a sterile place for all the wealth deposited there—marble lobby housing four teller cages, each behind bulletproof glass and topped by barbed wire so no bandit could get at the tellers and their cash drawers, behind the tellers the bank's safe, to the side a plain wooden desk behind which sat a secretary and, behind her, the doors to two offices, the bank president's and the head teller's—the men who handled the bank's loans and investments. Early headed for the desk.

"Marvelle," Early said in a greeting to Miss Marvelle Old-strum, a handsome woman who had guarded access to the bank president for as long as he could remember.

She looked up from something she was typing. "Sheriff."

"Is old Hi in?"

"And in what reference might this call be? Want to open an account or are you needing a loan?"

Early chuckled at that one. He did his banking at Randolph. "Just social," he said.

"I'll see if Mister Dodds will see you." She left her desk, walked less than five paces across the marble floor to a door with frosted glass, the gold lettering on the glass reading HIRAM DODDS, PRESIDENT. She opened the door, said something, and turned back to Early. "Mister Dodds says he will be pleased to see you."

Early peeled off his hat as he went around Marvelle's desk and on into the bank president's office, the door closing behind him before he could reach back to close it. "Hi," he said, extending his hand.

Hiram Dodds came around his massive walnut desk and, like a car salesman, pumped Early's hand, his face alight with an immense smile that showed well his highly polished teeth, one to the side capped with silver. "Jimmy, you don't get here often enough," he said. "Come on and sit with me on my couch."

To the side stood a leather couch that could accommodate the bottoms of four hefty men, but of greater interest to Early was a wildcat crouching on a shelf above the couch, looking as if it intended to pounce on anyone who came near.

Dodds noticed. "Got him last fall over in Geary County, didn't you know that? Bank client over there said the cat was spooking his cattle, so he and I went hunting, and I bagged him. By weight and his height at his shoulders, the conservation department people tell me that wildcat's the biggest one on record."

Early eased onto the couch. As much as he tried not to, he

still glanced up at the cat.

"Jimmy," Dodds said as he sat down, "I can assure you that one's quite dead. If he wasn't, don't you think he'd have eaten me by now?"

"Wildcat, huh?"

"Yup."

"Well, they are best when they are dead."

"As an old cowboy you understand that. So how social is this visit?" Dodds took two cigars from a humidor on a side table and offered one to Early.

Early studied the stogie. "This is not like the White Owls I get down at the drugstore. If you don't mind, I'll save this—give it to a judge who will appreciate its quality."

He slipped the cigar into his shirt pocket while Dodds flicked open a Ronson desk lighter. Dodds put the flame to his own cigar and puffed away, getting a good burn going. He expelled smoke between each puff, changing the hue of the air in the office.

"Hi," Early said, "you wouldn't by chance be holding the paper on Bill and Judith Smitts's house?"

The banker tapped some ash into a silver tray on the side table. "Shame, isn't it? She was a nice person. Her death's really destroyed Bill's life."

"I expect it has. . . . But the paper?"

"You know I don't like discussing the business of my bank's customers, but yes, I hold the mortgage." Dodds blew smoke from the side of his mouth as he glanced at Early. "You already know that, don't you? You checked with the registrar of deeds."

"Hi, as near as I can tell you loaned Bill and Judith the full value of the house. Bankers don't do that."

"Might as well know I also increased their loan so they could buy the new car."

"You'd never get that by a bank examiner, not without hav-

105

ing some kind of collateral beyond the house and the car."

"How about five thousand dollars in a savings account?"

Early's eyebrows rose.

"I told Bill to make the loan work, I had to have something to fall back on if he failed to make his payments. Next day, he gave me five thousand dollars—cash, mind you, not a check— and promised not to draw on it until the day he could burn his mortgage."

"Were you curious where he got the money?"

"I'm not curious where anybody gets the money as long as they deposit it in my bank. Why are you so interested?"

"Oh, I don't know. But I'm going to ask you one favor."

Dodds sucked on his cigar.

"You handle most of the property sales your bank finances. If Bill asks you to sell his house, I want you to call me."

"And why should I do that?"

"May come a day you might want a favor."

Early strolled away from the Ranchers & Merchants wondering what he had learned. Why would anyone borrow a pile of money when he already had a pile? And where did the pile come from? Smitts hadn't worked for the U-P all that many years, and Judith's teaching check wasn't much. At the corner he crossed the street to the courthouse and went on to the side entrance where he found Pop Irving waiting on the liars' bench, feeding the squirrels.

"You sure got a like for the critters," Early said as he ambled up.

"They're free like me." Irving shucked a peanut. He tossed it out on the grass. "Why'dja ask me to come by? I'm not in trouble, am I?"

"You like football?"

"It's moderately interesting, though I don't profess to

understand it. Baseball, that's what I played as a kid. Not half bad."

"Nice afternoon like this, let's go up to the college and watch some football."

"Be all right." Irving jerked his head to the side, several vertebrae in his neck crackling like popcorn. He shuffled to his feet and gathered his bedroll from where he had left it at the side of the bench. "So whatcha been doin', Jimmy?"

"Oh, not a lot," Early said as they strolled around back to the parking lot where Early had left his Jeep. "Been out at Fort Riley to ask a few questions. You've heard about the murder in our county?"

"Talk o' the jail. You tellin' me someone out at the fort had something to do with it?"

"It's possible. Pop, at this point anything's possible."

Irving fitted himself into the passenger seat of the sheriff's Jeep, Early slipping in behind the steering wheel. He fired up the engine and rolled the one-time war machine out onto the side street and away, north to Bluemont and west to K-State, Irving riding at ease in the warmish air of late summer swirling about him.

"Reminds me of the time you an' me rode across Nebraska on top of them boxcars," Irving said. "It was a beautiful day."

"Thank God we had the sense to jump off before we got to Lincoln."

"Yup. The bulls was waitin' fer us. They thumped our buddies in the yard."

Early turned in at the graveled parking lot beside Kansas State's low-slung stadium built from cut limestone, the stadium's walls rising up into medieval battlements. Spectators could sit in the bleachers and imagine knights on horseback jousting before crowds from the king's court. The crowd this day was a rag-tag collection of students, Early guessed from their looks, with a scattering of somewhat better-dressed adults among them. He guided Irving across to the west side, to put the sun at their backs.

As they settled in, three rows up from the grass, someone walloped Irving. The blow whanged off the back of his head and knocked Early's hat away as it swept on.

"Why you bring that old man here?" a woman bellowed, her face red, mouth snapping into a harsh line.

Irving, a hand clasped over the back of his head, spun around before Early could recover his hat. "Ella? My, gawd, woman, it's a free country."

"T'aint free with you around."

Ella Irving launched herself at her husband's throat. He went over backward, down two bleachers with her on top of him, the tangle startling a number of spectators, horrifying others.

Early jumped after them. He got hold of the woman's shoulders, but she again swung her massive purse. Irving twisted away and the blow carried on to Early, whacking him in the side of his face.

"Ella, that's enough!" Early, staggering, hauled the woman back, and Irving scrambled out of her reach. "You looking to get arrested?"

"After what he did to me, you ought to arrest him."

"That's in the past. This is now."

"Not to me it isn't," Ella said, her eyes narrowing as she studied Early. "I come to watch my son play some football. If you're gonna let that mean old man stay, I'm leavin'. I'm going home."

She wrenched at the seat of her dress, straightening her hemline, then stomped down off the bleachers and away up the sideline.

Irving held out a shaking hand. "You gonna let her do what she done to me?"

"Don't you think you deserved it just a little?" Early touched his ear. "Think I took the worst. Can't hear too well."

He clambered back up into the bleachers and settled himself, gingerly feeling around his ringing ear. "Pop, get your butt up here and sit down before I arrest you just for something to do."

"I didn't do nuthin'."

"I don't care. Get back here."

Below, a gaggle of players charged onto the field. They ran toward the long bench in front of Early and Irving. And then came another gaggle, heading for the bench on the opposite side of the field.

Irving tapped Early's knee. "What's goin' on?"

"A scrimmage. It's a bunch of K-Staters who want to make varsity."

One of the players twisted around. He saw Early and waved up to him, and Early waved back.

"Know him, do ya?" Irving asked.

"Yup. He's your son."

The old man said nothing. He made a business of looking away.

"You gonna say something to him, Pop?" Early asked as he turned his attention to the bandage beneath his pant leg. He scratched around its edges.

"What do ya want me to say?"

"I don't know. I'm the man who made you, maybe?"

Irving turned back from his inspection of the several clouds in the quadrant of sky south of the stadium. "I wouldn't of known him if ya hadn't of pointed him out. He was just a tyke when last I seen him. Good lookin' fella, though, huh?"

"Cuts a swath with the girls, his sister tells me. Of course, Ronnie doesn't talk about it."

Irving nodded. "That's good. Some things a man ought to keep to himself."

The blue team—the team in front of Early and Irving—trotted out onto the field. They lined up to receive the kickoff, the one Irving now knew as his son in the front, toward the center of the formation. The gold team moved out to the other end of the field, on the forty-yard line. They held and waited, watching one of their players standing back on the thirty.

A whistle released the gold player. He ran forward, toward the center of his line and the football. He kicked it high. Early followed the ball, but not Irving. He watched his son squat, then spring forward low and uproot a gold player racing his way. His son rolled to the side and knocked another gold man from his feet, wheeled and raced forward, ahead of the player who caught the ball. He rammed his shoulder into another gold man, careening him toward the sideline, and ran on hard, throwing himself into a flying block that tripped a fourth.

Irving came up on his feet. He sucked his teeth, his face sheathed in worry. "He all right?"

The play moved on down the field, but Early ignored it. He, too, watched Ronnie Irving, watched him push himself up, watched him pull off his helmet and run a hand over his head, watched other players in blue jerseys run up and pound him on the back.

Early clapped Irving's shoulder. "Pop, if he can tackle the way he blocks, I'd bet the coach pulls him up to the varsity."

But neither the blue team nor the gold team repeated the spectacular opening play. They ground on one another, lines swaying forward one play, falling back the next, resulting in turnovers and short kicks that ended in fumbles. Irving picked at the threads in his bedroll each time his boy went down. "This sure don't look like much fun," he said.

A whistle blew and both teams backed away from the line.

"What's that about?" Irving asked.

"End of the first quarter." Early pointed across the way. "The

teams change ends of the field."

"But they're goin' off to the sides."

"Well, it's a water break too."

"How much longer is this thing?"

"Another three quarters, maybe forty-five minutes."

"We gotta stay fer all of it?"

"No," Early said, "but after what I've been through, let's watch a couple more minutes. Your boy might break open a play."

As the two teams walked back out onto the field, to the opposite thirty-seven-yard line and hunkered down for the snap of the ball, a man in a cowboy hat in the bleachers opposite Early and Irving worked his way down to the field, to where the gold cheerleaders stood waiting for the play to begin. He picked up a megaphone. The man aimed it across the field and bellowed, "Hey, sheriff!"

Early turned. He saw the man with the megaphone waving his hat at him, grinning.

"Sumbitch."

Early pushed between two people sitting in front of him, then hopped from the bleachers to the grass. He leaped across the blue bench and raced out onto the field, pursuing the figure making his way up the bleachers on the opposite side. Early didn't hear the roar of the crowd, people yelling, nor did he see the football thrown his way. Running all out he found himself in a swirl of players trampling by, and him scrambling across the current, spinning, dodging, getting slammed by a passing gold or was it a blue man? Early lost his hat but raced on free. He hurdled the gold bench and clambered up through the bleachers, people parting as if they were the Red Sea. Midway, Early saw the man go over the top of a battlement and disappear.

He pounded on up the bleachers. At the top, his chest heaving, Early looked over the outside wall and saw Sonny Estes

sliding down a rope.

When Estes hit the ground, he gazed up, hollering, "Hey sheriff, ain't this fun?" and hurtled off.

Early yanked down a banner. He wrapped his hands in it, grabbed the rope Estes had used, and kicked over the side and out, the rope ripping at the banner's fabric and his hands as he slid down. Early hit the sod hard. His knees buckled, and he went down, rolling, holding his hands out, his fingers curled, burning. Early forced himself up. He tore a bicycle away from a collection leaning against the stadium wall and pedaled off in the direction he'd seen Estes run. *Why wasn't the sumbitch hurting?*

And then it hit Early as he pedaled on. The bastard had gloves!

A car horn sounded. Early swerved and his front wheel struck the curb, somersaulting him. He came down on his wounded shin and rolled once more, clutching his knee to his chest.

Someone put a hand on Early's shoulder.

"You all right?" came a voice cutting through his pain.

Early forced his eyes open. "Sonny?"

Estes patted Early's shoulder. "Yer all right if you kin recognize me, old pard."

"Sumbitch."

"Aw, now don't get upset on me. Somebody be by to hep ya, meantime you excuse me. I gotta skedaddle." Estes pushed himself up and away. He grabbed a passing student, pointed him at Early. "Man needs help," he said and dashed into the street where he grabbed the slats of a passing freight truck. Estes pulled himself aboard. And he waved his hat at the sheriff one last time.

CHAPTER 11

August 26—Friday Evening
Suppertime

"Cactus, what the hell were you doing, sliding down a rope?" Doc Grafton asked as he daubed a disinfecting solution over the burns on Early's hands.

"Trying to catch a bank robber."

"Was it worth it? Look what you did to yourself."

"Wasn't thinking."

"That's for damn sure, and you an old cowboy who ought to know a bean or two about working with rope." Grafton brought out a sterile pad. He dabbed the solution away. "Look, I'm being hard on you so your lovely wife won't have to."

Thelma glanced over from where she sat at the side of Grafton's inner office, aimlessly turning the pages of a Saturday Evening Post. "Doc, I'm going to ding him and dent him good when I get him home. Can you imagine what that call did to me?"

"I've got an idea."

"Alice telling me a city police car brought Jim to you, telling me I'd better get in here, and me carrying his child?"

"And now you found out there wasn't much worth getting upset about. Your old bonehead of a husband here will heal up pretty well." Grafton went to a shelf in a side cabinet. He brought back a small jar, opened it, and patted some of the contents over the burns. "Stinks a bit like a mouse had crawled

113

in the back of your kitchen cabinet and died, but it's good stuff—a silver oxide salve."

"Wouldn't butter do as well?" Early asked, his nose wrinkling. He sneezed.

"Bless you, my son. Bad business, butter. Got salt in it."

"And until his hands do heal?" Thelma asked, interrupting.

"Old Cactus is going to find it a mite difficult to button and unbutton his pants." Grafton brought out a roll of gauze. He began the tedious process of wrapping the sheriff's hands.

"Can I say something?" Early asked.

"A smart man wouldn't." Grafton went to humming as he continued his ministrations. After he finished tying off the gauze, he hauled up on Early's pant leg. Grafton fingered around the bandage. "The patrolman said you were squalling about your leg. How'd you do this?"

"Went through a rotten step. Granny Weichselbaum patched me up."

Grafton peeled the bandage away and went to prodding in a serious manner.

Early grimaced.

"Pretty sensitive, huh?" Grafton asked.

"Yes. You have to do that?"

"Scabbed over, that's good. Bandage probably kept your shin from getting tore up worse when you came down on it. . . . Got a bruise that'll go black on you. Cactus, you're damn lucky you didn't break your leg." Grafton rummaged in the drawer beneath his examining table for a large gauze pad. He found one, tore it out of its sterile packaging, and laid the pad over Early's damaged shin. "Thelma, a couple days you throw this bandage away and let the skin heal in the air."

Early winced at the pain of Grafton slapping an adhesive strip across the pad. "You this rough on all your patients?"

"Aww, Cactus, everybody calls me 'the kindly old doc.' " He

slapped down a second strip. "That'll hold ya. . . . Thelma, get him back in here next week. I want to look at those hands."

"Anything I should do for him?"

Grafton went back to rummaging in his drawer. "We learned a few things about burns in the war. His aren't serious. I'd massage the tissues every night, make him work his fingers. It's going to hurt and he's going to complain something awful, but I want his fingers and hands flexible."

He brought out two packages of rolled gauze and several sterile pads. Grafton gave them to Thelma, and the disinfectant and the silver oxide.

"After you give his hands a workout, clean the burns like I did, then salve him up, but just a light coating. You're not basting a turkey." He gazed at Early, grinning at him. "Or maybe you are."

"Anything else?" Thelma asked.

"Wrap his hands in the morning. It's just a little protection, but at night, I want his hands unwrapped. Air and rest are the best healers. A shot of whiskey would help him sleep."

Early gazed up from studying the wrappings on his hands. "I'll skip that part."

"The whiskey or the sleep?"

"The whiskey."

"Your choice, Cactus. I'm only the doctor here."

Early held up his hands. "Thanks for what you've done."

"Yeah, well, why don't you get on out of here, so I can see me some paying customers?"

Early leaned on the stair rail as he limped down the front steps of Grafton's office to the sidewalk, Thelma coming along beside him.

"You can lean on me, Jimmy," she said.

"No, no, I gotta make my own way."

Gangly Hutch Tolliver, made taller by his tall Big-brim Alpine Stetson, waited for them at the end of the walk. The deputy pushed himself off the fender of his Jeep where he had parked his frame. "You all right, chief?" he asked.

"Guess so. The doc didn't take me out back and shoot me."

Tolliver helped Thelma into the backseat, then waited while Early struggled into the front. "Office or home?" Tolliver asked.

"Home," Thelma said before Early could open his mouth.

"Right it is." Tolliver hustled around to the driver's side. After he got the engine started and the Jeep rolling, he took down the microphone that swung from the mirror at the top of the windshield. "Alice," he said, pressing the transmit button.

"Go ahead."

"I'm taking the boss and Thelma out to Keats."

"He all right?"

"He's done with foot races and steer rassling for awhile."

Thelma touched Tolliver's shoulder as he turned the Jeep onto Anderson and headed out into the country and the Wildcat Valley, toward Keats some five miles out. "Tell Alice nobody's to call him tonight."

Tolliver pressed his transmit button again. "Alice?"

"Go ahead."

"Put up a note for the night dispatcher, would you? Nobody's to call the sheriff tonight. Call me instead."

"You get kind of owly when people wake you."

"I'll take my sweetness pills before I go to bed."

After they were well out into the valley's farming country, Early leaned in to Tolliver. "You find Pop Irving?"

"Vanished, just like Sonny Estes."

"He can travel when he has to. Maybe he'll come back to the jail tonight for a free sleep."

"I'll have Benny call me if he shows up."

"That'd be good."

Early fumbled with his knife as he attempted to cut the slab of beef roast on his plate.

"You want me to do that for you?" Thelma asked when she came by with a cup of coffee for him.

"No, I can do it." Earl sawed away. Then the knife slipped and the fork right after it, the implements scooting the beef off the plate and onto the table.

Thelma set the cup in front of Early. Then, with his knife and fork, she hauled the meat back on his plate where, with a practiced hand, she diced it. "Would it hurt you so much to let people help you? Goodness gracious, James Early. Stubborn? You're worse than the mule my father had. Know what happened to him?"

"Your father?"

"The mule, knothead. Dad sent him to the glue factory."

"You gonna do that with me?"

"It's tempting." Thelma raked the dozen bite-sized chunks together before she held the fork out to Early. He took it and stabbed a piece of beef into his mouth. Early chewed in silence.

Thelma took her seat across the table. She peered into his face after she picked up her own cup of coffee. She cradled it in her hands. "James Early, I have to teach my little kids to say thank you. Do I have to teach you?"

"Huh? . . . I'm sorry. Look, my hands hurt, my leg hurts, I can't hear all too well, I'm just not thinking too good."

"We can agree on that. So are you going to say thank you?"

Early released a lungful of air. His chin dropped to his chest. After a long moment, he peeked up and a thank you slipped from between his lips.

Thelma blew on her coffee, cooling it. "Didn't kill you, did it?"

"No. . . . Would you turn on the radio for the news? I can't do it with these fingers."

Thelma ignored him and went about ladling gravy into a depression in her mashed potatoes.

"Well?" Early asked.

"A companion word to thank you is please." Thelma set the gravy bowl aside. She picked up a slice of raisin bread.

"All right, please?"

She swiveled around to the Zenith on the kitchen counter. "That didn't kill you either, did it?" Thelma said as she twiddled the knobs. "The Friendly Neighbor's off the air. How about WIBW?"

"That'd be fine."

A crackle of static came from the speaker as she dialed in on the Topeka frequency, then a voice. *And now from New York, Lowell Thomas with the news* . . . A second voice followed. *Good evening, everybody* . . .

"I like him," Early said. "He's an old Colorado boy. Did you know that?"

"No." Thelma went to buttering her slice of bread.

"World traveler. Back in the first war, he traipsed off into the Arabian desert and found that English fella, Lawrence, leading an army of nomads against the Turks. Became a big story."

"Jimmy, you aren't that old."

"I read about it. We had Thomas's book in our high school library."

. . . *In Washington today, President Truman met with a delegation from the nation of Israel* . . .

"That reminds me," Early said, waving his fork toward the radio, "you found Judith's diaries, a stack covering her growing up and school years and teaching time. Where are the books covering her time in the war and in Palestine? Were the books numbered?"

Thelma set her knife aside. "No."

"If she was such a dedicated diarist, she wouldn't quit at such an important time in her life, would she?"

"So you think we're missing some books?"

"Gotta be."

"Could someone have taken them?"

"Why wouldn't they have taken them all?" Early leaned back in his chair. He massaged a sideburn as his mind churned. "What could have been so important in those books that someone would want them?"

"One thing's sure, Sherlock, you're not going to figure it out tonight, so finish your supper."

"No. No, my dad saved every letter I wrote home during the war. I didn't think they were much and my mother didn't either, but my dad kept them. When I came home, he brought out this box he'd made—polished walnut, tooled leather hinges—and he opened it and brought out all those letters for me to see. He even kept a scrapbook of stories he cut out of the Kansas City Star that took place where he thought I was. And he had this map of Europe where he marked when I was in this country and that. He had a real history there."

"I'd like to see that."

"You ask him, he'll bring it out. . . . Where's Judith's history?"

Headlights flashed up into the hackberry tree in the backyard as someone drove in.

"Who could that be?" Thelma asked when she saw the lights wink out. A neighbor's dog set to yapping. "Got to be a stranger for Huddy to go off like that."

Then came the sound of boots striding across the back-porch floor, and a sharp rapping at the doorjamb.

Thelma left the table. She flicked on the porch light.

The man on the other side of the screen door snatched off his campaign hat. "Trooper Plemmons," he said. "Cactus here?"

"Yes, but we're having supper."

"Kind of late for that, isn't it?"

"Well, this has been a very odd day, but come in." Thelma opened the door for the trooper. She stepped back, and Plemmons came in, blinking in the brighter light of the kitchen.

"Would you like coffee, maybe have some pie with us?"

"No thanks. I ate pretty hefty a couple hours ago, and coffee'd give me problems I don't need tonight. . . . Cactus," Plemmons said in greeting Early, "you ready to do it?"

Early pushed his chair back. When he struggled up, Plemmons gestured at the bandaged hands.

"Oh, it's nothing much," Early said.

"Somehow I don't believe that."

"Well, believe it." He pulled down his hat from where it hung next to the door.

Thelma put her hand on Early's arm. "Jimmy, you're not going out."

"I'm just going to ride with the trooper. I'd promised him."

"Gonna show him how we state police do traffic stops," Plemmons said.

"I won't have this, Jimmy."

"Look, this is a nothing thing."

"Then you can do it another time."

Early shrugged at Plemmons.

"I saw him at a bar in Junction City," the trooper said. "We could wait a week, but he might not be here in another week."

"He, who?" Thelma asked, moving into the doorway.

"The colonel Judith was seeing."

CHAPTER 12

August 26—Friday Night
The Traffic Stop

"Your bank robber?" Plemmons asked as he drove his cruiser through the Flint Hills, skirting the vast military reservation to the west. "How many times you gonna let the old boy get away?"

"Look, super trooper, I didn't plan it."

"Guess you didn't. Those hands of yours look to be pretty useless, so better hope young Mister Estes doesn't come trotting by where we're going to be."

Early squirmed in the shotgun seat. He glanced ahead into the light thrown forward by the cruiser's headlamps in time to see a skunk wander off the side of the road. "Watch—"

"I see him," Plemmons said. "I have no desire to get my car stunk up."

Early settled back. He twisted quarter to the trooper in the semidark of the cruiser's interior. "If Sonny does happen by, guess you'll have to catch him."

"I expect I will if I'm to save your reputation, which is getting about as tattered as your body."

Plemmons turned from the county road onto the main highway—US Eighteen—at Ogden and stepped down on the gas pedal. His cruiser ate up the miles as it rolled on to the southwest, toward the city—Junction City—that welcomed the soldiers from Fort Riley and the payday money they brought with them. Friday and Saturday nights, the Junction's main

121

street was thick with men in uniform, rambling from one establishment to the next. The city police and the post's MPs found business equally good and, on those nights, frequently filled their jails.

The trooper took his foot away from the accelerator when he topped a hill and the lights of the Junction opened out before him. At the bottom of the hill, he slowed and turned off onto a graveled side street, turned again, and parked under a maple tree, his car aimed out toward Eighteen. He cut the lights and the motor, then checked his watch in the glimmer coming from a street lamp on the corner.

"How much time we got?" Early asked.

"Oh, I'd say about ten minutes, assuming he's still there. The MPs ought to be making their rounds, telling everybody to close up." He rolled down his side window and stuck his elbow out.

Early worked at the handle on his side and did the same. With both windows open, the two officers of the law found themselves serenaded by a chorus of tree frogs.

"Little devils get kinda loud, don't they?" Plemmons said. He took a pouch of Red Man from his pocket and held it out to Early. "Have a chew?"

"You know I don't."

"Just being polite." The trooper stuffed a wad in his mouth. After he rolled the top closed, he put the pouch back in his pocket. "Want to listen to the radio?"

"You won't get much here."

"Never know. A night like this we ought to have some pretty good skip." Plemmons turned on his ignition, and the radio in his cruiser's dash. He rolled the tuner down toward the low numbers, where the fifty-thousand-watt stations were, catching a blip here and a burst of static there, then came a strong signal and big-band music, music that played on to a crescendo and applause.

That's the Benny Goodman Orchestra, said a voice from the radio's speaker, *and our concert under the stars, KCMO broadcasting from the Starlight Amphitheater in Swope Park.*

"Kansas City," Plemmons said. He spit a gob of tobacco juice out the window. "Tomorrow night, it's the symphony—Vivaldi. Wish I could be there."

"You like that stuff?"

"Cactus, you think I was a cowboy like you?"

"I just assumed."

"Look, you grew up with fiddles, I grew up with violins."

"I'll be damned."

Plemmons glanced at the traffic coming out on Eighteen, traffic passing under the street lamp. "Well, looky there. A black Ford."

"You really think that's him?"

"We'll find out when I get behind him and we see his license plate." The trooper flipped out a notebook and glanced at a number. He stepped on the starter button as he tossed the notebook aside. The engine roared and Plemmons rolled out into the intersection and the parade of vehicles moving toward the post.

"There's four ahead of you," Early said.

"Not to worry. I got a motor they don't have." Plemmons pressed the accelerator to the floor, and his cruiser's V-Eight responded, bellowing through cutouts that let him have maximum power. He swung into the passing lane, his attention on the cars as he shot by them, counting them . . . one . . . two . . . three . . .

"Truck ahead!" Early yelled, flailing a hand at headlights and an array of running lights looming up in the windshield.

Plemmons's mouth stopped in midchew. He tromped on the

brake pedal, throwing Early into the dash. Plemmons whipped the cruiser into the traffic lane, and the semi trundled by. He stepped down on the accelerator again, swung out around the fourth car, and held his speed while distant taillights grew. Plemmons slowed only when he came up within spitting distance of the black Ford's bumper.

" 'At's our boy. 'At's the license number." He flipped up the toggle switch for his bubble light, then popped his siren three times. Brake lights came on ahead of him.

"An honorable citizen. He's gonna stop." Plemmons slowed his cruiser as the car ahead slowed, and pulled off onto the gravel shoulder when the other car did.

"Watch how the big dogs do it," Plemmons said as he grubbed a long-barreled flashlight from beneath his seat. He stepped out and strolled forward, slowing enough to swing his flashlight at a taillight, and the taillight went out. Plemmons snapped his flashlight on as he continued up to the driver's window. There he shined his light in the driver's face. "Your license, please," he said.

Early opened his door. He slid off the seat and limped around to Plemmons's side of the cruiser, the bubble light rotating, its red light flashing across his back, the air smelling of exhaust coming from the rear of the black Ford. Early saw a hand come out of the driver's window, holding a wallet open. "I heard glass break," a voice said. "You bust my taillight?"

"Wouldn't think of it, sir," Plemmons said as he took the wallet. He put his light on it. "A colonel, huh? Name's Taggert I see. Sir, you ought to know better."

"What? I wasn't speeding."

"That you weren't, but you were running with one taillight, and you're drunk. I can smell liquor on you."

"A couple beers."

"Oh yes, I've heard that 'couple beers' stuff before. Step out here."

Plemmons moved back from the door. Again he held his light on the occupant as the man came out in Army tans and eagles on the collar points of his shirt.

The trooper studied the colonel, a bit shorter than he, thicker, and shoulders not quite as square as one expected of a military officer. "Having a little trouble standing, are we, sir?"

"Of course not."

"Turn around, sir, and face the car."

"This some kind of drunk test?" the man asked as he shuffled around, getting his back to Plemmons.

"Might call it that, sir. Put your hands behind you, please."

"Well, this is the damnedest—"

"That it is, sir."

Early saw the hands come out, and he watched Plemmons snap a pair of steel manacles around the man's wrists.

"What the hell you doing?" Taggert asked as he tried to twist around.

"Get your attention." Plemmons spun him the rest of the way. He slammed him back against the car and braced a forearm against the man's chest.

Taggert spit to the side. "I'll have your badge for this."

"Afraid not, your bird colonelship. You're not on the post. Out here you're on my state highway, and I've got the rank."

"Do I know you?"

"Yessir, you do. Trooper Daniel Plemmons. Met out at the Sunset Cemetery after the funeral for the Smitts woman, and that gimpy old man at the end of your car is Riley County Sheriff James Early."

"I'll have his badge too."

"Huh-uh," Plemmons said. "Not gonna happen. Last time we met, you didn't want to talk to us."

125

"Hell with you."

"Wrong thing to say, sir."

"You been in the military?"

"Gunnery sergeant, Marines. The sheriff an infantry corporal, last with the Big Red One in Germany. You get over there?"

"As a captain, yes." Taggert worked his face into a sneer. "Burns your butts, doesn't it, that neither of you two clods could get into the officer ranks."

"Sir, you're off the post. You're in civilian country. Careful what you say."

"You can't talk to me like this."

Plemmons leaned hard on the colonel's chest. "Sir," he said, an edge in his voice, "listen to me. If you have any desire to get home tonight, you talk to us."

Plemmons slammed the barrel of his flashlight down on the black Ford's roof, just to the right of Taggert, and the man flinched. Then Plemmons whipped his flashlight over the colonel's head and brought the barrel down a second time, on the other side of Taggert, grazing the man's arm before the flashlight sent paint chips flying from the car's roof. And again the colonel pulled away from the blow.

"We got an understanding now?" Plemmons asked. "If not, you smell that kind of rotten, garbagey smell? We got a swamp off here to the side of the road with a nice patch of quicksand in it, oh, about eight yards across. We march you into that, they'll never find your body."

The trooper again turned his light into Taggert's face, and Early saw fear.

"What do you want to know?" the colonel asked.

Plemmons, flushed, turned to Early. "What do we want to know, Cactus?"

Early hobbled up. "Colonel, Judith Smitts was pregnant. Is a blood test going to make that baby yours or her husband's?"

"Omigod."

"You didn't know?"

"It could be mine, but, no. No, I didn't know."

"You ask her to leave Bill?"

"Yes."

"And?"

"She wouldn't."

"That make you mad?"

"Yes. No."

Plemmons slammed the barrel of his flashlight onto the car's roof again.

"Yes," Taggert said, shrinking from the flashlight, "yes."

"You kill her?" Early asked.

"My God, no."

The sheriff studied Taggert, then turned to Plemmons. "You believe him?"

"Nope. I think he did it. Let's take the bastard out in the swamp and kick him in the quicksand."

"No trial?"

"Why waste the time?"

"Let him up," Early said. He leaned against the black Ford, his bandaged hands crossed at the wrists. "Colonel, you haven't made any friends here tonight. If you decide to ask for a transfer and skip, you will see how fast a U.S. senator from Kansas can get you yanked back here and into my jail. If we have an understanding, nod your head."

The colonel nodded, his head movement almost imperceptible.

Lights came along the highway from Junction City. As they neared, a bubble light flicked on, adding its sweep and rhythm to that of Plemmons's bubble light.

"Looks like we got company," Early said. "Cut him loose, Dan'l."

"Can't do that. He smells of booze. He's a danger to others on the road."

A vehicle pulled up beside the colonel's car, Plemmons, Early, and Taggert, a Jeep with MP markings. Someone in the passenger seat called out, "Trouble here?"

Plemmons turned to the voice. "You got that right," he said. "We stopped one of your boys, a Colonel Taggert. He's drunk. How about you drive him to his quarters?"

"We can do that."

An MP, a sergeant built like a wrestler, stepped out of the Jeep and into the light cast by the headlights of Plemmons's cruiser. He snapped to attention, bringing up a smart salute to Taggert. "Sir, Sergeant Russell. If you'll ride with my corporal, I'll drive your car back to the post for you."

Taggert mumbled something. Plemmons removed the handcuffs and nudged him toward the Jeep.

"Sergeant," the trooper said, "the colonel's car has a busted taillight."

"I noticed. I'll drive by the motor pool and have it fixed." He fingered the indentations in the roof, glancing at Early. "Something happen here?"

"How's that?" Early asked.

"These dents."

"Hail maybe. This is Kansas."

"Yes, sure." The sergeant slid in behind the steering wheel. "Does smell like a still in here. Sir? I didn't catch your name."

"Early, sheriff of Riley County."

"Well, thank you, sheriff, for stopping the colonel. We kinda keep an eye out for him. He's got a reputation for tipping a few too many."

The Jeep pulled away into the night, and the sergeant in the black Ford. Plemmons strolled up to Early standing in the glare of the cruiser's headlights, the bubble light still swirling away, the sound of it like someone grinding coffee beans. "What do you think?" he asked.

"Damn, you're rough as a cob."

"You don't tell anybody, I won't tell anybody. But I did get you some answers."

"Nothing that would warrant an arrest."

"Maybe, but I still like him for the deed."

"Dan'l, you're one suspicious sort."

"That's my job. That's where we're alike, Cactus, both of us damn good investigators."

Early turned toward the side of the road, the smell of the swamp, like cabbage moldering, more apparent as a breeze whispered in from that direction. "There really quicksand out there?"

"Yup."

"How do you know?"

Plemmons let off with a wicked laugh. "I've thrown a couple desperadoes out there. Of course, I had a rope on them at the time."

CHAPTER 13

August 26—Friday Night Late
Wasted Death

"You feel like a big man now?" Thelma asked as she laid the gauze-strip bandaging aside.

"I only asked a couple questions."

She manipulated and massaged Early's index finger. He ground his teeth.

"Can't you take it a little easy?" he asked.

"Doctor Grafton wants you to straighten your fingers. Now work with me." Thelma bent the finger back against the curvature it assumed after the rope had torn against the skin of Early's palms and fingers.

"Oh damn, it hurts."

"And I'm supposed to feel sorry for you? Come on, put your grit into it." She let off on the index finger and massaged the middle finger, sweat beading out on Early's forehead. "Your state trooper sure terrorized that colonel."

"Look, he didn't want to talk to us."

She pressed against the curvature of the middle finger, then attacked the next before he could cry out. "What he did was despicable."

"Bit extreme, maybe."

"You could have stopped him."

"I didn't let him throw the man in the swamp."

She pressed his pinky finger straight.

Early sucked wind. "Lord, woman, that's awful."

"Do you want help?"

"I suppose."

"Then don't get me upset. I'm pregnant." Thelma massaged at the thick muscles in Early's palm.

With his free arm, he raked the sweat from his forehead. "What's having a baby got to do with anything?"

"It makes some of us cranky."

"Ooo, I can attest to that."

"I want you to close your fingers into a ball, then straighten them."

Early, at the kitchen table, focused on his hand. He squeezed with all the effort he could muster, and his fingers moved together all of half an inch.

"Well, that's something," Thelma said. She glanced up into his face, her own features softening. "Now relax, then straighten your hand."

Early watched his fingers return to their clawlike curvature. Then he bore down. His hand shook as his fingers pulled against the curvature, not fully straight but something of a third of the way toward it.

"That's good for a first effort. Relax now, and let's work on your other hand."

"We gonna do this every night?"

"Every night for as long as it takes." Thelma unwound the wrapping on the hand that had avoided her attention. She examined the burns. "Jimmy, what you've done."

"Guess it's kinda like throwing a steer. You're committed once you start."

"I don't understand you," she said as she massaged one digit and then the next.

Early's jaw tightened. "Hon, ya know you're going to get beat up some, but if you let go, that steer's gonna kick your ribs in.

If I'd let go of the rope—"

"You'd have fallen, yes, I figured that out. Straighten that index finger."

"It don't wanna move."

Thelma pressed against the curvature.

"Oh jeez—"

"Buck up, mister."

She attacked the next finger and Early, his lips taut as cords, inhaled a world of air through his nostrils.

"You think he did it?" Thelma asked.

"Did what?"

She went after the third finger, massaging, straightening. "The colonel. You think he killed Judith?"

"Trooper Dan does, I don't." Early's eyes went large in response to the pain. "Heck of it is. . . . there's no proof either way."

Thelma went after the fourth finger, then his thumb and the palm of his hand, circles of sweat showing through Early's shirt beneath his armpits.

"You did good, Jimmy," she said as she spread on the cleaning fluid Grafton had given her. Thelma watched the fluid lift the salve out of the cracks and crevices of the burns, then dabbed the gunk away. She reached for the silver oxide, to reapply the ointment meant to hold down infection. "Wonder what your hands will look like when the scabbing comes off?"

"Probably not much different. Thel, these are rancher's hands. They been beat up for years. . . . What did you do while I was out?"

"Read Judith's diaries."

"And?"

She giggled. "I blushed."

"You? That's got my interest."

Thelma rubbed the silver oxide in but with a lighter, gentler touch.

"Feels good," Early said.

"Well, you earned a little care."

"And what was this embarrassing stuff you read?"

Thelma leaned back. "How can I put this?"

"Any way you want."

"Jimmy, you're not making this easy."

"Sorry."

"Um, sex . . ."

"Uh-huh."

"Quit grinning at me."

"All right."

"Jimmy, sex was a forbidden subject in my family, at least with my mother. My grandmother—my dad's mother—she took me aside after you proposed and did she give me an education. She and Granddad must have been wild in bed."

Early's eyebrows rose to his hairline, and Thelma's cheeks tinged pink.

"Look," she said, "sex was awfully important to Judith."

"With the colonel?"

"Yes, and with others, particularly back in college."

"And with Bill?"

"That's a puzzle. She didn't write about it. . . . Jimmy, it's late. I have to go to bed."

Early held up his hands. "With these, hon, I can't sleep. Maybe I'll read some." He pulled over one of Judith Smitts's diaries.

First light eased through the Earlys' kitchen window. It crept across the tabletop like a sleep-deprived beetle until it exposed a hand turned upright and then a head, down on crossed wrists . . . shoulders, still in yesterday's shirt, in a slow, rhythmic rise and fall. A fly, awakened from somewhere, buzzed out into the warmth. It settled on the tip of one of Early's fingers.

He responded to the trifling touch with a small movement that upset the fly. It lifted away, spiraled up in the sunlight, and, with a dive, buzzed into Early's ear.

He scrunched his shoulder.

Again the fly flew off. It bumped against the window screen in an effort to depart for the freedom of the outdoors. When that failed, the fly turned back. It rose, circled the room, then came once more to Early and put down in his hair. The insect's rustling about brought out a blackened hand with curved fingers. The hand and the wrist that supported it brushed around until the wrist rolled across the fly tangled in Early's hair, crushing it.

The business brought Early out of a fitful slumber. He rubbed the back of his hand at his stubble-covered cheeks as he yawned and stretched. And then it hit him . . . the pressure. A wrist went to his belt as he pushed himself up. He stumbled across the room and out, off the porch and down the path to the outhouse. Early hauled at the door latch until it gave way. He forced himself inside. Then he struggled with his jeans and his army-surplus shorts, cursing his hands for their uselessness.

Early got his jeans open and, using the backs of his hands, pushed them and his shorts down to his knees. He crouched over the one hole, relief coming in a flood of released water and waste.

When emptied, Early studied his hands and the Montgomery Ward catalog that hung on a nail to the side of the door. *How the hell am I gonna wipe myself?*

"Thelma!"

Early, his hands in new bandages, mashed blackberries into his oatmeal as a vehicle rumbled into his driveway. Thelma, at the kitchen window, sipping from a cup of coffee, glanced outside.

"It's Hutch," she said. "Anything supposed to be going on today?"

"Not that I know of." Early shoveled in a spoonful of well-berried cereal.

The hard sound of boot heels came across the back-porch floor and a call of, "Chief, you up for the day?"

"Better let him in," Early said, waving his spoon at the door.

Thelma opened the screen. "Hutch," she said.

"Howdy, Thel. It's business." The deputy raked his Big-brim Alpine Stetson from his head and ducked as he came inside.

Early went back to work, mushing in his oatmeal. "Thel's fixing to fry some eggs and bacon. Have a bite?"

"Can't," Tolliver said. "It's bad."

"Better sit and tell me."

"Just as soon stand."

"What is it, robbery? Bar fight in Aggieville spill out beyond the city limits?"

"No, it's Pop Irving."

Early put down his spoon.

"Last night . . . he was hit by a train. He's dead."

"Jesus H. Christ." Early pulled his napkin away from the front of his shirt. He threw it aside.

"From what the railroad people found, they think it's Pop. They can't be sure. Want you to come out."

"You call Ella?"

"She don't like me any more than she likes you. She wouldn't go."

"I don't suppose. Where?"

Tolliver's fingers twisted at a cuff button. "Ten east, out by Zeandale."

"That's Wabaunsee County. How about Irene?"

"Talked to her. She'll meet us there. Asked that we bring our coroner because she's without one at the moment."

"You call Grafton?"

"Yup."

"Well?"

"Well, he said some things he shouldn't. He was gonna go fishing up on the Blue, but said he'll meet us at the station. The U-P's got a speeder waiting for us."

Early looked over to his wife. What he saw did not warm his soul. "I gotta go," he said and pushed away from the table.

"Jimmy, you don't have to. Hutch can do this for you."

"Pop was a friend. I gotta go." From the peg by the door he lifted his cattleman's hat and settled it over his wild thatch as he pushed on outside. Tolliver came along behind. They split at the rear of the deputy's Jeep, Early going to the passenger side.

"She gonna be mad at you?" Tolliver asked after he got behind the steering wheel.

Early gazed away, deciding whether he should answer.

The deputy backed the Jeep around into the side yard, then scratched dirt as he bucked the machine out of the driveway and onto the county road. "Kinda glad I ain't married," Tolliver said as he shifted up through the gears.

"Come a time you'll change your mind."

"Not likely."

"Seems I said something like that, then I met Thelma. It became a stampede to the church. . . . What details you got?"

"The engineer of the Six-Ten westbound saw the shards of a body along the tracks. Stopped his train and walked back to confirm it. Figured it had to be one of the night expresses that hit him."

"And he could tell it was Pop?"

"No. But he found the old railroad cap and a wallet with a scrap of paper with your name on it, even a clipping about you investigating the Smitts's murder."

"That's not much."

"It was the shoes. The engineer stopped at the station to report what he'd found. The stationmaster—he had the engineer call me, and when he described the shoes, those old wingtips, not what you'd expect a bum to wear. . . . It's just got to be."

Early settled into silence, his gaze taking in the sweep of cornfields and hay fields as the Jeep rocked along. He waved a bandaged hand at a baler crew turning a windrowed corner just beyond the borrow ditch.

"What ya thinkin'?" Tolliver asked as he throttled back after he topped the hill on the west side of Manhattan.

"How mean life is."

"Seems to be in spells."

"This sure is one of them."

Tolliver cut off on a side street that carried the lawmen toward the Union-Pacific depot, a rococo affair kept painted and polished by a local crew proud to have the station in their town, the youngest employee a quarter-century with the line.

A big man, who could pass for Santa Claus were it not for his navy trousers and white shirt, the sleeves rolled above his elbows, paced the platform as Tolliver herded his Jeep into the U-P's graveled lot. He hustled over before the deputy could kill the engine.

"Hutch, sheriff," Fritz Hollister said, his hand out, "hate to rush you, but you got twenty minutes to get out there and get my section car off the tracks before an eastbound comes through."

"You could slow him down," Early said as he worked himself off the passenger seat.

"Can't. He don't stop here. He's hot—got the highball."

"Why's that?"

"Hauling Colorado peaches in those new reefer cars to the East."

Tolliver took his gun belt and holster from beneath his seat. He strapped on his sidearm, a Forty-Five, a twin to the one Early occasionally carried.

"Expecting trouble from a dead man?" Early asked.

"Snakes. That's snake country out by Zeandale."

"Cactus, he's right about that," Hollister said. "How them hands of yours?"

"Won't be picking any berries for awhile."

The three hurried across the platform to where a one-cylinder speeder sat idling on the mainline, a trackman in the driver's seat, gabbing with Doc Grafton and a second man, both sitting on the center section, over the motor, a trailer behind the speeder piled with baskets and a stretcher.

"You won't find the body intact," Hollister said. "Be a mess to pick up, and you may not find all of him. No tellin' what the coyotes got."

Early settled on the seat to the right of the driver. "You sure are a cheery fella, Fritz."

"Just warning you. Train/people collisions are bad. The man always loses."

Tolliver sat forward of Early, his back against the back of Randy Brown, the undertaker's son. "Randy," Tolliver said in greeting.

"Hutch."

"See you drew the short straw."

"Dad's got a funeral up at May Day."

Tolliver glanced over his shoulder. "Doc."

"I'm not talking to you."

"That'll save my ears."

The driver, with a three-day growth of beard, gazed around at his collection of passengers. "If you boys are settled in," he said, "we best be going."

He pushed the shift lever of the open section car into first gear and let out on the hand clutch. The driver rammed the throttle forward, leaning over to Early as he did. "This rig's not much more than a four-wheel motorcycle, only ain't got the power . . . five itty-bitty horses straining for all they're worth when we got six fat boys aboard."

"Only five today."

The driver, Heck Millard, came back on the throttle. He shifted the speeder into second gear and slammed the throttle full forward again. Grafton pulled down on the windward side of his fedora, to keep the breeze from blowing it away.

"How fast?" Early asked.

"Thirty, thirty-two," Millard said, his driving hand resting on the brake handle. "Be out there in, oh, twenty minutes."

"Isn't that when the express is coming through?"

"Yup. Sec we get there, we gotta horse this car and the trailer off the tracks or that Baldwin Pacific's gonna blast them off."

"And if we're a little late getting there?"

"That would make for a bad day."

Early leaned forward to the coroner. He nudged him.

"Yeah?" Grafton asked, twisting around.

"You as grumpy as Hutch says?"

"Wouldn't you be if you got robbed of a fishing trip? Had my tasters set on a couple pan-fried bass for lunch. Now I'll be damn lucky if I get a baloney sandwich. How're your hands?"

"Some better."

The timbre of the rhythmic clicking of the speeder's wheels over the rail joints changed as the little machine rolled out onto a bridge that took it across the meandering Kaw River, its water moving with no hurry under a cloudless, crystalline blue Kansas sky.

"Maybe you could throw a line in the Kaw along about where we'll be stopping," Early said to the coroner.

"Nope, nothing but damn mud cats in that section. Understand you knew this Mister Irving."

"Pop and I hoboed across the country before the war."

"Sorry. It's no good losing a friend, particularly this way."

"The old man did like trains."

The speeder rattled across a second bridge.

Millard leaned in. "Mile or two now. Engineer said he put a flag beside the tracks to mark the place. . . . Yeah, that's it ahead."

He pulled back on the throttle. Before he could reach for the clutch and the brake, a steam whistle moaned in the distance. Millard glanced back. "Oh shit, there he is."

He pulled hard on the brake, and steel screeched on steel as the speeder and trailer slid along the rails to a stop. Millard bailed out. He unhitched the trailer and hollered to the others, "Doc, Randy, grab the handles in the front. Hutch, back here with me! Let's lift this beast off the tracks. On three now. . . . One, two, three."

The quartet lifted, straining. They side-shuffled with their burden and set the speeder down when they were well clear of the tracks. The men ran back to the trailer and grabbed the sides of the flat bed. "Now!" Millard hollered.

Up, side-shuffle, side-shuffle, side-shuffle—Brown tripped on a rail—and down.

The express roared by. The wind blast whipped Millard's cap and Grafton's hat away while Early, Tolliver, and Brown scrambled to hold onto theirs.

"Cutting it a bit close, weren't you, Heck?" Grafton asked.

"Naw." The trackman walked off into the weeds, after his cap. He stopped. "Oh gawd, here's part of him."

Grafton and Brown each picked up a basket from the trailer. "Whatcha got?" Grafton asked.

"A leg."

Grafton, Brown, and Early moved into the bluestem and

burdock, Early to kneel beside the bloody limb and torn trouser leg, a shoe still on the foot. "It's Pop," he said. "That's one of the shoes he was wearing. He did love those wingtips."

Brown lifted the limb in his basket, twisting away as he did.

"You all right?" Early asked.

"I hate these accidents," the undertaker's son said. "Much rather pick up a body that died in bed."

"They do look better."

Three shots sounded, and Early snapped around.

Tolliver stood on the speeder's engine compartment, aiming his Forty-Five off into a hay field. "Coyotes," he said. "A mama and three pups lunching on something. Got the mama."

"The pups?"

"They ran. Guess I better get out there and see what they had." Tolliver scrambled off the speeder. He strode down into the ditch and hopped the fence into the field. Twenty yards out, he called back, "Doc, better bring yer basket."

"What you got?" Early asked.

"You don't need to see this. It's a head . . . what's left of it, and a shoulder."

Early sat back on the gravel ballast. Grafton touched his arm as he passed. "Sorry, Cactus."

Early watched them—his friends—work like rag pickers, parting the weeds with the toe of their shoes or a stick, crouching down, putting something in a basket, and moving on. A stubby speeder, half the length of the one that had come out from Manhattan, putted into Early's view from the east, coming out from Wamego, five miles over the horizon. The two-person vehicle rolled to a stop.

"Jimmy," the hefty woman in the passenger seat said.

"Irene."

She held out a pack of White Owl blunts.

"No thanks," Early said. "You didn't get run over by the east-bound?"

"Nope. Old Talley here had us off on a siding before she came by." Irene Bolton took a short cigar from the pack. She stuck it between her lips, then raked a match across the metal housing that covered the speeder's motor. The Wabaunsee County sheriff wore tans, like Early, but not a cattleman's hat, instead a battered fedora. And like Early, she did not carry a sidearm. Irene Bolton favored a night stick, and one hung from her belt.

"He who Hutch thought he was?" she asked, blowing smoke from the side of her mouth, away from Early.

"Yup."

"So he's one of yours."

"Guess you can say that."

Bolton took another drag on her cigar. "You want the investigation?"

"Irene, it's your county." Early pitched a stone into the weeds.

"Well, I'm gonna call it an accident and be done with it."

"Don't know what else it would be way the hell out here. Pop was always riding the rails or walking along a road bed if it was a long wait between trains."

"But at night?"

"Coulda been drunk."

"I'll sign off on your coroner's paperwork then, keep it legal."

A blast came from beyond the tracks, near a concrete culvert that let a creek flow from north of the tracks to the south, to join the Kaw at the base of the Flint Hills a mile on. The sheriffs and the driver of the second speeder twisted around.

Tolliver held up a snake. He flung it away, into the hay field. "Rattler," he called out to his audience, all staring at him.

"Hutch! Get outta there in case he's got family."

"Right, chief. . . . Wait a minute." Tolliver ducked from sight.

When he came up, he held a bundle high. "Bedroll."

"Bring it up here!"

Early pushed himself to his feet as Tolliver, a distance away, hop-stepped through the weeds and up the side of the grade. When he got to the tracks, he shambled on, a rolled-up calico blanket over his shoulder.

Early and Bolton eased over to the trailer.

"Heard about your hands and the bank bandit," she said as she flicked ash from her cigar.

"Bet that got a laugh around your office."

Bolton covered a snicker. "Jimmy, it sure did. . . . That bedroll."

"Yeah, calico. That's Pop's. He's been toting that everywhere since he come back home."

"He got family?"

"A wife who doesn't want him. Guess I'll buy the funeral."

"You could let the county do it."

"Pop deserves better than the potter's field."

Tolliver flopped the bedroll down on the trailer. "Hate to break up your gab fest," he said.

"It's all right." Early motioned at the leather laces that secured the ends of the bundle. "Let's see what he's got."

The deputy's nimble fingers danced around the knot at one end of the bedroll and then the other. He laid the laces aside and unrolled the blanket to reveal a straight razor, a shaving mug, toothbrush, a comb with some teeth broken out, and a wad of bills. Tolliver picked up the money. He counted it. "All fives it seems . . . two hundred sixty, two hundred sixty-five, two hundred seventy dollars, if a couple bills didn't stick together."

Early rubbed his chin with the back of his hand. "Pop said he had enough money to buy a grave. Guess he did."

"Where'd he get it?"

"Said a job out in Denver."

"Yeah, right." The deputy stuffed the wad in Early's shirt pocket. "I'm not gonna be responsible for this."

Early motioned at a smaller bundle, something wrapped in a red bandana.

Tolliver picked it up. He turned the bundle over and let the ends of the handkerchief fall away. "What the heck are these?"

Bolton squinted through the smoke from her cigar. "Figurines, looks like two're broken. Hummels. I buy myself one every Christmas. Have a pretty fair collection."

Tolliver glanced at Early. "You thinking what I'm thinking?"

"If you're thinking these are Judith Smitts's, how the hell did Pop get them?"

"Killed her, maybe?"

CHAPTER 14

August 27—Saturday Afternoon
The Hummels

Early opened his mailbox after Tolliver let him off back at his house in Keats. He pawed out a newspaper, a letter, and three magazines.

"Kansas Sheriff's Digest, oughtta be a fair read," he said of the magazine on top of the modest load cradled in his wounded hands. Early carried the mail around the side of the house to the kitchen door. The kitchen door . . . He wondered why carpenters bothered putting front doors on small-town and farm houses. Nobody ever used them.

Early wedged the screen open, got his butt inside and pushed, letting himself into the cool. The shades had been pulled, to keep the sun and the baking heat of the day out?

"Thel?"

"Bedroom. I'm worn out."

"What is it, only three, four in the afternoon?" Early asked as he made his way into the gloom of his house's sleeping quarters.

"I weeded the garden. Too hot. I shouldn't've done that."

Early laid the mail on the dresser. "Can I get you something?"

"You're hardly able."

"Well, I saw the sun tea on the porch. If we got ice in the icebox, I can get it cold for you."

"Be nice," Thelma said, her voice leaden with exhaustion.

Early didn't feel much better, but he rambled back out into

145

the kitchen. He got out a jelly glass and went to the porch, humming an aimless tune as he did. There Early set the saucer off the top of the Mason jar of amber liquid. He daubed the tea ball in it up and down before he set the ball—dripping—on the saucer. Using his hands like the grips of pliers, Early lifted the jar. He spilled some of its contents onto the porch rail and down onto a patch of rain-starved grass as he filled the grocery-store glass.

When Early got the assemblage back in order, he worked his way into the kitchen. Still humming, he turned on the radio . . .

. . . thermometer outside the window of Your Friendly Neighbor reads ninety-three degrees . . .

"Lord, who needs that," he muttered and turned the radio off. Early went to the Frigidaire. He brought out an ice tray and banged it against the side of the sink until half the cubes fell out. Some he scooped into the jelly glass, the rest into the tray that went back in the Frigidaire.

Early hummed on into the bedroom, the jelly glass squeezed between his hands, tea splashes slopping onto his bandages and the linoleum as he went.

"Here ya are, hon."

Thelma recoiled when cold tea dripped on her. She rose to an elbow and took the glass as Early sat down on the edge of the bed. "I suppose I'm going to have to mop the floor," she said.

"Hhmm?"

"Don't you notice anything?"

"What?"

Thelma swallowed some of the contents. "Mint," she said of the tea, "from my herb garden. You want a taste?"

She held out the glass. Early took it in that pliers-grip of his hands. He lifted the glass to his lips and drank down the contents—drained the glass except for the ice cubes—then set the glass on the night stand.

"Jimmy, you got your head on?"

"Huh?"

"The tea."

"You want some more?" he asked.

"You're hopeless. . . . Come on, talk to me. What is it?"

"It's in my shirt. You'll have to get it."

Thelma curled around her husband. She unbuttoned his shirt at the bulge above his belt and removed a bandana-wrapped bundle.

"What is this?" she asked. Thelma turned on the lamp on the night table, then looked at what her fingers had unwrapped. "Broken pieces? Wait a minute, there's a good one in here. . . . Jimmy, these are Judith's. Where'd you get them?"

"They were in Pop Irv's bedroll."

"Where'd he get them?"

"I don't know. He's only talking to the angels now."

"Could he have taken them?"

"You mean, could he have killed Judith? There wasn't a mean, vindictive, or envious bone in Pop."

"You sure you're not being blind on this, because he was a friend?"

Early did not answer.

"Could he have gone in the house after?"

"And seen that blood and mess? Pop would have told me."

"What else is there?"

"Hon, I don't know."

CHAPTER 15

September 15—Thursday Morning
The Journey

Early studied his hands. He could almost ball them, but not quite. He picked at the scabbing beginning to peel away. Another week, he thought, maybe two weeks. At least he didn't have to wear the bandages anymore.

Gladys, Early's blue-haired secretary, interrupted by dropping a stack of file folders on his desk.

He gazed at them, pained, then at her.

"First one has three tax-sale orders you have to sign, next one subpoenas the judge wants served."

"Give 'em to Hutch. I'm going to get out of here for a couple days."

Gladys rested the knuckles of her hand on her massive hip. "Well, you didn't check with me."

"I don't have to. I'm the sheriff."

"My point exactly. There's a whole lot of things in that stack you got to tend to." Gladys's jaw jutted out and the wattles beneath her chin shook.

"There's nothing in that stack Hutch can't do."

"How do you know? You haven't even looked."

"My God, woman, Hutch's John Henry will work on any of those papers as well as mine. He's got the same authority I have."

"And if he makes a mistake?"

"Who's to say I wouldn't?"

"Well, we certainly agree on that. You've messed up some."

"Thank you, Gladys, you surely know how to build my spirits."

She backed away, toward the door. "So where you going?"

"Kansas City."

"When were you going to tell me?"

"I wasn't."

"Why not?"

"Because you put me through this every time I have to leave the county."

"But your job is here."

Early leaned back in his oak swivel chair, its springs squalling, the chair worn from having served the bottoms of three previous sheriffs. "My job is wherever my job takes me."

"This got something to do with that Smitts woman?"

"Two points for your side."

"What about your wife?"

"What about her?"

"Jimmy, she's what, four, five months pregnant with your first child? Who's going to look in on her? . . . You didn't think of that, did you?"

Early pulled his pasteboard suitcase from the backseat of his Jeep, then strolled on to the platform of Manhattan's Union-Pacific depot.

Fritz Hollister met him with a ticket. "Round trip to the big KC. I left the return open and charged the whole mess to the county."

Early stuffed the ticket in his shirt pocket.

"See your hands are some better," Hollister said.

Early flexed his fingers. "Good enough I can take care of myself."

"So you can do your sheriff business all right?"

"Yes. Guess I can."

An air horn sounded three times in the distance. The station-master pointed west along the tracks, toward where they disappeared around Bluemont Hill. A sleek silver and red locomotive, and a sister trailing it, nosed around, the twins pulling an express car and a dozen passenger coaches.

"You're in for a treat, Cactus. Two diesels on The Portland Rose today."

"Where's my steamer?"

"Gone the way of the your dad's Model T, to the scrap yard. Diesels, we got 'em coming on the line fast now."

"Progress, I suppose."

"Oh, it is, Cactus." Hollister waved to the engineer as the lead locomotive rolled past, the train slowing to a stop. A mail truck backed up to the open door of the express car, and a man inside threw out bags of mail.

A dozen people boiled out of the depot with suitcases and handbags. They milled around the steps of the first passenger car, filling time while a gaggle of passengers came down and off.

When the new group could go up, the chief conductor stepped away. He shot a look up the platform and down, then bellowed, "All aboard, Topeka, Kansas City, Saint Louis, and Chicago! All aboard!"

"That's me," Early said.

"Anybody asks," Hollister said, "where'll you be staying?"

"The Muehelbach."

"That's pretty good. You pay yer dues to the DP?"

"Pardon?"

"The Democrat party. President Truman's going to be there tonight, speaking at some kind of shindig. Oh, that's right, you're one of those 'R' people, aren't you?" Hollister chortled.

He slapped Early's back as he pushed him on toward the conductor.

Early showed his ticket before he clambered up the steps and inside. When he saw all the seats occupied, he pushed down the aisle toward the second car, stepping around a child chasing after a teddy bear that had gotten away from him. The second car held the same story—no vacant seats—so Early shuffled on to the third. The dining car.

He felt the train move as he went on, grinning sheepishly at a crew of waiters in pressed white jackets eyeing him while they set tables with silverware and china embossed with the Union-Pacific logo. Early glanced at his watch.

"Excuse me," he said to the nearest waiter. He peered at the brass nameplate above the man's jacket pocket. "Tony, it's not quite noon, I know, but suppose I could get a sandwich and beat the rush?"

The black man, a bit thicker than Early and moving with grace, pulled out a chair. He motioned Early into it. "And what may I get for you, sir?"

"What do you recommend?"

"If it's a sandwich, the chef makes a turkey BLT that's mighty outstanding."

"Can I get sweet tea with that?"

"Absolutely, sir."

"By the way, wouldn't happen to be a newspaper around, would there?"

"Denver Post, yessir. It's yesterday's." The waiter bobbed away to return a moment later, holding out a paper folded in quarters. "Pretty interesting front-page story on that Berlin airlift thing, if that interests you."

Early unfolded the paper as the waiter moved away to the galley. There it was, the headline, BERLIN AIRLIFT ENDS, and a secondary headline, MORE THAN 2 MILLION TONS

OF SUPPLIES FLOWN IN. Early scanned through the story, stopping at the recap of something called Operation Easter Parade, the day, a half-year earlier, when American and British cargo planes landed in Berlin at the rate of one a minute. Early let out a low whistle when he contemplated that, then turned inside, to the sports pages.

Another headline caught his attention, NEWCOMBE WINS 17TH, DODGERS SWEEP TOWARD PENNANT. In a companion story, a columnist speculated on a Red Sox/Dodgers World Series, but concluded a Yankees/Cardinals matchup wasn't out of the question.

The waiter set a sandwich plate and a glass of tea to the side of Early. When he noticed, he closed his paper.

"That Berlin thing," Early asked, "Tony, were you in the war?"

The waiter folded his hands in front of him. "Yessir, Navy. Steward on the battleship Missouri. You, sir?"

"A mud soldier in Europe."

"You get to Berlin, sir?"

"The Elbe. The high-ups called it quits and gave Berlin to the Russians. You get to Tokyo?"

"Tokyo Bay, yessir. Saw General MacArthur collect the Japs' signatures on the surrender."

Early grinned. "That had to be something."

"Certainly was. You'll have to excuse me, other people are coming into the car."

Early pulled the sandwich plate in front of him, the sandwich a mammoth thing on rye bread with roast turkey slices, bacon, and slabs of tomato hanging over the sides. And the aroma, it made Early's mouth water. He bit in and chewed, and returned to the Post's front page, to a lesser story about Israel petitioning the United Nations for membership.

Early, eating and reading, ignored the other diners swirling around him, only becoming aware of them when the waiter stopped at his table.

"Excuse me, sir, we're about full up. Would it be all right if I seated someone here with you?" he asked.

Early touched his napkin to his lips. "Tell you what, I'm finished. Why don't I let you give the table to someone else and I'll go back to one of the passenger cars?"

The waiter placed the lunch ticket next to the tea glass. Early glanced at it, then covered the ticket with two one-dollar bills. As he walked away with his suitcase, the waiter called him back.

"You got change coming, sir."

"Tony, it's yours," Early said.

"Well, thank you. Thank you, sir."

Only when Early entered the fifth car did he find a plethora of empty seats. He selected one on the aisle halfway down, put his suitcase on the seat to the side, and settled in. Where was that seatback thing? The release?

Early felt around. He found it and let his seatback recline to where he found himself yawning when he laid back on it. Early set his cattleman's hat aside and closed his eyes.

He felt a tapping at his knee and opened an eye, the rhythmic clicking of the train's steel wheels reminding him where he was. A blurry shape took form before Early as he opened his other eye. "What the hell?"

A cowboy, seated across from him, raised the barrel of a Forty-Five in a let-us-have-silence gesture. "Just you and me, sheriff. Everybody else in the car, they've gone to lunch."

"Sonny?"

"None other."

Early jerked toward him, but something stopped his left arm—a handcuff manacling his wrist to the arm of the seat.

Estes made a clucking sound. "Now, sheriff, that's got to be embarrassing. Those are your handcuffs, from yer suitcase where I found this here pistol. Mighty nice gun." Estes waggled it at Early. "When you sleep, man, you surely do sleep. Snore something nasty."

Early grabbed for Estes with his free hand, but the cowboy spun out of his seat, away from Early, beyond his reach.

"What the hell you want?" Early spit the words out.

"Nothing really, other than to let you know what a pleasant surprise it was to find you here. I'd like to stay and chat, but people are going to be coming back to the car soon." Estes placed the Colt on a seat two rows away, then made work of taking something from his shirt pocket. He dangled it for Early to see before he put it down beside the gun. "The handcuff key. Yer gonna need it to get loose."

"Sonny—"

Early had hardly got the name beyond his lips when Estes dashed toward the front of the rail car. He rammed open the side door and dove out. Early watched him through the windows, watched Estes arc out beyond the side of a bridge and down. He grabbed for the emergency cord, triggering the train's air brakes. The wheels locked up in a ruckus of squealing, flinging Early forward, the handcuff near yanking his arm off, steel screeching on steel for the longest time, until all forward motion and sound ceased.

A conductor, an average man in all respects except for his massive mustache, appeared at the head of the car. He clung to the frame of the doorway. "You all right in here, mister?"

Early, on the floor in the aisle, jerked at the handcuff. "Does it look like it? I'm the guy who pulled the cord. Sheriff of Riley County."

The conductor trotted up. "What you doing all handcuffed up like that?"

"This bank robber from back home got the drop on me while

I was sleeping. He threw the cuff key on the seat up there."
Early motioned toward it. "Get it and my gun."

"Not here," the conductor said.

"Maybe slid off. Look on the floor."

The conductor got down on one knee. He spotted both several rows ahead and crawled after them. When he came back, Early took the key. He fumbled it into the lock and twisted on the key until the cuff fell away.

"Where's this fella?" the conductor asked.

"Went out the side door. Dove over the bridge."

"Into the Kaw River?"

"Damn lucky. If he'd gone head first into a ditch, Sonny'd broken his neck."

"Could still have. Water's shallow in this stretch."

"Let's go look for him," Early said as he stuffed his pistol in his belt. He grabbed his hat and hustled up the aisle, down the steps, and out onto the gravel, the conductor close on his heels.

"I got a trainload of passengers I got to look after," the man in the black uniform said as he hot-footed it to keep up with Early running back along the tracks toward the bridge.

The waiter who had served Early leaned out of the door of the dining car. "Hey, boss!" he called out.

The conductor twisted back, stumbling.

"What's the trouble?" the waiter asked.

"Passenger jumped! Went in the river."

"You gonna need help?"

"Won't turn you down, Tony!"

The black man hopped down. He ran after the conductor already hustling away.

Early, first to the bridge, scrambled down the embankment to the water's edge while the conductor, on the tracks, continued past him, out onto the trestle.

"See anything from up there?" Early hollered as he waded

into the knee-deep water.

"Nothing. . . . Wait a minute."

"What is it?"

"Hat in the middle of the river, drifting downstream."

"A body?"

"Not that I can see."

The waiter plunged down the embankment and into the water. He sloshed after Early, who waded on, holding his pistol high to keep the gun from getting wet as the water rose to his waist.

He glanced up toward the conductor. "What do you guess the fall?"

"Thirty feet, maybe."

"Man could crack his head open just going in the water."

At midriver, Early yelped. He splashed from sight, a swirl of water taking his hat away. The waiter dove after him. Several moments passed, then the two surfaced, the waiter with his arm under Early's shoulder, Early flailing, spluttering. "There's a damn hole here!"

"Deep?" the conductor asked.

"Deep enough I didn't feel bottom." Early, again established on his feet, stuffed his wet pistol in his belt. He twisted around to his savior. "You didn't have to come out here, but thanks."

"Admiral back there on the Mo made us all learn how to swim."

"Could the body be in the hole?" the conductor called down.

The waiter touched Early's arm. "Only one way to find out." He arched himself into a dive and disappeared.

Early launched himself after his hat drifting away. He recovered it, slapped it on his head, and waded back to near where he felt the hole had to be. Early glanced up to the conductor. "How long he been down there?"

"Minute. Minute and a half."

"I don't like this."

"You dive after him?"

"My only swimming's been in a stock tank."

The water roiled and the waiter burst through the surface, sucking for wind, spitting. He swam to Early and let his feet down. "Nuthin' in that hole I could feel wasn't supposed to be there."

Early squeezed water from his shirtsleeve. "Then where the heck is he?"

"Hole's big enough, deep enough a man could dive in and kick back up without ever hitting bottom, if he hit it just right."

"You think he swam away?" Early twisted around. He peered back up at the conductor. "You don't see nuthin' in the river?"

"Just that hat floating sixty yards on."

"Damn. . . . Banks of the river?"

"Lot of weeds, could hide an army. A couple cows down a ways. What you gonna do, sheriff?"

"Search, I guess. How much time I got?"

"Ten minutes and we have to have this train out of here to make a siding for a pass at Lawrence."

"When's the next eastbound?"

"An hour." The conductor pointed off to the side. "Sheriff, there's a water snake swimming your way. Big one."

Early twisted around. He saw a triangular head above the surface of the river, the head the size of a dime at the distance, propelling toward him. He brought his pistol up in one motion and jerked the trigger only to hear a click, then a second click when he jerked the trigger again. Wet powder in the cartridges. Early backpedaled. "Dammit, Tony, let's get outta here."

Both men turned. They high-stepped it for the opposite shore, churning up a froth of water as they ran. When they hit dry ground, both fell forward into the grass, breathing hard, Early wheezing. "Snakes. Gawd, I'm gonna have nightmares."

Early banged into an overhead compartment when he straightened up. He rubbed at his smarting scalp. Then as he had one leg up, to step into dry trousers, the railcar lurched. It threw him against the door of the men's lavatory. Early ooched and massaged his bruised shoulder. And he felt the clicking of the wheels slow.

"Tony, we at that siding?"

"Yessir," came a voice from the other side of the door.

"Sure not much room for changing in here, is there?"

"Wasn't intended for that purpose. Hand your wet clothes out. I'll hang them where they can dry some."

Early gathered the pile he'd dumped in the sink—his suit pants, white shirt, undershirt, socks, shorts, and necktie—unlatched the door and passed them to waiting hands.

After Early closed the door, he pulled on a tan shirt, his only spare, and, while fumbling with the buttons, caught his reflection in the mirror—a picture of hair spiked out from being towel dried. Early finger-combed his thatch into some semblance of order.

Socks? Where'd I put my socks?

Early poked through his suitcase on the toilet seat. Nothing. He peered around over the floor, then—Ahh!—he slapped his back pocket. The wad Early felt gave him his answer. He pulled his socks out and, doing a one-legged stand, got the first over a foot. A repeat of the one-legged stand—only the other leg—and Early had that job done. A rumble broke through his concentration. Early leaned down. He peered out the side window, at a westbound passenger train roaring past on the mainline, less than an arm's reach away. And then the train was gone, its absence revealing a vista of farmland and, perhaps half a mile away, the Kaw River, its waters, where they rippled, reflecting quartzlike glints of the late afternoon sun. Could Estes be out there?

Early shrugged. He dumped water from his boots into the sink, gathered up his suitcase, and stepped out into the passageway, suitcase in one hand, boots in the other. Early padded back to his seat, sensing through the balls of his feet the train moving, picking up speed. It lurched through a switch onto the mainline, a lurch that threw Early to the side. He grabbed a seatback to keep from going over, twisted around as he did and found himself staring into the face of a woman, startled, into whose lap he had fallen.

"Sorry," he said, getting up. "Kinda dangerous here, isn't it?"

"Certainly appears so."

"Well, again I'm sorry."

He moved on, away. At his seat, Early tossed his suitcase into the seat opposite, next to the one on which he'd left his not-too-wet hat. He dropped into his seat and there drummed his fingers on his knees and wiggled his toes in his lone pair of dry socks, and gazed about.

The waiter—he, too, in dry clothes and, to Early's envy, dry shoes—came down the aisle. "Mister Early," he said, "I got your things hanging in the pantry. Your pants, I'd get them to a cleaners when you get to Kansas City. They're going to wrinkle and smell of river water. Shirt, you can always wash that out in your hotel room. Room service might even get you an iron."

Early motioned to the seat across the aisle.

"No, it wouldn't be proper," the waiter said. "Mind if I ask a question?"

"Go ahead."

"Why are you going to Kansas City?"

Early rubbed his chin as he wondered how much he should say, then thought better of even wondering. "Investigating a murder," he said. "I'm to meet some people who may be able to

159

help me understand the woman who was killed."

"Got to be interesting."

"No, your job is interesting. My friend, you get to travel the country, and you get paid for it."

" 'Fraid it gets old. I'm away from home a week, two weeks at a time." The waiter steadied himself against a seatback as the passenger car rocked through a low spot.

"Where's home?"

"Bronzeville . . . South Chicago."

"Family?"

"Wife and three children. You, Mister Early?"

"Wife and a first child on the way."

A beaming, prideful smile spread across the waiter's face. "That little child's going to change your life, sir. . . . Well now, you'll excuse me, I have to get back to the dining car. I'm kind of behind in my work getting ready for supper."

"Supper served before Kansas City?"

"No, after. When you get off, come by the dining car. I'll have your clothes for you." The waiter brought two fingers up to his brow in a salute, then he left.

Nice fella, Early thought as he gazed out the window. A town flashed by. Early thought he read Linwood on the sign on the end of the depot.

"Your clothes," the waiter said, handing Early a package wrapped in butcher paper. "I triple wrapped them so you can put them in your suitcase. The wet shouldn't come through."

Early opened his suitcase on a chair. He put the package in. "Don't know how to thank you," he said as he buckled the flaps.

"You don't have to."

"Tony, I don't even know your last name."

"It's Haskins, sir. Anthony George Haskins Junior."

"That's a mighty proud name."

"Thank you. Yessir. Where are you meeting these people?"

"Under the big clock in the Grand Hall."

"It's—"

"I know where it is. Been here years back on layovers when I was riding troop trains."

"Yessir. Perhaps I'll see you again, sir."

Early nodded and went on, carrying his boots, his suitcase under his arm.

"Excuse me," the waiter called. He gestured to the boots.

"Still pretty squishy," Early said. "I don't mind walking in my socks."

"Very well, sir."

Early moved back into the flow of passengers making their way forward to the exit door and the steps down to the platform, others oblivious of him as they hurried away. He had time, at least half an hour, before he was to meet the Silverbergs. Early ambled on.

Someone fell in beside him.

He glanced over. "Tony?"

"Said I might see you again. I'm stopping over, to see my sister and her family." The waiter, hatless before, wore a cleaned and blocked fedora and a suit coat rather than the white jacket of his occupation. "Mind if I walk along?"

"Not at all."

The two went over to the broad concourse on the west side of the terminal.

"Sister, huh," Early said. "Where does she live?"

"On the Kansas City, Kansas, side. Twenty, thirty blocks from here."

"She waiting for you?"

"No, I'll catch a city bus."

"Why not a taxi?"

161

"Taxi drivers pick up Coloreds where you come from, Mister Early? They sure don't here."

"That shouldn't be."

"Maybe not, but that's the way it is."

They moved from the concourse through an entryway and into the Grand Hall, a magnificent specimen of a waiting room of rose-brown marble with a ceiling high enough that the room could enclose a seven-story building. In the swirling crowd, someone rammed into Haskins, sending him sprawling.

"Hey. Hey!" Early called after the retreating figure. When the man failed to stop, Early dropped his suitcase and boots and raced after him, dodging and dancing through the crowd. He grabbed the shoulder of the man's coat and spun him around, swarthy, bulked like a professional wrestler in his black suit, tie, and black fedora.

"Git yer hand off me!"

"Whoa, wait a minute," Early said, breathing hard. "You knocked my friend down back there. You need to go back and apologize."

"You're friend's nothing but a damn nigger. I don't apologize to you, and I sure as hell don't apologize to damn niggers."

"Oh, now you've gone and done it," Early said. He brought his wallet from his back pocket and let it fall open, revealing his star.

The man reached in his inside pocket. He, too, brought out a wallet and let it fall open. It revealed a gold shield. "Secret Service trumps county sheriff. Now if you don't mind, I'll be on my way."

"What's your all-fired hurry, mister?"

"I'm with the president. His train's due in in five minutes." The man moved on.

"Hey, what's the name of your supervisor?"

The federal man turned back, his lip curling. With one hand

he slapped his biceps, the other hand shooting up as a fist. The man stepped away, into the crowd moving toward the east concourse.

Early pushed his hat forward. He rubbed the back of his head. *Maybe if I had my gun . . . Ah, he's probably got one too. Been a Mexican standoff.* He turned and shambled back and found Haskins sitting on his suitcase, Early's suitcase and his boots between the waiter's feet.

"You shouldn't have chased after him," Haskins said.

"He shouldn't have done what he did."

"White men been running over us for generations."

"Doesn't make it right."

"Didn't say it did. But there's change coming. We've got Mister Truman in office."

"You know who that was?" Early asked, gesturing back toward the east concourse. "Secret Service man assigned to your Mister Truman."

The muscles in Haskins's face went slack.

"Anyway, thanks for watching my stuff," Early said. He sat and pulled on his boots, then pushed himself up. "Not the first time I've marched in wet boots. Let's get you to your sister's."

"You don't have to do this."

"Tony, I'm a tad upset. Let's get you to your sister's, and we're going to take a cab."

"What about your people?"

"When they get here, they'll wait." Early grabbed up his suitcase. He marched off toward the doors that opened out of Kansas City's Union Station onto Pershing Drive, nine blocks south of the central city, Haskins moving at his side.

"Mister Early, I wish you wouldn't."

"Well, by God, somebody's got to do the right thing here." He waved at a Circle cab.

The driver waved back and pulled over to the curb.

Early opened the back passenger door. He leaned down. "I want you to take this man to—"

The cab drove off.

"I told you," Haskins said.

"Well, fool me once . . ." Early waved at a Checker and that driver, too, pulled up to the curb.

Early opened the back passenger door. He pushed his suitcase ahead of him and got in. "Come on," he said to Haskins.

The driver glanced in his mirror. "I don't take niggers."

"Just a minute, let me get my money out," Early said. He pulled his suitcase up on his lap and grubbed inside until he found his Forty-Five. Early slapped his pistol and his star in his gun hand, and held them out. "Will this do?"

The driver swallowed his gum. "Do just fine," he said, his voice cracking.

"Come on, Mister Haskins," Early said, "lets us go for a ride."

As the black man settled in and pulled the door closed, Early asked, "The address of your sister's place?"

"Ten twenty-eight B West Fifteen Street."

Early waved at the driver to start. "That's in the Kansas side of Kansas City. How long it take you to get us there?"

The driver, a ragged mustache like Early's warming his upper lip, glanced in his mirror. "We got some traffic. I'd say twenty, twenty-five minutes."

"That's fine. Mister, you'll be bringing me back here."

Early trotted up the several steps of Kansas City's Union Station and inside, through the oak and brass doors. He worked his way in against the flow of others leaving the terminal for waiting cars, taxis, and city buses idling at the curb. Inside, he glanced up toward the midpoint of the hall, to a half-ton clock suspended from the ceiling . . . *a half-ton of machinery, six feet*

164

across the face of it. Amazing the stuff you gather, passing the time waiting for a train. Once, during the war, Early had waited here for two days for a troop train that would take him to Savannah by way of Memphis, Chattanooga, and Atlanta.

Before he got to the clock, he recognized them, the man studying his pocket watch, chatting with the woman beside him.

"Mister Silverberg, Missus Silverberg," Early said as he came up, his hand out, "didn't mean to keep you waiting, but another matter kind of busted in. I'm sorry about that."

Silverberg clasped Early's outstretched hand. "Your train got in some time ago, didn't it? We were worried. I had them page you twice."

"I wasn't here to hear it, I'm sorry. The why, that isn't important."

Ethel Silverberg, wearing a broad-brimmed summer hat, slipped her arm around her husband's arm. "You will be staying with us, won't you, Mister Early? We have a room ready for you."

"Oh, now that would be an imposition. I got me a room at the Muehelbach."

"You should cancel it," Mishka Silverberg said.

"No, I wouldn't think of that. Tell you what, the hotel's got a fine restaurant. Let me make up for you having to wait by taking you to supper there."

Silverberg, chuckling, turned to his wife. "Should we tell him?"

"Yes, dear."

"Mister Early, we were planning to take you there. We even made reservations—a table for four."

"More company?"

"A friend of Judith's you should meet."

They rambled out the east entrance, onto Main Street, the Silverbergs gesturing to their right, toward a massive structure on a rise to the south of Union Station.

"They tell us that's the largest memorial to the First War in the country," Silverberg said. "Of course, it was built before we got here. Dedicated in Nineteen Twenty-One by your President Coolidge."

Early gazed up at it. "Always wanted to ride the elevator to the top of the tower, but never got around to it. You ever do it?"

"I'm afraid of heights, but Ethel has."

Missus Silverberg touched Early's arm. "Quite a sight of our city from up there. Two hundred seventeen feet high. Judith and I read that number on a plaque by the elevator door when she and I went up. Perhaps we could do that tomorrow."

"Well, now I'd like that."

Early waved at a taxicab, a Checker. The driver pulled to the curb, and Early opened the back door for the Silverbergs. After they climbed in, he took the front passenger seat.

"Not you again," the driver said.

Early grinned. "Sure 'nuff. Jews in the backseat this time. Got a problem with that?"

"And if I did?"

"I still got my money in my suitcase."

"Uh-huh. Where to?"

"The Muehelbach."

The driver stuck his hand out the window, signaling to passing traffic, then U-turned on Main Street to go north. "Short jog," he said as he leaned forward on the steering wheel. "Be thirty-five cents."

Early grubbed out a pocketful of change. He sorted out two quarters and flipped them into the cup on the taxi's dash.

The driver scowled as he said, "Not in my coffee."

"Sorry. I thought it was a tip cup."

"You're not from around here, are you?"

"Manhattan."

"You got dirt clods behind your ears, huh?"

"I said I'm sorry."

The driver glanced up at a traffic light going yellow. He stepped down on the gas and swung his Nash around a city bus, Early grabbling for the door handle, to keep from sliding across the bench seat, the driver counting down the streets as he shot on. At Twelfth, he threw the taxi into a hard left as the yellow light clicked over to red.

Two blocks on, at Wyandotte, the driver bumped the taxi's tires up onto the curb and braked to a stop. "Muehelbach Hotel," he said.

Early peered out and up, the brick building so many stories tall that the muscles in his neck twinged as he looked up.

A doorman hustled over, gold epaulettes and braid on the shoulders of his knee-length red coat. He opened the back door for the Silverbergs. After he helped them out, he opened the front door for Early and took his suitcase.

Early held a quarter out to the driver as he slid off the seat.

"What the hell's that for?" the driver asked.

"Getting us here alive."

The driver snatched the coin away. "May I never see you again," he said and stomped on the gas, the car doors slamming as he swung out into traffic.

Silverberg elbowed Early. "You have that effect on everybody?"

CHAPTER 16

September 15—Thursday Afternoon Late
Stephanowitz
"Name, sir?" the Muehelbach's doorman asked.

"James Early. They got a room for me."

"Right, sir." He waved a bellhop over, gave him Early's suitcase, and pointed him inside.

"This way, sirs, ma'am," the bellhop said, a young black man, smooth faced, by Early's guess no more than twenty-one. He moved away with the same hustle the doorman had shown, only to stop and hold open the door for Early and the Silverbergs. "Welcome to the Muehelbach. Your first time here?"

"As a guest," Early said.

"And you good people?" he asked the Silverbergs.

"We live in the city," Mister Silverberg said. He pushed his spectacles up on the bridge of his nose. "We're here to have dinner with this gentleman."

"May I recommend the Kansas City strip steak? The Muehelbach is known for it."

As they went up the steps into the lobby of royal oak paneling and leather furniture that spoke of wealth and comfort, the bellhop asked Early, "Are we holding a room for you, sir?"

"Yes."

"Name, sir?"

"James Early."

"Mister Early, if you wish, you can go right in to dinner. I'll tell them at the desk that you've arrived, and I'll take your bag up to your room for you."

"Well, that's unexpected, but thank you." Early slipped the bellhop a dime.

"Thank you, sir. All part of the service at the Muehelbach."

The bellman started away, but Early called him back. "I understand the president's staying here tonight."

"Yessir, we're holding a suite for Mister Truman. He's speaking to a steel manufacturers convention at The Johnson."

"Couldn't get a room there?"

"The President always stays with us," the bellman said, pride beaming through his words.

Early tugged at his earlobe. "He'll have breakfast here in the morning, I expect."

"I expect so, sir."

"Again, thank you."

"Not at all, sir." The bellhop backed away a step, turned, and went on to the front desk.

Early gandered around at the vastness of the lobby, perhaps three times as long as it was wide, people—men mostly—clustered about talking, some smoking cigars, a few reading newspapers. One of the newspaper readers glanced toward Early and the Silverbergs. He folded his paper and drifted after the trio as Mister Silverberg pointed the way toward the main dining room. "Table for four in the name of Silverberg," he said to the maitre d'.

The man, in stature a double for the doorman except for his vest and swallowtail coat, consulted the notes at his stand.

"Are you?" Early asked, thumbing toward the front of the hotel.

A smile spread across the man's face. "Yessir, that's my brother. There are three of us working here. You met Elroy. My brother Nathan is an accountant in the back office. . . . Follow me, please."

The man moved away with the same brisk pace as the doorman. Early loped along, the Silverbergs hurrying to keep up. At a table in front of the window on Twelfth Street, the maitre d' pulled out a chair for Missus Silverberg and held it. After he seated her, he pulled out a chair for Silverberg. Early merely plopped himself onto one of the velvet chairs across the table from them and tossed his cattleman's hat on the seat of the spare.

The maitre d' gathered the hat. "If it's all right with you, I'll check this in the cloakroom. Your name, sir?"

"James Early."

"Shall I take yours, too?" he asked Silverberg.

The older man handed over his Panama as he said, "Silverberg, just Silverberg."

"Very well."

The maitre d' waved a waiter to the table and hurried away.

The waiter, a smallish man in a tuxedo, came up carrying three goblets of water on a silver tray. He placed a goblet forward and to the side of each of the three. "I'm Terrance," he said. "Anything you need I can get for you."

Early winked at the Silverbergs. "Money?" he asked.

"Except that. But I can tell you where a very reputable card game is, should you wish to win some." He gazed at Missus Silverberg. "Of course," he said, "you never heard it from me. Dinner for three, then?"

"We're expecting a fourth," Silverberg said.

"Very good. Do you wish to order now or would you rather wait?"

A slim man in a white summer suit, a newspaper sticking from his jacket pocket, slipped into the empty chair. "No need to wait," he said.

"Very well. Do you wish menus?"

Silverberg shook his head. "The house specialty for everyone."

"Excellent choice."

While the waiter leaned down to Missus Silverberg, to get the details for her order, Silverberg pointed from Early to the stranger. "Sheriff," he said, "this is Mister Isaac Daniel Stephanowitz from our new nation of Israel."

Early extended his hand, but it was Stephanowitz's left hand that met Early's, making for an awkward shake.

"You'll have to forgive me," Stephanowitz said and brought up his right hand, a clawlike structure, "this one doesn't work very well. Souvenir of another time."

"War?" Early asked.

"You might say that."

The waiter moved to Silverberg where the two discussed in whispers the choices of sides that went with the strip steak.

"You knew Judith?" Early asked.

Stephanowitz leaned in close, his chin resting on the back of his crippled hand. "In Palestine at the time it was becoming Israel. I got there a year earlier courtesy of Mister Churchill."

"You're British?"

"Hardly. Polish—Warsaw. I was studying in London when the German Panzers invaded my country. I couldn't get back home."

"So you—"

"Yes, with a British regiment. The Royal Fusiliers liked my company because I was sexta-lingual—spoke Polish, Yiddish, Hebrew, some Arabic, German, and English the English way."

"I speak it the Kansas way."

"Is it different?"

Early held up his thumb and index finger, a half-inch apart.

The waiter came to Stephanowitz. "And how would you like your steak, sir?" he asked.

"However Mister Silverberg is having his is fine."

"And the sides?"

"Again, whatever Mister Silverberg is having."

The waiter turned to Early, his pencil poised over his pad.

"The same," Early said. "Ah, just a minute. How are they having their steaks?"

"Rare."

"Oh no, I don't want mine bawling when I cut into it. Well done, please."

The waiter raised an eyebrow. "And to drink, sir?"

"Sweet tea now. Coffee later."

"So it shall be," the waiter said and whisked away.

"Did I say something to offend him?" Early asked Stephanowitz.

"Can't imagine what."

Silverberg sipped from his water goblet before he set it aside. "It took a number of cables to maybe twenty people to learn that Mister Stephanowitz was the person closest to Judith in the movement."

"The movement?" Early asked.

"The Zionist movement, and another half-dozen cables to convince him to come to Kansas City."

"Some reluctance, Mister Stephanowitz?" Early asked.

"My name's a mouthful. Call me Steph." He glanced around the room, giving Early the impression he was checking to see whether anyone might be eavesdropping. "I resigned from the British army to join the Haganah."

"And what would that be?"

"In your army, the Rangers. We operated in enemy territory."

"Kill and destroy."

"And get out before the Arabs or the British could catch us, yes. One of my team's jobs was to meet the leaky old ships landing Jewish refugees and get the refugees off the coast, inland before the British could intercept them."

"And Judith?"

"She was one." Stephanowitz paused, as if he were sorting through his words. "She and three friends came in one night," he said. "Their boat capsized in the breakers, and my team fished them out of the water."

Early fiddled with the corner of his cloth napkin. "What did they want to do?"

"The Dutchies? Live and work on a kibbutz—be pioneers, you would say. Judith thought she might like to teach." Again Stephanowitz paused, and again it appeared to Early the man was weighing his words.

Once more the Israeli resumed. "We were talking, Judith and I after we were well inland and safe, and she said she had been an ambulance driver. So I recruited her."

"She drove ambulances for you?"

"No, Land Rovers we liberated from the British, desert cars with machine guns mounted on them." Stephanowitz glanced at Missus Silverberg who had gone blanch white. "Your daughter was a soldier, a very good one."

"We didn't know," Silverberg said.

"She didn't want you to worry." Stephanowitz smiled.

To Early, the smile lacked emotion, as if it were given as a courtesy. He rolled and unrolled the corner of his napkin. "What ended it for her?"

"A nation being born needs money, more money than it has," Stephanowitz said. "My colonel thought Judith would be of greater value to us if she were to return to your country and be a fund-raiser for Israel. The Silverbergs know she was very good at it."

"How good?"

"Ten thousand a month. A third of a million in three years."

"I'm impressed," Early said. "So I have to ask could anyone from what was once Palestine have killed Judith? They can't

173

have loved her."

"It's possible. A year ago, we picked up word she had become a target, so I dispatched one of my men to shadow her, to be her bodyguard if necessary."

"And?"

"Nothing ever happened, so we called him home."

"When was this?"

Stephanowitz pulled a small, black notebook from his inside pocket. He paged into it, reading down. "Your Valentine's Day, February Fourteenth."

"Perhaps too soon?"

"It would appear so."

"You came all this way, eight thousand miles, to tell me so little?" Early asked.

Stephanowitz closed his notebook. "I'm a soldier. I go where ordered."

"Uh-huh."

The waiter hustled up with a serving tray he carried high over his shoulder. He swung the tray down and set off plates of steaks and baked potatoes. As the waiter gave Early his plate, he announced, "And one extremely dead steer for you, sir."

CHAPTER 17

September 15—Thursday Evening
Meeting at the Memorial

Early stood back, studying the frieze that comprised much of the north wall of Kansas City's War Memorial. Twilight deepened, putting the words and the life-size figures into ever-increasing shadows until a series of floodlights flicked on, making the wall, the halls at either end, and the monolith in the center appear as in daylight were it not that the sky beyond them had gone from deep reds to purple in the time Early had been there. Overhead, he heard the thrumming of motors and gazed up to see the wing and taillights of an airplane, an airliner. A DC-Three, Early guessed, bound for—where else could it be?—the island airport on the north side of the city. Some way to travel, he thought. Where had the passengers come from? The pilots, the crew? Where would they go tomorrow?

Something else took his attention, the near silent steps of someone crossing the Memorial's lawn a quarter to the rear.

"Mister Stephanowitz," Early said without turning, "wondered when you'd come away from the trees."

"You knew?"

"Saw you in Union Station, in the lobby of the Muehelbach, even coming up the hill."

"And I thought I was a pretty good spy."

"One of the better ones, I expect. Of course, I didn't know who you were at the train station or the hotel until you joined

175

us in the dining room."

Stephanowitz, his suitcoat slung over his shoulder and his necktie pulled loose, sidled up next to Early. "Have you seen me anywhere else?"

"Come to think of it, the cemetery, yes, after Judith's funeral. As I remember, you weren't in your white suit that day."

"White would not have been respectful. You are very good, Mister Early. . . . Some memorial, isn't it?" Stephanowitz said, gesturing at the frieze.

"Indeed."

"I wonder what kind of memorial we will build in Jerusalem someday, to remember those who died in making the new Israel?"

"Know many of them?"

"Only those on the ground in the small area where I moved. Not one died a hero, Mister Early. None of us really wanted to be there, certainly not with a gun or a grenade in our hand."

"That's not what your prime minister and your president say."

"Stories old men tell. They didn't have to lace on boots in the morning or look down a gun barrel at an enemy intent on killing them." Stephanowitz shook a cigarette from a pack. He put the cigarette between his lips before he offered a stick to Early. "Do you know what the real tragedy is?"

Early, intent on the frieze, did not answer, not immediately, nor did he take a cigarette. He gazed at a bareheaded soldier carved into the granite, to the side of the Angel of Victory, the soldier standing next to a cross. "Don't know what it was for you," Early said, "but for us, it was the fact that we never stayed long enough to bury our dead. I didn't see the cemeteries until the war was over. The one on the bluffs beyond Omaha Beach— acres and acres of crosses."

Stephanowitz flicked open a brushed-steel Zippo. He lit his

cigarette. "I have seen it and the British cemetery above Gold Beach. . . . You know one day, thirty, forty years from now, we will be the old men. Our grandsons will say the same things of us because we took our nations to war." He blew a plume of smoke toward the night sky.

"Perhaps there won't be another war."

"And perhaps you and I won't wake every night, screaming from our nightmares. War, my friend, it's a condition of mankind. Read it in your Old Testament. Read it in our Torah."

"War is holy?"

"No, it's killing someone you do not know before he can kill you." Stephanowitz pointed his cigarette at a cannon and gun crew and a group of charging infantrymen carved into the east end of the frieze. "That is what war is, deafening and bloody."

"And peace like we have now?"

"Merely an intermission."

Early swept a hand toward the women sculpted into the frieze at either side of the center. "Tell me about Judith. Could she be one of them?"

Stephanowitz shook his head. "Mothers and nurses, no. She would be on the far end with the charging soldiers."

"You did mention that to the Silverbergs. Is there something you didn't want to tell them?"

"You noticed."

A half grin prodded at Early's mouth.

"Yes. We were lovers."

"Really."

"War does that to men and women, when you doubt you will see the next day."

"So it wasn't serious?"

"We thought it was at the time." Stephanowitz shambled up to the broad sweep of steps that fronted the frieze. He dusted an area on one and sat down, the concrete warm, still holding a bit of heat from the day. The man from Israel glanced up at Early.

"Let me tell you a story," he said. "One night in a mortar attack on us, we lost our Land Rover. A direct hit. We saw the car go up in the biggest damn ball of flame." Stephanowitz took a heavy drag on his cigarette. He blew the smoke away. "We had a plan. We all went to screaming like we had been hit, and, one by one, we went silent. . . . They did what we never would. After some time, they walked into our camp to survey their victory."

"And you slaughtered them," Early said.

Stephanowitz turned his cigarette up in his claw of a hand. He studied the glowing end in a manner that suggested it was something he'd never seen before. "They were the enemy," he said and tapped ash away. "We disposed of them, threw their bodies in the fire. But here we were in the desert, not all that far from the Sea of Galilee and no car. We occasionally employed a scout—Mustafa. He told us where a British patrol was camped, where we might, um, liberate another Land Rover. Judith volunteered to go."

"Did you let her?"

"Of course. She took two others and said she would meet us at a point some miles away, at a place called Hannah's Well, an hour before dawn."

Early settled next to Stephanowitz. He set his cattleman's hat on the step and finger-combed his hair. "She didn't show, did she?"

"No." Stephanowitz stubbed out his cigarette. "I never really liked Mustafa, so I questioned him . . . persuasively. . . . Had his hand strapped to a table and proceeded to cut off his fingers one joint at a time."

Early glanced away.

"When he had only stumps and a thumb left," Stephanowitz said, "he told us between soul-wrenching cries that he had sent 'that woman' into a trap, that the British camp was a Palestinian camp. They were waiting for her." He shook another cigarette from his pack and lit it. "I slit his throat, and we went after Judith. Found her wandering alone not far from Hannah's Well."

Early turned back. With elbows on knees, he cast a sideward glance at Stephanowitz, wondering, then asked, "Was that the knife in the boot top?"

"The one bit of truth we allowed Judith to put in a letter to home. Every parent needs to know his child is fearless. It is a fiction, but it is an important fiction."

Early tapped the claw that clutched the burning cigarette.

"Yes," Stephanowitz said, "everyone asks, and you I shall tell."

"Why?"

"Because you've been a soldier at war." He rose and went to the broad, waterfall-like fountain at the far end of the steps. Stephanowitz sloshed a hand in. He raked the water across his forehead and the back of his neck. "It's hot for nighttime. . . . I got a message to report to Haifa for a briefing of some kind. If you are a stranger in a strange land—"

"It's safer to travel at night," Early said, finishing Stephanowitz's words.

"Yes. Somehow on the second night, I became lost, terribly lost. We Haganah did not have uniforms. We fought in civilian clothes, often in robes and head rags we stole from those we killed. It is better not to look out of place. I saw a light in this mud hut and took a chance."

"You told us you could speak Arabic."

Stephanowitz again dabbled his fingers in the water. He fractured the surface, half grinning. "I went to the door and said I was separated from my men and could they direct me to the Haifa road, said I was Abdul Saleem. There must have been magic to the name because the family welcomed me as if I were a lost cousin."

"Invited you in?"

"And sat me down, and served me the strongest coffee ever and, before I could take a second sip, the woman put a knife to my throat. The robe I wore was her husband's, she said." Stephanowitz took a last puff on his cigarette. He ground it out under his shoe and kicked the butt into the grass. "So the torture began—Who was I? Where was I from? Was I Haganah or Irgun? Her son, not ten years old as I am living, wielded a rock that he had to lift with both hands. With each question and a nod from his mother, he hammered my hand, starting at the tips of my fingers. I heard myself screaming as Mustafa had done, and, when the rock came down on the back of my hand, I heard myself blubbering out the most fantastic lies. . . . And I suppose God took mercy on me. I passed out."

Stephanowitz again dabbled in the water. He flicked the cooling beads away from his fingertips. "When I woke, I found myself in some kind of dog pen, my good hand tied to a stake, the sun high in the sky."

"How did you get away?"

"As you would say, the cavalry arrived. A Land Rover roared past with my second on the machine gun, firing, tearing up the camp. Judith vaulted the fence. She cut me loose. Two minutes, I swear, and we were gone."

"Jeez."

"Yes. My second was shot as we raced away. We buried him at Hannah's Well that night."

"And you?"

"Desk job in Haifa."

"Judith?"

"A month later, she came to see me, walked in when I was in what we shall call a compromising position with my male nurse.

That was the last I saw of her. She left Haifa and Israel in such a hurry that she left behind her diaries." Stephanowitz took a wrapped package from the pocket of his coat. "I give them to you. I do not think you will want to give them to Judith's parents. I certainly would not."

"Would it surprise you that you're in an entry in her last diary?" Early asked. "Oh, not by name, but as a man from Israel. You came to see her."

Stephanowitz's lips stretched tight across his front teeth.

"You want to tell me about it?" Early asked.

"I'm a diplomat now."

"Earlier, you said you were a soldier."

"I am that, too. But as a diplomat, I can courier money out of your country. . . . I had heard Judith was getting careless, reckless in her fund-raising, drawing attention to herself. So I went to see her, to caution her, and to apologize for our last time together."

"Three years later?"

"What can I say? I am a man, and we men are sometimes slow in doing the proper thing. I sensed something was not right with Judith. She wouldn't tell me what it was."

"I gather you had your suspicions."

"And still do. That Gentile husband of hers."

"But he was nowhere around when Judith was killed."

"Have you not heard of friends lying for friends?"

CHAPTER 18

September 16—Friday Morning
The Man from Independence
Early sat on a window ledge of sandstone on the Muehelbach Hotel's Twelfth Street side, one leg thrown over the other, studying the Kansas City Star's livestock market page. The long time between rains had dried pastures, and ranchers in the Flint Hills, those who couldn't lease pastures in Nebraska, were shipping their cattle to the stockyards. A glut of beef. Prices down for the sixth straight week. He turned to the sports pages, hoping for better news.

A gaggle of men poured out of the lobby of the Muehelbach onto the sidewalk, led by one in a light gray suit—double-breasted—and an equally light gray fedora, the brim shaped like a cattleman's hat, like Early's. The man, chuckling with the others, wore wire-rimmed glasses.

Early glanced up as the group neared. He folded his paper and pushed off the ledge, taking a moment to brush grit from the seat of his pants. Then he swung in beside the man in the lead. "Mind if I join your Early Risers Walking Society, Mister Truman?" he asked.

"If you can keep up," the president said. "Most of the boys are newsmen. You a newsman?"

"County sheriff."

"Whoops, Harry," one of the walkers called out, "you get yourself jammed up with the law?"

Truman turned to the man, a muscular fellow in shirtsleeves and a duffer's cap. Truman showed him a long face before he swung about and continued on. "Am I in trouble?" he asked, laughing, the other walkers laughing with him.

"Not at all," Early said.

"Sheriff, where?"

"A bit west of here. Riley County, Kansas."

"Think I can count the number of votes I got there on one hand. Yours one of them?"

"No, but my dad's was."

Truman, moving at a pace to do a ten-minute mile, aimed his cane to the left at the intersection and all did a "to the left march" onto the Wyandotte Avenue sidewalk. "We usually shoot the breeze on world events," he said to Early. "You up for that?"

"Could one of those be the poor treatment of a black man?"

"Possibly. Here at home last year I ordered the Army to integrate."

"That was the right thing to do, sir," Early said, the fast walk nagging at his leg of shrapnel.

"You been in the Army?" Truman asked.

"The Big Red One."

"Damn fine division."

"About this ill treatment, sir—"

"I get the feeling this is going to be close to home or you wouldn't be talking to me."

"Yessir. One of your Secret Service detail."

Truman's smile fled. He turned to the other walkers. "Boys, why don't you go back to the hotel and have breakfast. Tell 'em I'm buying."

One in the middle of the pack waved a notebook. "But, we gotta find out what you're gonna do if there's a steel strike."

"Same thing I did when there was a coal strike, bust it. Steel's too important to the country."

"Can we quote you?"

"Hell no. Now get along. This fella and I have to talk private, soldier to soldier."

"And you're buyin' breakfast?" a man with a camera asked.

"Didn't I say so, Johnny?"

"Just checkin'."

The group turned and mumbled away. One swung back. "Harry?" he called out.

"Yeah, Ted?"

"Can we ask about this conversation?"

"You can ask. Probably won't tell you anything."

Truman set off once more toward the levy district at his ten-minute mile clip. One of those among the Early Risers, a man in a white summer suit, broke away from the others. He fell in some twenty paces behind Truman and Early.

A Checker taxi swung over. It idled alongside the president, the driver tapping his horn.

Truman waved his cane, and the driver grinned. "Give 'em hell, Harry."

"Did last night. Told those steel men where to get off."

"Attaboy. You got my vote if you want to run again."

"I'll remember that."

The driver, his grin bringing light to the canyon that was Wyandotte Avenue, waved and wheeled his taxi back into the proper lane. He drove on.

"Anybody you don't talk to?" Early asked.

"Give me two minutes with that man and I'll know more about what concerns this country than talking all day to the United States Senate."

"But you were a senator."

"And one of the few who never forgot who sent us there, who we were working for."

The light changed from green to red, and Truman stopped at

the intersection. He tapped a staccato beat with his cane on the curb while he glanced one way, then the other. "No traffic," he said. "Dammit, let's go."

Early stepped out fast to catch up with Truman already at the middle of the crosswalk. "You should have waited."

"I'm out to walk, not stand around. So what's this thing eating at you?"

Once more in lockstep, the men hopped the curb and continued on, a towering bank building to the right, blocking the morning sun, and Bernard's Department Store to the left, neither yet open.

"At the train station yesterday afternoon," Early said, "one of your Secret Service men knocked down a black man. Called him a nigger and refused to apologize."

Truman glanced at his fellow walker. "You know this how?"

"I was there with Mister Haskins, the black man. We were talking when it happened. I ran your man down and he showed me his badge."

"What's his name?"

"He didn't say."

"That's not very helpful, sheriff. Anyone see this?"

The man trailing behind quick-stepped up to flank Truman. "I did," he said.

"Saw you back there," Truman said without slowing. "Wondered who you might be."

"Isaac Stephanowitz—Israel, diplomat."

"And I'm supposed to know you?"

"No sir. Very minor functionary, but an able pickpocket." Stephanowitz brought out a wallet. He let it fall open to a gold shield. "Your man never missed it. It's yours."

Truman stopped at the next traffic light. He took the wallet and opened it to a driver's license. "Wally Andrews," he said, reading the name. "Works the graveyard shift. Saw him when I came out of my room this morning. Pretty good man. . . . None of this convinces me."

"But sir," Early said.

Truman gave him a fish-eyed stare. "I'm not saying you're not telling the truth. I'm just saying the word of a pickpocket isn't worth much for support."

"Would pictures help?" Stephanowitz asked.

Truman turned to him.

Stephanowitz held out a camera only slightly larger than a package of chewing gum. "It's a Leika, German-made. I have three pictures of the incident in here and three more of the sheriff and your Mister Andrews arguing."

"Mind?" Truman asked as he took the camera. "Never saw one this small."

"There aren't many around."

"So if I have this film developed?"

"It will show you what Mister Early told you."

"Sonuvabitch." Truman slipped the camera into his side pocket. He turned back toward the hotel and again set off at a ten-minute mile pace. "I'll call Wally in. If he says he did what you say he did and what this film is supposed to support, he's on the street. I'll not have that attitude in any of the people who work for me. . . . A diplomat, huh?" Truman asked Stephanowitz. "What were you doing at Union Station?"

"Observing the sheriff before our meeting last night."

"Perhaps I should know why."

"Let me just say it is a security matter for the new nation of Israel."

"In Kansas City?"

"Do you know Mishka and Ethel Silverberg?"

"They've captained one of my wards since I was elected to the Senate."

"They can tell you."

Truman, with a studied glance, once more took the measure of Stephanowitz. "You registered with your embassy?"

"Yessir."

"So they can track you down, get this camera back to you?"

"I would appreciate that. It was hard to come by."

"How so?"

"I had to kill a man for it. . . . It was in the war, sir."

Truman peered at Early as the trio stepped off the curb at the next intersection. "And the man at the center of all this, he a good man?"

"Yessir, waiter on a Union-Pacific dining car. Before that, a steward on the battleship Missouri."

"Well, now that's impressive," Truman said. "And should I want to get in touch with this Mister Haskins?"

Early stopped. He took a small notepad and a pencil from his shirt pocket and scribbled. When he finished, he tore out the page and handed it to Truman. "Full name. Lives in Chicago. I don't have that address, but on the note, that's the address of his sister in Kansas City."

"Missouri?"

"Kansas."

"That's almost as good."

"Some of us would say it's a mite better, Mister Truman."

"By 'us,' you mean sheriffs from Kansas?"

CHAPTER 19

September 16—Friday Afternoon
Home Again

Early drove absently through the Wildcat Valley, toward Keats, toward home, wondering whether anyone would believe him if he said he had talked to the president, got him maybe to fix a problem. At best, he thought, the response would be what's a good Republican like you doing talking to a damn Democrat?

He slowed for half a dozen dairy cows ambling along in the borrow ditch and waved to the boy herding them toward their home and milking time. He chuckled. Not every cattle drive is a massive thing. Early drove out of the shadows cast by a patch of hickory trees, squinting when the late afternoon sun, low in the sky, smacked him in the face, a squint he held until he came up on Keats and drove into new shadows from the hackberry trees on his lot.

Early wheeled his Jeep about, into the driveway, surprised that two cars were there, an Oldsmobile, parked square in the drive near the kitchen, a car that looked like Gladys Morton's—it was, he was sure of it, he remembered the dent in the rear fender—and a Cadillac, crosswise in the front yard, Doc Grafton's Cadillac.

Screams ripped from his house as he cut the Jeep's engine.

Early bailed out. He raced for the back porch and the screen, whipped it open and plunged inside. Thelma, in her nightgown, barefoot, her hair unkempt and wild, slashed out with a butcher

knife at a blue-haired woman—Gladys, Early's secretary—
crouching at the far side of the table.

Thelma slashed again, screaming, "You'll never kill me!" She
sliced through Gladys's upper sleeve, and the woman yelped.

Gladys grabbed for her arm. "Sheriff, she's crazy!"

Thelma turned, her knife in front of her, her eyes filled with
terror and confusion. "Jimmy? Jimmy? They said they'd killed
you. They said you were dead."

She rushed to him, threw herself at him, sobbing. Early
caught her and her wrist, held the butcher knife up, away from
himself.

Grafton, harried and hurrying in from the front room, syringe
in hand, plunged the needle into Thelma's shoulder.

"Jimmy," she said, her eyes going wide, "you let them kill
me."

"Thelma," Grafton said, "it's only gonna make you go to
sleep."

"Jimmy?" Her voice and her eyes pleaded with Early.

A knee gave way, and he felt her weight increasing as she
clung to him. "What the hell's going on here?"

"Sedative. Enough to knock a horse down," Grafton said. He
wiped the needle on his sleeve before he dropped the syringe in
his breast pocket. "You gonna help get her into bed or are you
gonna stand there like some dumb yahoo gaping at the moon?"

"I still want to know what the hell's going on."

"Put her in bed, and we'll tell you. It's damn complicated.
Gladys is cut, and I got to look after her."

Early shook the butcher knife from Thelma's hand. He then
turned her, got an arm behind her back and his other under her
knees and swept her up—carried her out of the kitchen, leaving
in his wake the parched smell of a coffeepot boiled dry. Early
went through the front room and into the sleeping room, a
room spared the coffee stench, a room where a slight perfume

of lilac claimed the air. He lowered Thelma onto the bed.

She worked at keeping her eyes open, yet they seemed not to focus. "Jimmy, why they doing this to me?"

"Who's doing what to you?"

"People outside. Got a hearse with them."

"Thel, there's no one outside," Early said as he drew a sheet over her. He thought better of it—too warm a day, too warm an evening, gonna be too warm a night—and drew the sheet back. Early sat down on the edge of the bed. He ran his fingers through Thelma's hair, brushed it into place, taking care not to pull too hard at the snarls.

"Jimmy," she said, words slurring, "can't keep awake."

"You don't have to."

". . . afraid."

"It's all right. I'm here."

"Jim . . ."

Thelma's eyes closed. The lines in her forehead that had been trenched there by anguish softened.

"Jimmy," Gladys said from behind him, from the doorway.

He turned. Her sleeve had been cut away and a bandage taped to her upper arm.

"Jimmy, I came out to check on Thelma like I told you I would, and you're not going to believe it."

"I sure don't believe what I saw," he croaked out.

"Jimmy, I know. I found her hiding in your little pantry. When I called her out, she rushed at me with that knife, screaming I'd killed you."

Early shook his head. "Couldn't be."

"I swear it was, Jimmy, I swear it was. I ran out of your kitchen as fast as I could and next door and used their phone to call Doctor Grafton. Stayed out of the house until he came."

"Where's Ellis and his wife?"

"Who?"

"The people next door."

"There was nobody there. I just went in and used their phone, and waited."

Grafton pushed past Gladys. He hauled a kitchen chair with him and parked it beside the bed. He slumped down, the chair squeaking under his weight.

"Anything happen like this before, Cactus, anything remotely like it that you didn't tell me?" Grafton put his fingertips on Thelma's wrist and counted the pulse.

"Hell, I don't even know what happened this time."

"Gladys told you." He caressed the pale skin of Thelma's forehead and temples. "Well, she's gonna sleep now."

"How long?"

"The night. Maybe longer." Grafton peered up at Early. "Now tell me how she's been doing."

"I don't know, maybe worried about the baby some. Judith's murder was getting to her."

"Yes."

"Yes, what?"

Grafton leaned with his elbows on his knees. He stared up into Early's face. "Cactus, I doctor the body, not the mind. What we got here is way beyond me. We got three choices. You can do as my grandfather did when his sister went off her nut— hide her away in the attic and never let the world know anything." He raised two fingers. "Second, we can bundle Thelma off to the Menninger boys over in Topeka. They know a helluva lot about the mind."

Early drew down on his mustache. "I've heard they demand big pay. On my salary, I can't afford that."

Grafton brought up a third finger. "We wait and see. Maybe it's just what the Menningers would call an episode, and it won't repeat itself."

"You believe that?"

"Cactus, I don't know what to believe."

"Jimmy," Gladys said. She came up beside Early and put her hand on his shoulder. "I can wait with you. I can stay the night."

He touched her hand. It had a warmth he had not expected. "No, Henry's going to worry as it is. You'd best get on home."

"You sure?"

"Yes. You drive all right?"

"She didn't hurt me that bad, and I'm sure she didn't mean to hurt me at all. You be in in the morning?"

"I'll call and let you know."

Her hand went to the back of Early's neck. She stroked his hair, then left.

"She's never been so nice to me," Early said.

"Gladys is a better soul than you give her credit for."

As if they had run out of words to share with one another, Early and Grafton went silent, a silence broken only by the squeak of a screen door's hinge, then a car's motor starting, and the whine of a transmission as a car backed around and drove out. Silence again until crickets and tree frogs filled the void with their night music.

Grafton roused himself. He pushed up and rubbed his face, his whiskers rasping like sandpaper against the skin of his hands. "Think I'll boil us up some coffee if the pot isn't burned too bad," he said. "You had any supper?"

"No."

"Me neither. I'll see what your good wife's got in the fridge and the cupboard."

He wandered out, leaving Early alone in the gloom. Early thought about turning on the lamp on the night table, but . . . He let his shoulders slump.

He felt something shaking his forearm.

"Cactus?"

Early opened his eyes, and he massaged the heels of his hands over his brows. "Yeah?"

"Coffee here and something to eat," Grafton said.

Early took the mug and the plate offered him.

Grafton slipped a knife and fork into Early's shirt pocket. With his hands free, Grafton turned on the lamp, a Tiffany, on the night table. "Nice," he said.

"That was Thel's grandma's."

Grafton touched the glass shade. "They're not making these anymore, old friend. You'd best take care of it." He went back to the kitchen.

Early sucked on the coffee before he tried the main course— scrambled eggs with chopped onion, pepper, meat of some kind, and fried potatoes thrown in, and a slab of well-buttered bread that Thelma had baked before he went to Kansas City.

Grafton returned with his own plate and coffee. "The way you're putting it down, it can't be too bad," he said.

Early pointed his fork at his plate. "You put cowboy round steak in this."

"Pardon?"

"Baloney. My granddad always called baloney cowboy round steak. . . . Doc, didn't know you could do kitchen duty."

"Worked my way through college as a short-order cook. Never had much time for it since medical school. You?"

"Fair hand. Batched for years. My momma taught me well."

"That's good."

"Why?"

"If Thelma doesn't come back, you may be doing the cooking again. . . . Gladys told me you went to Kansas City. Learn much?"

Early fiddled with the food remaining on his plate. "A lot about some things and not much about others."

"Tell me about the not much. It's probably more interesting."

Early scooped a forkful of scrambled—well, he didn't know what to call it—into his mouth and chewed. After he swallowed, he waved his fork at Grafton. "Met this fella who knew Judith in Israel, well, Palestine as it was then. He said he'd heard the Arabs had sent someone to kill Judith, and he dispatched one of his men to protect her."

"Good bread," Grafton said, pointing to the quarter slab he had left.

"Thelma baked it."

"Figured. Probably the only thing you ever baked was biscuits."

"Catheads, biscuits the size of a man's fist."

"Ooo, that's good. . . . So whatever became of this international conspiracy?"

"Nothing. He called his man home. He thinks the person who killed Judith is in the neighborhood."

"Oh?"

"Bill."

Grafton, working on his coffee, stopped. He stared at Early. "You said people told you he was with them at the time, in Abilene, wasn't it?"

"Judith's friend thinks they're lying."

"You gonna check it out?"

"Guess I'll have to."

Early, long asleep, felt something flop over his chest. He opened an eye and peered down at it—Thelma's arm. She had rolled onto her side and thrown her arm across him. "Hon," he said.

Thelma mumbled.

Early rubbed the arm. "Hon?"

"Yes."

"You awake?"

"Little. When you get home?"

"Last night. You all right?"

"Shouldn't I be?"

"Can we talk?"

Thelma turned her face to him, a world of exhaustion showing in the trenched lines. "Feel like I been hit with a board."

Early kicked at Grafton snoring in the kitchen chair.

"What?" he said.

"Thelma's awake."

Grafton itched around his dome of thinning hair as he yawned. He pulled a watch from his pants pocket and squinted at it. "Seven-ten. Good God, it's morning."

"What's he doing here?" Thelma asked.

"You had a bad day, yesterday. He came out to help you."

"Don't 'member."

Grafton slipped his fingertips under Thelma's wrist. He counted the pulse.

"What you doing that for?" she asked.

"Dammit, you made me lose count."

"Jimmy, shhh," Thelma said, putting a finger to his lips.

"That's right, it's my fault."

"Pulse is right where it ought to be," Grafton said. He put his hand on her forehead. "No fever."

"Am I going to have my baby?"

"Not today. Not for three months if everything goes as it's supposed to."

"Good, 'cause I'm not ready." Thelma yawned.

Early's nose wrinkled. "Morning mouth. You need to brush your teeth."

"Bet you do, too."

"Thelma," Grafton said, interrupting, "if Cactus helps you,

195

you think you can get up and come in the kitchen? We need to talk a bit."

"Can try."

Grafton slapped at Early's leg as he made his way out of the room.

Early slipped from under Thelma's arm. He rolled out of the bed in stockinged feet and the tans he'd worn yesterday. Early let the window shade up as he came around to the other side of the bed. There he helped Thelma turn onto her back and sit up. "Ready to put your feet on the floor?"

"I'm not helpless."

"All right." Early threw up his hands in surrender and stepped back.

Thelma twisted around. She brought her feet out and down. "Where are my shoes?" she asked, peering around.

Early hunkered down on all fours. He looked under the bed. "These old beaters?" he asked, raking out a pair of cracked leather shoes Thelma wore to work in the garden.

"They're fine." She slipped her feet into them. As she and Early came up, she fell against him, giggling. "My legs don't work too well, do they? Guess that comes from being pregnant."

And then Thelma groaned. She leaned on Early, clutched at his arm. "I got to go to the toilet."

"Slop jar or the outhouse?"

"Jimmy, I haven't peed in a chamber pot since I was a kid."

"All right, let's go," he said and helped her along, out into the brighter front room and the even brighter, sunshine-filled kitchen. Early gestured at the screen door.

"I can guess that one," Grafton said from the counter space where he whipped away at something in a mixing bowl.

"Now will you really tell me why Doctor Grafton is here?" Thelma asked when she and Early were outside, stepping off the porch and onto the dew-drenched path that led to the house of easy rest. Early had painted the thing and put in a new padded seat when he and Thelma bought the place at Keats.

"Thelma, you had a bad night."

"I don't remember it. Truly, Jimmy, I don't."

"Do you remember Gladys being here?" Early asked as he opened the door. He helped Thelma up the step and inside.

"No," she said.

Early closed the door and hummed around outside, waiting. A mockingbird and its mate winged into the hackberry above his head. He watched them, marveling at the complex songs of the male, none of them his—the redwing blackbird's, the robin's, the chipping sparrow's, the wood thrush's. The male even mewed like a cat. That drew the attention of the neighbors' calico wandering through Early's backyard. The cat glanced up, its gaze searching the branches of the tree. It answered the call, turning its mew up at the end, as if asking, who are you?

Early didn't have time to react. The two mockingbirds threw themselves from the tree. They dove toward the cat, the cat shocked and surprised. It raced away, to save itself from the gray fiends that rose, twisted, and dove again.

And then it was over. The birds swept back up into the hackberry where the male resumed his mewing.

"Is that cat out there?" Thelma asked through the cracks in the board wall.

"Not anymore," Early said. "It's a mockingbird."

She stepped outside, straightening her nightgown. "Where is it?"

He pointed up, and Thelma twisted to follow the direction of his index finger. "Oh, isn't he pretty. And look, there's two of them."

"Man and wife."

"Isn't that nice?"

Early took Thelma's hand. He placed it over his arm. "You

197

hungry for breakfast?"

"Unusually hungry. I can't explain it."

"You are eating for two."

"I suppose. Wouldn't it be amazing if I were eating for three? Wouldn't you like to have twins, husband?"

That thought hadn't occurred to Early. He wasn't all certain he could handle one baby, but two? He choked on the idea, went silent.

They walked together back to the kitchen porch, Thelma's gaze flitting from the English rose bush to her herb garden, her smiles and "oohs" suggesting to Early that she was seeing them for the first time, enjoying their perfumes. And they went on inside.

Grafton flopped a crispy-edged pancake onto a plate. "Sit the both of you and enjoy the great doctor's corn cakes. Found some sweet corn in the fridge and threw it in the batter."

He handed Early an amber jar. "Cactus, you lucky fella, you managed to get hold of a jar of Homer Greene's sorghum syrup. You're gonna live rich this morning."

Thelma slathered her pancake with butter before she accepted the open jar from Early. She drizzled some of its contents over her pancake. "Sorghum, doesn't that smell wonderful?"

"Doc," Early said, "she doesn't have any memory of last night, not even Gladys."

"That's good." Grafton slipped a china mug of coffee in front of Thelma and one in front of Early. "There are some things that aren't worth remembering." He went back to the stove and poured fresh batter into the skillet, the batter's edges hissing and snapping in the hot bacon fat.

Thelma cut a bite from her pancake. "You know, Jimmy, I really ought to hurry. I'm going to be late for school."

"It's Saturday."

"It is not," she said and fit the bite of pancake into her mouth.

Grafton lifted the edge of the pancake in his skillet. He studied the underside before he worked his flipper under and turned the pancake over to fry on its second side. "Thelma, what day is it?" he asked.

"Friday."

"That was yesterday."

"No, it wasn't."

"What do you remember of yesterday?"

"Everything I had my students do in class, then coming home and finding Jimmy's note on the table saying he'd gone to Kansas City and would be home Friday." She laid her fork aside as she turned to Early, her eyes widening. "You told me you got in last night. Have I lost a day?"

Grafton came over. He shoveled a pancake from his skillet onto Early's plate. "It appears so."

"What happened?"

"Probably nothing important."

"Why can't I remember yesterday? Why can't I remember Jimmy coming home?"

"It's a mystery, Thelma," Grafton said. "We don't really know. And if that's the only day you lose, well, that's really not so bad, is it?"

CHAPTER 20

September 19—Monday Morning
Abilene

Early, rolling out of Chapman for Abilene, fiddled with the frequency selector on his police radio. Satisfied he'd found the Dickinson County crystal, he squeezed the transmitter button on his microphone.

"Dickinson County Sheriff's Department, this is Riley County Sheriff James Early, come on?"

A crackling came back through his speaker followed by the voice of someone who could sing bass in a church choir. "Who the hell's on my frequency?"

Early pressed his transmitter button again. "James Early."

"Cactus, you got my crystal in your radio?"

"Sure 'nuff, Ronnie."

"That's gawddamn illegal, doncha know?"

"You gonna report me?"

After a long silence, the Dickinson sheriff came back. "Manhattan's too far out for your signal to reach my tower. Where the hell are you?"

"Chapman. Just topped Indian Hill. Be in your office in fifteen minutes. I need your help."

"The hell you say."

"Ronnie, you in a mood? Wife kick you out? You sleeping in the jail again?"

"Cactus, that's got nothin' to do with the world."

"Right. I'm fourteen minutes out, going off the air."

Early thought better of that last statement. He pulled off onto the shoulder and clicked his frequency selector to Riley County. From the high ground of Indian Hill, he thought he had an off-chance of hitting his tower on Bluemont Hill.

Early spoke into his microphone. "Sheriff's office, anybody in?"

A voice came back, faint. "Go ahead, sheriff."

"Alice, ask Gladys when she comes in to call Thelma, would you, see how she's doing?"

"We'll take care of it."

"Sure was bull-headed when I left. Intends to teach today."

"Got it."

"So you know, I'm on my way to Cowboy town. Be back in the afternoon. Early out." He hung his mic over the mirror at the top of his Jeep's windshield. Early rolled onto the highway and down Indian Hill, clicking the frequency selector back to Dickinson County. That done, he picked up the RC bottle tucked between his thighs and chugged a swallow. He had left Keats at sunup, driven south across country until clear of Fort Riley, then headed west to Junction City where he had breakfast with the Geary County sheriff. There he worked out a deal to put a repeater on the Geary tower so he could broadcast to and monitor the radio calls from the three sheriff's departments to the west. State law forbade the sharing of frequencies, but Early and the Geary sheriff—and the Pottawatomie County sheriff to the east—called it intercounty cooperation.

Early gazed about at the parched milo fields that bordered US Forty. Rain, he concluded, was as desperately needed here as it was at home.

A truck appeared on the horizon, rolling his way, wavering through the heat shimmering up off the concrete. As the truck came closer, Early could see it, the snub nose of a GMC semi huffing along, a trailer behind. Before he met the truck, he put his thumb over the top of his pop bottle. The driver sounded his air horn, and Early responded with a wave. And the Humphrey's freighter rumbled by, roiling up dust from the gravel shoulder, swirling it around Early and his Jeep.

Early coughed. He spit and, after he popped out of the far side of the freighter's storm, took another slug of RC and spit that overboard, too.

When Early topped the rise over which the freighter had come, he saw wheat fields harvested and more fields of milo, and on the horizon two grain elevators, gray concrete sentinels arrayed against a cloudless azure sky. This, Early felt, is Kansas . . . you see the elevators long before you see the towns that cluster around them. An elevator also meant a railroad track lay nearby because wheat grown here was railed out to markets in Chicago and Minneapolis where the great grain millers had their factories. Abilene's railroad was the U-P, the same that went through Manhattan, Topeka, Kansas City and beyond to the east, and Salina, Goodland, Denver and beyond to the west, the railroad that employed Bill Smitts.

At Detroit City, US Forty veered from southwest to due west. Early passed a star route carrier stopped on the shoulder, stuffing a newspaper and letters into a rusted mailbox at the end of a rancher's lane. And he waved to a mess of kids at the end of another ranch road, kids he knew were waiting for the school bus. A bus appeared a mile later, pulling onto the highway from a side road, a county highway—a single track of dust and dirt.

Early spoke into his microphone again. "Ronnie, countdown begins. I'm at the edge of town."

"Already?"

"Your road's as straight as a bee's flight home."

"S'pose you expect some hospitality."

"I'm drinking RC today. Like it on ice."

"An' I'd like a pay raise."

The Jeep jolted, and Early grabbed for his hat to keep from losing it as his vehicle bucked through a pothole vacated by broken concrete. Less than half a mile on, he slowed and turned left onto Abilene's only other paved thoroughfare, State Fifteen, the north/south main street of Abilene—Buckeye Street—and ahead saw what he was looking for, Abilene's ice plant. Early parked in front.

As he came in, he asked a woman reading a newspaper, "Could a fella get a bucket of chipped ice here?"

She, built wide for work and dressed in Montgomery Ward overalls, glanced up, then barked over her shoulder. "Archie! Got a man out here wants a bucket of ice." She eyed Early from the toes of his dusty boots to the top of his equally dusty cattleman's hat. "Not seen you in here before."

"From Manhattan, here to see your sheriff." Early parked his butt against the wall. "Thought I'd take him some ice. Got to be darn hot in that courthouse."

"Darn hot everywhere, but that's good for business, mine at least."

Early motioned at the squat red box-cooler across the room. "Got anything other than Coke in there?"

"Grape Nehi, Orange Crush, a root beer we make here, and RC. Root beer's awful good if I say so myself."

A man in a leather work apron, hugging a bucket of ice, came through the door by the counter.

"How about stuffing a half-dozen bottles of RC and a half-dozen of your root beer in with the ice?" Early asked.

The woman pointed at the pop cooler, and her helper went to it. He pulled the cover up until it leaned against the wall. One by one, he rattled bottles along and off the tracks that suspended them in the cooler.

"Nickel each if you tell Ronnie to bring my bottles back,

dime if you think I got to run him down," the woman said.

"And the ice?"

"Quarter, and you tell Ronnie I want my bucket back, too." She took the dollar Early held out, and punched keys on her black and gold National cash register. When she pulled down on the register's handle, a ka-ching sounded and up went a dollar sign, a zero, a decimal, and an eight and a five in the window at the top of her machine.

Early accepted his fifteen cents change. As he pocketed the coins, he asked, "Who should I tell Ronnie wants the bottles and bucket back?"

The woman grinned, a gap showing between her front teeth. "His wife."

Early trotted up the limestone steps to the propped-open doors of the redbrick Dickinson County Courthouse, the ice bucket and drinks cradled in one arm. "Sheriff's department still in the back?" he asked the first person he met, a young woman coming out of the county agent's office.

She gestured down the hall, and Early went on in no particular hurry. He stopped halfway. There he studied a huge photo of a stockyard at trail's end eighty-two years ago, the rangy, horned cattle in pens nothing like the sleek grain-fed, red-and-white Herefords ranchers in the area now trucked to market. Early could taste the dust of the Chisholm, knew it wasn't much different from the dust of the state's highways and county roads except the dust now lacked the smell of cattle and sweaty horses and cowboys three months without a bath.

"Cactus, that's the life you were cut out for," came a rumbly voice from the end of the hall.

Early pushed his hat onto the back of his head as he turned to the hog-fat giant who filled the doorway. "Ronnie, when I was a single fella, yup. But I'm married now. And speaking of married, I met your wife," he said as he pressed the bucket into the meaty hands of the Dickinson sheriff. "She wants the bottles and the bucket back."

Sheriff Galt grinned, the gap between his front teeth matching that of his wife. "Just like my Ruthie to say that."

He stepped aside and held the door open for Early. Once inside, Galt banged a bottle of root beer down on the desk of his secretary. He grabbed out two more bottles before he set the bucket in front of a small, elderly man at the counter, the man bald as a honeydew melon. "Curly, take these out to the jail and let our two prisoners have a cold one courtesy of our guest, the high sheriff of Riley County."

The little man, in bib overalls and an undershirt, bobbed his head. He gathered the bucket and went toward the back door that would take him outside to the jail.

"You got bad people in your county?" Early asked.

Galt put the crimped edge of a bottle's cap against the edge of the counter. He struck down on his hand holding the bottle, snapping the cap away. "Oh yeah. Caught me two boys who would be rustlers, but they weren't very good at it." He gave the root beer to Early. "Sad souls. Feed in the jail is probably the best they've had in a month."

"Your judge going to send them to Leavenworth?"

"Not if I can help it." Galt whacked the top from his bottle. He clicked it against Early's before he chugged half of it. "You like it?" he asked, aiming his bottle at Early's, also half empty.

" 'S'all right."

"My own recipe. When I quit this damn job, Ruthie and me, we're thinking of franchisin' this stuff. We could make us a nice little bundle."

"Your bad boys?" Early asked.

Galt set a stack of wanted circulars off a straight-back chair and gestured for Early to sit. For himself, Galt settled on a well-worn horsehair couch. "The rancher got his cows back, so there was no real damage done. I'm on the judge to give them boys to me for six months. Have them work for the county, sleep in the jail at night. We get some things done that need doin' and all it costs us is a couple meals a day. But you didn't come here to talk about my bad boys."

Early squinted at his bottle.

"It's the murder, idn't it?" Galt said. "You finally figured out who done it, an' the old boy's got an alibi."

Early rubbed the coldness of the bottle against his wrist. "Tell me about the manager of your elevator."

"Gilly? Everett Gilson? 'Bout the most honest man ever walked God's green earth, least most folks here think that."

"And you?"

"I got a doubt or two."

"How so?"

Galt chugged the rest of his root beer. After a belch that rattled the windows, he set his empty on the floor. "When I heard what he told yer caller, I went to asking a few questions around. No one saw yer man in town that day except Gilly."

"So he wasn't here?"

"I didn't say that. It's possible yer man could have hopped off the train at the elevator when it slowed for its stop at the depot, he and Gilly talked in Gilly's back office, then he hopped the next train drifting by a couple hours later. It's possible. . . . You want to go talk to Gilly?"

"Better. Want to come along?"

"Tell you what," Galt said with a wink, "let's make it a three-some." He twisted toward his secretary. "Hezzy, get the head bull of the town police for me, wouldja?"

She took the receiver from her desk phone and dialed.

"Dickie Eisenhower," Galt said, turning back to Early, "he's as mean a sonuvabitch as I am."

"Eisenhower?"

"Yeah, got some shirttail relative who was a big-time general in the war, now president of some fancy-assed college in New York City, if you can believe that. Dickie says he's gonna run for president someday and we all gotta vote for him." A laugh rolled out of Galt that shook his body to its rhythm.

"Got him, sheriff," the secretary said. She held out the receiver, and Galt took it. He stretched the phone's cord to its limit.

"Dickie?" he said into the mouthpiece. "I got the sheriff of Riley County in my office. Gilly over at the elevator alibied the man who killed that schoolteacher in Leonardville. We're gonna sweat him. You wanna come along? . . . Oh, say, five minutes . . . See ya there."

Galt tossed the receiver back toward his secretary's desk. The receiver bounced off a stack of file folders, and the secretary snatched the receiver from the air before it could bang against her typewriter. She gave Galt a tired look that he ignored.

Galt leaned hard on the arm of the couch as he pushed his bulk up. "You're not still drivin' that dinky Jeep, are you, Cactus? 'Course you are. You're too cheap to buy a real car. You wanna ride in my Hudson?"

"I'm for that."

"Hezzy," he called back when he got near the door to the outside, "be over at the Midland if you need me."

"You got a meeting with the county commissioners at eleven."

"Give 'em any sody pops left in Cactus's bucket. That'll hold 'em 'til I get back."

The lawmen went out and rattled down the steps to a car as dust covered as Early's Jeep. Might have been green underneath, but Early couldn't be certain. What he was sure of was that Galt's Hudson Hornet was one aerodynamically designed car, perhaps the best looker of the postwar vehicles. He opened the passenger door and climbed in, shocked when he sat down that he couldn't reach the dashboard. Someone had jacked the seat so far back that anybody in the backseat had no knee space.

Galt got in and the car sagged to his side. "Pure comfort, ain't she?" he said as he fired the engine. "Got a cousin in Kansas City who got me a deal. Then I turned around an' sold it to the county for full retail. Profit got me an' Ruthie a nice little vacation last year."

He wheeled out of the dirt lot, his hand out the window, Galt waving as he talked. "My gawd, this had to be some town in Eighteen and Sixty-Seven when the railroad first terminated here. All those Texas cows and cowboys comin' up the trail, had to be wild. See that dog over there?" He gestured toward a tan mongrel flopped down on the sidewalk. "Times he sleeps in the middle of Buckeye an' nobody disturbs him."

"He's gonna get run over, Ronnie."

"Not by any of our locals. Dog belongs to the judge an' everybody knows it."

Galt herded his cruiser off onto Northeast First Street, a graveled road that paralleled the Union-Pacific's tracks. Less than two blocks on stood the grain silos of the Abilene Flour Milling Company and, beyond, the silos of the Midland Grain Elevator. Galt pulled up in front of the Midland's office, white paint peeling from the structure. As he and Early got out, a pickup truck came up and parked behind the cruiser. A tall man in pressed tans stepped out. He touched two fingers to the bill of his police cap in salute to Galt.

"Dickie," Galt said, "this here fine fella is Jimmy Early, sheriff over in Riley. Guess you two have never met."

"Not had the pleasure," Eisenhower said. He shook Early's hand. "You think our man might be fibbing some?"

"We got to find out."

"This is your case, so I'm here as a courtesy. If it's all right with you, I'll just lean against the wall and keep my mouth shut."

"Eisenhower," Early said, mulling the name as the three strolled toward the office door.

"Yes," the police chief said, "that name'll get you elected to anything in this town."

"I worked for the general in Europe kinda, several levels down as a two-striper toting a rifle."

"I was Navy myself. Thought I'd see the world. Just saw a lot of water."

Galt opened the door, and the three lawmen tramped inside, the air of the office permeated by the sweet smell of warm wheat. "Mavis," Galt said to a brunette beating out a drummer's tattoo at a typewriter, "Gilly in?"

She nodded toward a frosted glass door without breaking her typing speed.

"Guess that's an invitation." Galt opened the door. He pushed on in, Early and Eisenhower behind him.

A nondescript man waved while he both talked on the telephone and fanned himself with a sheaf of papers. He gestured to the captain's chairs against the sidewall of the office.

Galt dragged one over to Everett Gilson's desk and shoehorned himself into the chair. Early pulled a chair over too, but not Eisenhower. He instead did as he said he would—leaned against the wall, his thumbs hooked through his belt loops.

Early gazed around. A chalk price-board on one wall took his attention. Before he got too deep into it, a teletype to the side clattered to life. It rattled on for less than half a minute and shut down. Weather information? Early wondered. Shipping news? Updated prices from a buyer at a distant destination? Then words of Gilson drew him back. . . . "So that's six railcars for Amsterdam. Is that firm? . . . I can fill four cars and get the

209

rest from a couple other elevators."

Gilson dropped his fan. He pulled over a booklet that, to Early, looked like a railroad timetable. "Give me three days to get them out of here. You willing to pay for fast freight to New Orleans or do you want me to ship to Saint Louis and barge from there? . . . Barge it will be. . . . Gotta go now. Got company."

Gilson set the receiver on his telephone's cradle. He glanced up at Galt and reached for the man's great mitt of a hand. "To what do I owe the pleasure?" he asked with a salesman's smile.

"A matter's come up we gotta check out," Galt said.

"Can I get you all a soda?" Gilson asked as he stood, the back of his shirt ripping away from the wooden slats of his swivel chair. He held out the front of his shirt, airing himself, wet circles under his arms and a wet band above his belt. "This heat, water's just running through me."

"You need to get yerself a fan, Gilly."

"Burned ours out yesterday. The Montgomery Ward store's got one on backorder for me. . . . Sodas, gentlemen?"

"Jimmy and I tanked up before we come over," Galt said. He twisted around to Eisenhower. "Dickie?"

"I'm fine."

"Well, I'm going to get me one," Gilson said. He left by a side door and, a moment later, returned with an Orange Crush, the bottle dripping water. Gilson took an opener from his center drawer. He jacked the top off, pitched it in a wastebasket, and drank, his Adam's apple bobbing with each swallow. When Gilson stopped, he rubbed the cold bottle across his forehead.

"Feel better," he said as he sat down. "Now how can I help?"

"This is the sheriff from Riley County," Galt said, thumbing at Early. "You remember a month or so ago telling somebody from his office that the husband of that murdered gal over there was here with you the day she was killed?"

Gilson set his bottle aside. "That would be Bill Smitts, yes."

"There's a problem, Gilly."

"What's that?"

"Nobody else saw that Mister Smitts in town that day, not even Mavis out front."

"But he was here." Gilson picked up a pencil. He poked the eraser end at some of the papers on his desk.

Galt again thumbed at Early.

Early took a notepad from his shirt pocket. He paged into it and studied an item. "How well do you know Bill?" he asked.

"Pretty well, I guess," Gilson said. "He calls on me about once a month to discuss freight rates and schedule railcars."

"Like the cars you need for that wheat shipment to Amsterdam?"

"Well, I only need them to get the wheat to a river terminal at Saint Louis, but, yes, I arranged for those cars back in July. I've had them on my siding for a week."

Early glanced again at his notepad. "Don't you two go back to college? . . . At Fort Hays Normal?"

"Yeesss. You been doing some checking?"

"Made a few calls. You were in the same fraternity together, weren't you?"

"Phi Delta Gamma, uh-huhh."

"That last year, he was the president and you were his vice president, right?" Early peered at Gilson when he didn't answer. "You two pretty tight?"

"I wouldn't say that."

Galt came forward in his chair. He thumped Gilson's desk. "Gilly, let's get down to where the rubber meets the road. Nobody but you saw that man here that day. How do you explain it?"

Gilson turned away. When he glanced back, his mouth had drawn into a tight line. "Ronnie, we talked outside. After a bit, we got in that junker car of mine, and I drove Bill out into the wheat country, and we watched the harvest."

"Talk to anybody?"

"We just watched from the road, Ronnie."

"Then after some time, you brought him back an' put him on the train?"

"You got it right."

"Gilly, that doesn't work for Jimmy. He thinks yer lyin'. Frankly, I do too." Galt pulled a tobacco pouch from his back pocket. He grubbed out a wad, stuffed it in his mouth, and settled back to chew.

Early turned a page in his pad. He studied it before he looked up. "Mister Gilson, if somebody from your old fraternity called and asked for your help, you'd help him, right?"

"Sure, if I could."

"And if Bill called?"

"I wouldn't lie for him."

"So you'll tell a grand jury what you told us if you're subpoenaed over to Manhattan."

"You're going to charge Bill?"

"That's not up to me. The county attorney wants to present the case to the grand jury. They'll decide whether to indict."

Galt hauled Gilson's wastebasket over. He spit a stream of tobacco juice into it. "You lie to a grand jury, Gilly, they gonna put your butt in jail."

Gilson resumed prodding at papers.

Eisenhower cleared his throat. "How's your card game, Gilly?"

Startled, Gilson turned to the police chief. "Fair," he said.

"Does your wife know you lost twelve-large the other night, that you had to take out a second on your house to pay the debt?"

Gilson's pencil slipped.

"The banker and I sing in the church choir, Gilly. Gossip like that's just too sweet for old Carl not to let it slip."

"You'd tell Helen?"

"Might," Eisenhower said.

"What's it going to take to keep this from her?"

"A little truth telling."

Gilson threw his pencil across the office. He swiveled away from the others, to the window that looked out on the truck scales and the hopper beyond where someone's red Reo was dumping a load of grain. "Shit."

He inched his swivel chair back around. The muscles of his face sagged and, to Early, the man looked to have aged a decade.

"All right," Gilson said, "Bill called me that afternoon."

"Where was he?" Early asked as he scribbled in his pad.

"I don't know."

"What'd he say?"

"That someone had killed his wife and, if anyone asked, would I say he was with me that day. Well, he was scheduled to be in, but he missed his appointment."

"What did you think?"

Gilson hefted his Orange Crush. He took a long, slow drink before he set the bottle aside. "I didn't know what to think, so I asked him, 'Bill, did you do it?' "

"And?"

"He said no. Said he'd spent the night and most of the day with a woman he'd been seeing, and he didn't want to get her involved."

Early glanced up. "Who's this woman?"

"My God, man, you think I'm gonna ask a frat brother who he's running around with behind his wife's back? There are some questions a friend doesn't ask a friend, and that's one of them."

Early closed the cover on his notepad. He slipped it back in his pocket. "I thank you for your honesty, Mister Gilson, no matter how delayed you were in finding it."

"Your county attorney going to call me before your grand jury?"

"I wouldn't think so. You don't have anything particularly useful to tell them."

Outside, the three lawmen stood together, Galt with his elbow on the roof of his cruiser. "Would you believe it? Mister Chamber of Commerce a gambler?"

"You'd have more respect for him if he'd won," Eisenhower said, "but he lost big."

"And you knew about it."

"Hey, I know where the games are, even play a hand now and then."

"But never with Gilly?"

"Naw, his bunch bets more than I can afford. I play with Leroy and a couple others at the back of the barbershop. Ronnie, you ought to sit in some night."

"If I want to gamble, I'll take up ranchin'." Galt puckered and spit a stream of tobacco juice to the side.

Early reached for the police chief's hand. "For one who wasn't going to say anything, you were a mighty big help and I thank you."

"Thank Ronnie. He invited me. Now if you'll excuse me, I got to go roll around town, let people know I'm on the job." Eisenhower went to his truck and left.

Galt and Early got into the cruiser, Galt spitting his gob of well-chewed tobacco out the window. "So now you can arrest the husband," he said as he twisted the key in the ignition.

"If your Mister Gilson's right, Bill's still got an alibi."

"Cattin' around with some woman? You believe that?" Galt spun his cruiser's tires, throwing up dust and gravel as he whipped the car around and headed back for the courthouse.

"I believed this," Early said.

"No, you didn't, or you wouldn'tna come over." Galt turned his cruiser onto the paved main street.

"Can I ask you a question?" Early said.

"Sure."

"Did you know the general's mother?"

"Ida? Sure. Grand old gal. Died a couple years back in that little house of hers. You never saw so many big names in town as when all her sons come home for the funeral."

"Anybody living there now?"

Galt massaged his whiskers as he drove. "Nope. Dwight and Milton made the decision for the brothers not to sell the place. They locked the front and back doors an' left it pretty much the way it was. Talk is they're going to set up a foundation to look after the property. You ever been over there? It's two blocks down and to your left," Galt said as he guided his cruiser over to the curb. He stopped behind Early's Jeep.

Early slid out the passenger door. When he closed it, he looked to Galt coming around the front of the cruiser. "Think anybody'd mind if I was to go over and look? I got a lot of respect for the general. Be nice to see where he grew up."

"Don't be surprised if the neighbors sic the police on you. They're pretty protective of the place."

Early grinned. "I got a leg up. I know the chief."

Galt clamped his arm around Early's shoulders and squeezed. "I'd go with ya, but I got a meetin'."

"Ronnie, I appreciate your help."

"Hell, if we sheriffs don't look out for one another, who's gonna? You hurry on back. Next time we'll swat flies an' tell lies."

Early watched Galt hustle his bulk up the steps and into the courthouse. After the Dickinson sheriff disappeared, Early settled himself behind the steering wheel of his Jeep. He fired the engine, glanced over his shoulder for traffic, and U-turned back toward Southeast Fourth Street. Moments later, Early made the turn and watched the house numbers roll up as he drove along. He stopped at the end of the second block, eased through the intersection, and parked in front of a house where an elderly woman swept the porch. Early stepped over to her walk.

"Excuse me?" he asked.

"Yes?" The woman stopped and leaned on her broom's handle.

"Is the Eisenhower home around here?"

"Why do you ask, mister?"

"I was in the war in Europe. Kinda feel I know the general a little."

"Dwight?" the woman asked.

"Yes, ma'am."

She set her broom against the wall and came down to the edge of the porch, her hands going into the pockets of her gingham apron. "He and his brothers were a handful for Ida, but she sure raised them right, and I liked them all. That's their house, right across the street."

Early glanced at the two-story, white-clapboard structure, the lawn and a one-time flower garden starved for water. When he turned back, he asked, "You going to call the police on me?"

"You going to do something you shouldn't?"

"No, ma'am, just look around, maybe sit a spell."

"As long as you don't disturb anything," the woman said. With that, she went back to her sweeping, and Early ambled across the street.

He expected there to be a picket fence around the place, he didn't know why. There was none. The walk was graveled, as was the street in front of it, no surprise there. But it was such an ordinary house, and lonely, as if it missed the family that had once lived there. Early strolled around back. He peered through the glass of the kitchen door. Early could picture the kitchen on bath-night Saturday night, six hulking boys taking their turns in a washtub by the wood-fired stove, getting clean for Sunday church. He had done it, too, still did because his and Thelma's little place didn't have a bathroom . . . fill a copper boiler on the stove for hot water, then bucket it into the galvanized tub . . .

He shambled around the side. There he stepped around an old-fashioned rose bush rich with bloom that perfumed the air. Early peered through a window. He rubbed the dust away from the pane with the sleeve of his shirt.

Hmm. Back parlor . . . rocking chair, another chair, carpet on the floor—couldn't tell the colors for sure—and an upright piano, the varnish gone black. Did the general ever play it? His mother had and Early had heard stories that she had taught Milton, now president of Kansas State Agricultural College . . . well . . .

Early stepped back. He went around front, to the porch, as unremarkable as the house. Its roof, though, provided a porch for the second floor, and Early could picture the brothers sleeping out there on hot summer nights. Using his hat for a broom, he swept the dust from the steps and sat down. After some time Early became aware that he was not alone, and cold prickled at his skin. He could see them—Tom Rodgers, Alf Debbs, the kid they called Frenchy because of the accent he faked, Carson Wills, Ned Townsend who lied to get in the Army—a big kid but only fifteen, best sniper in Early's squad and he had kept the boy's secret—Dutch Collins and Stumpy Collins, his brother, inseparable even in death. Stumpy had stepped on a land mine and Dutch was beside him . . .

"You look like you've seen a ghost," a voice said from the end of the porch.

Early jerked around, his eyes blinking, trying to focus.

"You all right?" the Abilene police chief asked.

"I guess. Neighbors call you about me being here?"

"No." Eisenhower held up a bucket. "I come by every couple days to water Ida's rose bush. It was my time today. If we'd get some rain, the lawn would green up and I'd mow it."

"You the caretaker?"

"Kinda. I got the right name. If you don't mind me asking, you looked like you were in another world, sheriff."

"Guess I was. It comes back at the strangest times."

CHAPTER 21

September 19—Monday Afternoon
Someone Else's Other World
Early rounded Sunset Hill on US Eighteen, coming in from Abilene. He went under the U-P's viaduct and back out into the sunlight. Early had stopped for lunch at a café in Chapman, meatloaf and fried potatoes and, as advertised on the menu board, Mom's apple pie, then drove on in silence, enjoying the time to think, but it was over now. He took down his microphone and pressed the transmitter button.

"Alice," he said into the mic. "Early here. I'm in town."

The voice of his dispatcher came back. "Go ahead, sheriff."

"Hutch in?"

"Up at Randolph. Couple yahoos in a fist fight, broke up the grocery."

"When he comes back on the air, tell him to run down Bill Smitts. We need to talk to him."

"I can make some calls for you."

" 'At's a good start. Anything else going on?"

"Um . . ."

"Spit it out."

"Gladys wants to talk to you."

Early drove by the cement plant. He waved to one of the drivers.

A new voice came on, hysteria in its pitch. "Jimmywhere-youbeenthepasthour?"

"Whoa, slow down. Chapman, getting lunch."

"It's Thelma."

"What do you mean?"

"She's at the department store, now. Mose Dickerson's keeping an eye on her 'til you can get in here."

"She's not at school?"

"Jimmy, what'd I just say?"

"All right, I'm four minutes away." Early pitched his microphone to the side. He stepped down on the gas and swerved his Jeep around a hardware delivery truck, skidded onto Eighteenth Street and, four blocks on, cut over onto Poyntz. Early pushed the accelerator all the way to the floor. He watched for teenagers coming out of the high school as he sped by, slowing only when he came up on the courthouse. A block past and he slid his Jeep into a parking place in front of Hall's Department Store, banging his right front tire up over the curb.

Early bailed out. He ran toward a bench in front of the display window where Mose Dickerson sat, bobbing his lame foot, fanning himself with his sweat-stained Stetson.

"Jimmy," Dickerson said without making an effort to rise, "no need to go rushin' in there. She's all right."

"She's supposed to be teaching today. Why isn't she at the school?"

"I don't know."

"Well?"

"Look, I was out on my mail route an' saw her hoofing it toward Manhattan. I stopped, said, 'What's goin' on?' An' she said she had an appointment at the beauty shop and I don't know what all else. Couldn't talk her out of any of it, so I figgered the wise thing was to bring her on in, kinda stay with her. Jimmy, there's something not right with your wife."

Early stepped up to the glass. He shaded his eyes as he scanned the interior. "I don't see her."

"Well, she's got a new look. What's this about the governor calling her, asking her to take a job in Topeka?"

"Damned if I know." He went to the door and plunged inside, glancing at the face of each woman shopper he came to.

From the stairway up to the second floor, Thelma called to him, "Jimmy, you're just in time. I've all these purchases for you to carry to Mose's car." She held two packages. Behind her and three steps above stood a man, a horseshoe of hair around an otherwise bald head, balancing half a dozen more packages.

Early trotted up the steps. He relieved the man of his burdens, greeting him with, "Owen."

"Sheriff," the storeowner said. Owen Hall straightened the front of his shirt. "Four new outfits here, and they're really something. She's going to make a dandy impression on that new job. This mean you're moving?"

"Could be. We gotta talk a little."

"Well, I put everything on an account for you. Know you're good for it."

"How much?"

"Better part of seventy-five."

Early winced. He turned and started down the stairs. "What's this all about, Thel?" he asked from behind his pile of packages.

"Jimmy, it's just the most amazing thing," she said as she handed her parcels to Dickerson, who had wandered in. She led the parade toward the front of the store, Owen Hall and two of his clerks trailing in the wake. "The governor heard about my work at the school, and he called me and asked me to take a position in his administration. He wants me to head up elementary curriculum planning in the state department of education. Isn'tthatsomething?"

At the last moment, Hall slid around the group. He wrenched open the front door.

"ThankyouMisterHall," Thelma said as she passed by, her

hair poofed out and in a wave Early had never seen before. And a new hat and white gloves, and she had never worn gloves, not even at her wedding.

"Owen," Early said as he stumbled out, Dickerson hop-stepping after him, hurrying to get to his coupe before Thelma and Early got there. He opened the trunk, shoved a tire out of the way, and threw his two packages in. With space open, Dickerson added the parcels Early carried.

"Sure is a lot of stuff, Missus Early," he said after he banged the lid down.

"And I'll need every bit of it. My clothes are just so worn."

"I always thought you looked right smart."

Thelma smiled at Dickerson. She patted his face.

"Thel, is this it?" Early asked.

"I really need to go to Dobson's Jewelry Store."

"Why don't we go across the street first, to the Wareham, get an iced tea in the restaurant?"

Thelma turned to him, a quizzical expression on her face replaced in an instant by an overly generous smile. "That would be lovely."

She turned and, without looking for traffic, marched across the street. Early jumped out. He waved at a school-bus driver fast approaching, stopped him before his bus could flatten Thelma. The driver glowered, and Early shrugged, as if to say, it's not my fault.

The maitre d' met them at the hotel door. He squired them into the dining room, bubbling. "Sheriff and Missus Early, it's always so good to have you here."

The bubbles stopped when he saw Dickerson limping in. "And youuu."

"I always pay," Dickerson said, raising his hands.

"Don't you have any decent clothes? And that hat, it's disgusting."

The constable snatched off his elderly Stetson. "I'll put it under my chair. Nobody'll see it."

"Very well." The maitre d', in his swallowtail tuxedo, pulled a chair out for Thelma. "And what will you have today?"

"An iced tea."

He pulled out a chair for Early. "And you, sheriff?"

"The same."

The maitre d' left Dickerson to wrestle his own chair. He peered over the top of his half-moon glasses at the constable. "Your order I know. Coffee, blaaack." He whisked away.

Early came forward, his elbows going up on the starched white tablecloth. "Thel, what's this all about?"

"I already told you, the governor called me."

"At school?"

"Of course, where else?"

"And you just took off like a big bird?"

"They understood this was important."

"But you walked."

"I don't have a car."

"On what I make, we can't afford one."

"On what I'll make, we can afford two," Thelma said. She patted Early's hand.

"Jimmy, she didn't walk far," Dickerson said. He rubbed a hand over his thinning hair. "Maybe only—"

Early raised a finger in warning.

"All right," Dickerson said, "all right."

Thelma took off her hat. She primped her new hairstyle. "What do you think?"

Early studied her for a moment. "It's different."

"Is that the best you can say?"

"Ahhh—" But before he could say more, the maitre d' swept in with a tray. He set a beading cut-crystal glass of iced tea in front of Thelma, another in front of Early, and a white china cup of steaming coffee in front of Dickerson.

"Will there be anything else?" he asked. "Dinner menu, perhaps?"

Early waved him away.

"This is good. Thank you, Jimmy," Thelma said after she sipped from her glass.

Dickerson slurped his coffee. "This idn't bad either."

Early again raised his finger in warning. When he looked across the table to Thelma, her happiness and enthusiasm appeared to have drained from her. She slouched in her chair.

"Jimmy," she said, an ancient weariness entering her voice, "I'm tired. I think we should go home."

He nodded. Early slipped a quarter on the table and helped Thelma up. They walked out of the restaurant at a measured pace, Thelma carrying her hat at her side, Early with his hat at an angle on his head. Dickerson trailed along behind. The three stopped before they stepped off the sidewalk, and when traffic cleared—a prewar Dodge and a pickup truck—they strolled across. Early helped Thelma into the passenger seat of his Jeep and, after he came around, there stood Dickerson, waiting by the back bumper.

"She all right?" he asked.

"Mose, I don't know. Would you do me a favor and take all those packages back into the store? Tell Owen I'll work it out with him."

"What about what she needs for Topeka?"

Early scratched at the back of his head. "You think the governor really called?"

"Well, she said—"

"Look, the governor doesn't know Thel. Hell, he doesn't even know me, and I worked the county for his election."

"I was with you when he shook yer hand at the courthouse."

"Didn't mean horse apples to him. Knew it when he kept

calling me Sheriff James."

Dickerson shrugged and limped away to his car.

Early got in the driver's seat of his Jeep. When he glanced at Thelma, her head had slumped forward and her chin rested on her chest. He sighed, started the engine, and backed out into the street. Early herded his Jeep east, then north on Fourth. At Bluemont, where he should have turned west for Keats, he instead continued on through the intersection to US Twenty-Four that went north and then west to Clay Center in the next county. Early grubbed his microphone out from where it had fallen between the seats. He pressed the transmitter button.

"Alice?" he said, holding the mic just beyond his lips.

"Go ahead, sheriff."

"Is Gladys listening?"

"Yes."

"I've got Thel. Something's going on here I don't understand, so I'm going out to the Estes place, see if Walter and Nadine will help keep an eye on her when I have to be away."

"Got it."

"Call Doc Grafton, wouldja? Ask him to come out to Walter and Nadine's when he can."

"Gladys is on it now."

"Where's Hutch?"

A new voice came on, Hutch Tolliver's. "Coming out of Randolph. Two drunks made a helluva mess of Morgan's Grocery. They're passed out in the backseat. Taking them to jail."

"Stay on the radio. I'm going over to the state police frequency, see if I can raise the super trooper, get him on the air with us."

Early scrunched down for a better look at his frequency selector as a Humphrey's semi motored past him in the opposite lane. He turned the selector two clicks and spoke into his microphone. "Daniel, you out there somewhere?"

Static answered, followed by, "Junction City. That you, Cactus?"

"Right. Switch to my frequency so you, Hutch, and me can talk."

"Changing frequencies."

Early turned the selector back two clicks. "Dan, you on?"

"Roger."

"Hutch?"

"I'm here."

"Spent the morning in Abilene, boys," Early said as he guided his Jeep around a bend and onto a grade that took the highway up out of the Big Blue Valley. "Bill Smitts's alibi collapsed in the dust. We gotta find him."

"This is Alice. I called his house. No one answered. Constable Dickerson just came in, so I asked him to drive by, see if he's outside or in his shop."

"Could be at work," Early said.

"I called a Mister Larson in Topeka, Mister Smitts's supervisor. Says he's taken a leave of absence."

"Cow flop . . . I don't like this."

"Sheriff, there's more. Mister Larson said the railroad's got a detective looking for Mister Smitts."

"What's that all about?"

"He wouldn't say other than the detective's on the way here, to see you."

"Any idea when he'll get in?"

"Mister Larson didn't know."

"You know where I'll be."

"Right."

"Hutch here. Chief, what do you want us to do?"

Early topped the high ground. He steered his Jeep around another bend that took the road on north. "Hutch, get to all our constables. Tell them who we're looking for. Give them

Bill's license plate for that Ford Woody he bought. Alice, do the same with the neighboring sheriffs. Call Pott County, Wabaunsee, Geary, and Clay."

"Cactus, this is Dan. Sounds like the U-P's already looking for Bill. I got a couple buddies who're railroad bulls with the Santa Fe. A couple calls and I can have eyes out all along that railroad."

"Do it." Early slowed for the turn onto the county road that would take him west, into the ranching country around Leonardville. "This may all be for nothing. Could be Mose will find Bill out in the garden, digging turnips. You need me, I'll be at the Rocking Horse E."

"Hutch again. Walter doesn't have a telephone."

"I'll leave my radio on. Early out." He hung his microphone over the mirror and motored on. Early waved his hat to a cowboy riding beside a fence next to the road, a crowd of Hereford yearlings rattling along ahead of him. Beats chasing people, Early thought.

He glanced at Thelma. Still she slept.

A mile on and Early slowed for the turnoff onto the lane that led to the Estes ranchstead. When he stopped for the gate, Thelma woke. She massaged her temples and yawned. "We home?"

"No," Early said as he got out. "Going to stop in on Walter and Nadine, visit a bit."

"That's nice." She stretched and shook her shoulders.

Early swung the gate wide. He drove through, then closed the gate. When he returned to the Jeep, he found Thelma studying her hands.

"Why am I wearing gloves?" she asked.

"Bought them at Hall's."

"I did not. I don't even like gloves."

Early fished the new hat from the backseat. He placed it on

Thelma's lap. "You bought this too."

She studied the hat with the same curiosity she had her gloved hands. "Well, I might have bought this. It's nice."

"Thel, you bought a whole lot of things."

"When?"

"Today."

"Jimmy, don't tease me."

"I'm not teasing you."

"I know you, Jimmy, you are."

"Have it your way." Early let out the clutch and drove on.

Thelma turned to him. "Did I really do that?"

"Yup." Early hunched forward. He leaned his forearms on the steering wheel as the Jeep rolled on toward a dip in the lane.

"You think I'm dotty, don't you?"

"Thel, I don't know what to think. All I know is you've been doing some strange things, and you don't remember them. I'm getting afraid for you."

"You think I could hurt someone, don't you?"

"I didn't say that."

"You said I attacked Gladys with a butcher knife, and I can't remember that happening."

"Do you remember walking out of school before lunchtime today because you believed you had to get to Manhattan?"

"But I wouldn't do that."

"Thel, you did. You know what I think you should do? I think you should quit teaching until after the baby comes, just take it easy."

"But we need the money."

"We can get by," Early said as the Jeep topped the rise on the far side of the wash. Ahead laid a spread of buildings and a corral.

A black dog, lapping water from the stock tank, twisted

around at the sound of the Jeep approaching. He galloped out toward Early, his great bush of a tail whipping the air.

"Wish we had a dog," Thelma said.

"How about him?"

"He's Walter and Nadine's."

"What do you think of us asking the Esteses if we could move in until the baby comes? They're alone and needing help, and I'm pretty fair at cowboying . . . and you wouldn't be alone during the day."

"But what about our house?"

"The neighbors would watch it for us."

Thelma gazed at the swaybacked roof of the one-story ranch house set back in the cottonwoods as Early drove past the corral and around the barns. "It'd be nice, wouldn't it?" she said.

"The worst they could say is no, and you know Nadine isn't going to say that." Early swung the Jeep about and stopped in front of the dirt walk that led to the house. He strolled around to the passenger side where he helped Thelma down, both greeted by the dog slobbering on their hands as they reached out to pet him.

"Your people around?" Early asked the Newfoundland.

The dog jerked his head toward the house.

"You're pretty good," Early said, then called out, "Nadine! Walter!"

After a moment, a woman pushed out a screen door onto the porch, her hands richly white with flour. She shaded her eyes with her forearm. "Jimmy? Thelma? Well, aren't you two nice to come by, and just in time for supper. I got biscuits rolled out."

"Walter around?" Early asked as he helped Thelma along toward the house.

"Oh, he's off in that truck of his, checking on the cattle back in the creek pasture, only pasture that hasn't been burned off by the sun. He'll be home directly. You come on in." Nadine took Thelma's hand. "You surely do look nice, white gloves and all. You're just the best thing that ever happened to Jimmy."

"You're sweet to say that," Thelma said as she went on inside.

"Oh, I'm just tellin' the truth." Nadine eyed Early as he came in. He raked off his hat. "You're lookin' good, too, Jimmy. Come back to the kitchen and we'll talk while I get the biscuits in the oven. Know what we're gonna have for supper?"

Early scratched at his head as he thought about that one. "A ranch, I'd say beef."

"Barbecued brisket, yessir. Got it slow-cooking at the side of the oven, basting it with the best barbecue sauce you ever laid a tongue on."

Thelma pulled off her gloves. "Better than the sauce Jimmy makes?"

"Honey, after you taste mine, Jimmy's will only be second best." Nadine grinned and went to picking up the circles she had cut from her patted-out dough. She laid them in a greased pan. "Good day at school?" she asked, glancing at Thelma.

"Jimmy says I walked out this morning."

"Well, I suppose you had things to do." She opened the oven door and a wave of sugary-sweet heat rolled into the room. "Makes you hungry, don't it?" Nadine said as she slid the biscuit pan in.

"Jimmy says I went to Manhattan. I don't remember it except for him and Mister Dickerson and I having iced tea at the Wareham."

"Well, we women, when we get babies inside us, they do sometimes make us change, do unusual things that we can laugh about later." Nadine went to the sink. She wrung out a rag and came to the table. "Thelma, you know where the plates and glasses are. How about you set the table while I scrub the counter? Jimmy, you could make yerself useful, too."

"How's that?"

"I got a mixing bowl and stuff in the sink. You could wash them."

All were at their work when someone clomped in the front door bellowing, "Hey, we got the sheriff here?"

"There's my Walter," Nadine said. "Walter? Thelma's here, too, isn't that nice?"

"Just like sunshine," the old man said as he rambled in, whacking his misshapen Quigley hat against the leg of his denim pants. He slapped Early's back as he passed by the sink, hung his Quigley on a peg, and hugged his wife. "Glory, don't it smell good in here."

"Barbecue brisket."

"Oh my, we do know how to eat, don't we?"

"You clean up before you come in?"

"Splashed a bit in the stock tank." Estes eased his arthritic frame down onto a chair at the head of the table. He gazed around. "What brings you good people by?"

Early turned as he worked a drying towel around a granite-ware mixing bowl. "Walter, could you use a little help around the Rocking Horse?"

"Lord, could I ever. I thought we could get on without Sonny, but it's wearing me down."

"Maybe we could do a little trading."

"You want my ranch?"

"No no. With this baby coming on, I've asked Thel to quit teaching and take it easy. If you were to invite us to live with you for a couple months, you could keep Thel company when I have to be away. Evenings and weekends, I can wrangle cows for you."

"Well, now that's some offer." Estes held out his glass as Nadine poured it full with lemonade. "What do you think, Mother?"

"I think it would be awful nice to have young people in the

231

house. I worry about you, Walter, and Jimmy would be an awful good hand."

"Then I think we got us about the sweetest deal around." Estes splashed sugar in his lemonade. He glanced up at Early wiping dry Nadine's mixing spoons. "When you wanna do this?"

"Maybe Thelma could stay the night, and tomorrow I could bring up what few things we need from our house."

A hard rap came from the screen door. Nadine Estes slipped away to see who might be there and returned a moment later, a man at her heels—heavyset, buzz haircut, dark suit, a brown fedora in his hand. "Jimmy," she said, "this is a Mister Guerney. Says he needs to see you."

Early tossed his drying towel over his shoulder before he shook hands. "My wife," he said, indicating Thelma—making introductions, "and Walter Estes."

The visitor nodded his greetings.

"Something I can help you with?" Early asked.

"Maybe I can help you. I'm with the Union-Pacific. Got in your office right after you went off the air. Your dispatcher was kind enough to write me directions so I could drive out. Maybe we should talk outside."

Early glanced at Nadine.

"Jimmy, it's all right," she said. "But don't be too long. Ten minutes and supper'll be on the table."

Early motioned for Guerney to follow him as he led the way back through the front room. "You the dick Mister Larson said was on his way?"

"Guilty. Got a badge if you want to see it."

"Your haircut says you're ex-military."

"Military police. Came out of the war a sergeant, and the railroad was hiring. They put me in Topeka."

"How much territory you cover?"

"Lawrence to the Colorado line. Gets busy, I can call in help from Kansas City or Denver."

Early pushed the screen door open. He stepped out and held the door for Guerney. "You want to sit?"

"No, I'd just as soon stand."

"So what do you have to tell me?"

"Do you know what bearer bonds are?"

"Bonds issued by a business that are payable to whoever turns them in."

"Yup, just like a check and just as good, only there's no name on the 'pay to the order of' line. The bonds are numbered, so we know who bought them initially."

"By 'we,' you mean the railroad?"

"Right."

"And this involves Bill Smitts?"

"We think so. Couple months ago, seventy thousand dollars worth of bonds disappeared from our Topeka office. We shouldn't have had them at all, but a bank had bought them, and we were holding them overnight."

"Break-in?"

"No."

"So you figured it had to be an employee."

"It's the only thing that made sense. I grilled everybody and confirmed where they said they were that night. Bill was in Lawrence. When I couldn't find anyone guilty, my boss figured it had to be me, but I was in Wamego, checking on pilfered freight. Caught the little bastard who was stealing it too."

"But Bill?"

Guerney rubbed the palms of his hands together, and it appeared to Early he was stalling, perhaps trying to decide how much detail he wanted to share.

"Couple weeks ago," Guerney said, "someone cashed in some of the missing bonds at a Goodland bank—seven thousand dollars worth."

"Bill?"

"He was out there at the time, though the teller and the bank officer couldn't give a description that would allow me to arrest anyone less than half the population of Kansas. . . . I'm thinking if I could find Bill, I could haul his butt out west, stand him up in front of the bank people, and they're gonna know it was him or it wasn't him." Guerney pushed the toe of his boot around the dust that coated the porch floor. After a moment, he glanced up at Early. "So you're looking for him for the murder of his wife?"

An elderly Chevy coupe came around the barns and stopped at the end of the dirt walk that led to the house. Mose Dickerson leaned out the window.

"Jimmy," he said, "Bill's gone, and the boy with him."

CHAPTER 22

September 21—Wednesday Morning
Wakeeney
Early made his way through the side entrance of the courthouse and on down to his office, his tan trousers wrinkled from the long ride in. Before he could park his hat, Hutch Tolliver glanced up from his morning coffee and the report left by the night deputy.

"You look tuckered," he said.

"I guess," Early said.

"So?"

"Walter and I spent yesterday afternoon till dark fixing fence. Lord, his place is run-down. To top that, we found one of his cows down with the bloat, got in that dab of alfalfa his neighbor has."

"That can be bad," Tolliver said.

"I had to stab a knife through the old girl's side, into her stomach. All that gas and mess blasts out all over me. Gad."

Gladys, Early's secretary—her hair in a new permanent that had a faint emerald coloration—snorted as she opened the mail. "Least you did something useful. Beats sitting on your fanny listening to Tom Mix."

That pained Early, but he ignored it and went to his desk. "Anything on Bill?" he asked Tolliver.

"No sightings. Mose goes by his place every couple hours on the off chance he's come home."

The telephone set to jangling. The dispatcher picked up the receiver, listened for a moment, then turned to Early. "You'll want to take this, sheriff."

"Who?"

"Mister Dodds at the bank."

Early took the receiver from his phone. "How can I help you, Hi?" he said as he pressed the receiver to his ear.

"You told me to call if anything happened concerning Bill Smitts's house."

"He's gonna sell it?"

"No, paid off the loan and then some. I got twelve five-hundred-dollar bills in the morning mail from him."

Early came forward, pulling a pencil from his pocket, about to write on the back of a wanted circular. "Still got the envelope? What's the postmark?"

"Ahhh, could be Wakeeney. Can't be sure, it's kind of messed up. This help you?"

"It's possible. You call me if anything more happens."

"Right."

Before Early could free himself of his telephone, Gladys came to his desk with a letter, deep concern having replaced her sniggering smile. "You need to read this, Jimmy."

He took the letter. Early leaned back in his chair and placed the crook of his arm over the top of his head as he scanned down the lines of pencil scratch on paper torn from a Big Chief tablet.

"Sumbitch."

Tolliver peered up from his report, and the dispatcher twisted away from her radio monitor.

"Bill did it." Early spit the words out as if he were spitting grains of sand. "He told his dad."

Tolliver hustled away from his desk. He read over Early's shoulder. "Dated Thursday," he said.

236

Early pulled the envelope from behind the letter. He glanced at the postmark. "Mailed the next day."

"You think this is for real?"

"It's a Wakeeney postmark. That's where Bill's family is."

"You think he's still there?"

"Only one way to find out." Early sailed the envelope to Gladys. "Get the dad on the line for me. Howdy Smitts, probably Howard. Could be Harold."

She turned to her telephone.

"Now all we have to do is catch him," Tolliver said.

"Not going to be easy. If Bill's got half a brain left, he'll keep going west. He could be out of the state already. Time we conflabbed with the county attorney." Early went to the office closet. He brought out a broom and, grinning like a raccoon fresh from a field of sweet corn, banged the handle against the ceiling.

Moments later, a rotund man clattered down the stairs and into Early's office—coatless, his necktie, hand-painted with a fish jumping from a stream, pulled loose, plaid suspenders keeping his trousers around his girth. Carl Wieland's right sleeve hung empty, the cuff pinned at the shoulder.

"Jesus H. Christ, Cactus," he said, "can't you pick up the telephone like anybody else?"

"Broom handle never fails."

Wieland mopped his forehead with a handkerchief as Early handed him the letter.

"Hold on, man, I only got one hand," Wieland said. He stuffed the handkerchief into his back pocket and recovered his spectacles. After he hooked the bows over his ears, he squinted at the letter.

"Sonuvabitch." Wieland raised the letter to his lips. "You probably said that already, didn't you?"

"Can we use it?"

"The letter? Got to authenticate it, either get an affidavit from the old man or call him to testify. But I tell you, there's nothing I like better than a confession, even if it's secondhand."

Early went back to his desk. He sat down and swung his boot-clad feet up on top of the morning mail Gladys had placed there. "Let's think about this a minute. Listen to me, Carl, what if Bill denies ever saying this? Then it's his dad's word against his—it's a standoff."

"Was Bill's mother in the room at the time?"

"Don't know."

"If she was and she heard it, then, boom, Bill's off to Leavenworth and the gallows."

"Well, now think about this. If she heard it, do you really believe she's going to let her only son be convicted?"

Gladys turned from her desk, her hand over the mouthpiece of her telephone's receiver. "Jimmy, I've got the Wakeeney operator. She doesn't have a listing for a Howard or a Harold Smitts."

Early aimed his finger as if it were a pistol. "Get the sheriff for me."

Wieland parked his bulk in a side chair, the chair's joints stressed, squalling under his weight. "Where are you on catching the bastard?" he asked.

"As I was telling Hutch, if Bill's smart, he kept going west. He's left the state. But it's amazing how many dumb criminals there are. We might find him."

"Better get out some wanted circulars. You got a picture?"

"The only picture I know of was Bill and Judith at their wedding . . . stolen from their house."

"Well, isn't that convenient? Parents might have a picture."

"I intend to find out."

Gladys again turned back, her hand once more over her

telephone's mouthpiece. "Pick up, Jimmy. The sheriff is Adam Clark."

Early winked at Wieland. "Adam, the first man." He pressed his desk phone's receiver to his ear. "Sheriff Clark? Sheriff Early."

"How can I help you, sheriff?" The voice sounded as distant as Wakeeney was from Manhattan—half the length of the state away.

"You know Howdy Smitts?"

"I do."

"What's that?"

"Yes, I know Howdy. Lives about twenty miles south, down in the Smoky Hill River country. Got a nice little ranch out there."

"He got a telephone?"

"Oh, I'm sorry on that one."

"We haven't got the best line. Would you say that again?"

"Maybe you want me to shout?"

"Would help."

"I said the phone line doesn't get any closer'n about seven miles to Howdy's property. We got a dozen ranchers down that way don't have phones. Don't have 'lectricity either unless they got wind generators. Why you ask?"

"Got a letter from him. Got some information I got to check out."

"This got something to do with the murder of his daughter-in-law?"

"You know about that?"

"We read the papers."

"Say again?"

"I said we read the papers. You think his boy did it?"

"It appears so." Early rummaged in the center drawer of his desk, then the side drawer. He brought out a railroad timetable and paged into it. "Sheriff, if I were to come out there, would you drive me down to his place?"

"Always glad to help. Know you'd do the same for me."

"My timetable says we got a hot train coming through in twenty minutes. That would put me in Wakeeney at twelve-oh-eight."

"I'll be at the depot."

"Pardon?"

"I said I'll be at the depot."

Early slumped in his seat, reading a paperback, his hat on the next seat, when the conductor leaned down to him.

"Know you're in a hurry to get to Wakeeney," he said, "but we're going to make a stop at Dorrance to pick up some express freight. We shouldn't lose more than five minutes."

Early mumbled and turned a page.

"What you reading?" the conductor asked, his face leathery, showing age.

"Zane Grey." Early closed the book, with his finger serving as his place marker. He held the cover out.

The conductor nodded as he read the title. "Yup, my dad's favorite, Riders of the Purple Sage. He got every book Grey ever wrote through the Sears-Roebuck catalogue. I have to read that one sometime."

The conductor went forward. Early felt the train slowing, so he dog-eared a page and put the book in his valise on the aisle seat. Early leaned to the window. He gazed ahead—wheat country close to the tracks, grazing land on the slopes and in the draws that led up to the flat land of the high plains that extended to the Colorado border, dry country that depended on windmills to lift water from wells. The Saline River to the north and the Smoky Hill to the south provided for a little irrigation—darn little, Early knew—and none further west where the headwaters were hardly a trickle. A tree out here was a rare thing and only grew in a creek bottom.

Early saw the Dorrance sign hanging askew on a telegraph pole and felt the brakes grab, dropping the train's speed to a slow coast. Ahead he saw a grain elevator, then a depot, and a water tank destined to be abandoned as progressively fewer steam locomotives made the runs on this long line. Early would miss it, the lonely wail of a steam whistle drifting across the plains. Call it nostalgia. Call it romance. The bleat of a diesel's horn just wasn't the same thing.

Lost in his reverie, he failed to notice the train had stopped until he found himself staring at a parking lot beside the depot. A car drew his attention, a well-dusted Mercury, one of its rear tires flat. Early pulled his notepad from his shirt pocket. He opened it and paged back to July, and there it was—a license number. Early peered again at the Mercury. He read the license plate, and the numbers matched.

Early jumped out of his seat. He hustled toward the front of the railcar and the steps down to the gravel ballast beside the tracks. There Early ran to the lot and the automobile. How long had it been here?

He glanced around until he saw a man with a sheaf of papers talking with the weary conductor. "Hey, fella!" he called out.

The man, a nebbish, turned to Early. "Yeah."

"You the stationmaster?"

"That's right."

Early held up his badge. "Sheriff of Riley County. How long's this car been here?"

The stationmaster, in jeans and a checked shirt, the sleeves rolled to his elbows, gave a paper to the conductor, said something, and came over. "Couple months," he said.

"That didn't concern you?"

"Not particularly. We got a rancher leaves his pickup here all winter when he goes to California to see his daughter and twin grandkids."

With the heel of his hand, Early rubbed a hole in the dust of one of the side windows. He peered inside. "Know who left the car?"

" 'Fraid not. Think I was off the day it showed up."

"You got a constable? I want this car impounded."

The nebbish grinned as he folded his arms across his chest. "The constable would be me. Dorrance is a real small town. As for impounding, nobody's going to drive that car away with that tire flat."

The diesel's horn sounded and sounded again. The conductor came trotting over. "Sheriff, we have to go," he said.

"Look, I'm not going anywhere and that train's not going anywhere. This car belongs to a man who murdered someone in my county. I want to get inside it before we leave."

The horn sounded a third time.

The conductor kicked at the gravel. "I'm sorry, sheriff, the railroad doesn't wait for anyone. We're leaving."

Early caught hold of the man's lapel. "You leave me and I'll have the next sheriff up the line pull you and your engineer off, and jail you both for hindering an investigation. How's that going to make you look with the railroad?"

The conductor's face went from gray to ash. He stepped away and wigwagged his arms over his head in an all-stop gesture to his engineer.

Early gripped the Mercury's door handle. He pulled on it, but the door refused to yield. "Who locks a car?" he asked as he tried the handle again.

"One person, I guess," the stationmaster said.

Early stepped to the side. He picked up a whitewashed rock from among those that bordered the parking lot. He hefted the rock and found it a good fit for his hand.

"What you going to do?" the stationmaster asked.

Early came back to the car. He whanged the rock into the wing window on the driver's side, shattering the glass, releasing a rush of dry, musty air seeking escape from its long captivity. Early reached inside. He lifted the lock and opened the door. "Always a way," he said as he climbed in. Early rifled the glove box and found nothing more than an Esso highway map, a railroad timetable like the one in his desk, only several months out of date, and a melted Hershey bar.

He got out. Early pulled the driver's seatback forward and clambered into the backseat. There, kneeling on the cushion, he got a grip on each side of the rear seatback. Early wrenched at it and pulled, and the back popped free of the clips that held it. He set the back aside and peered into the dark of the trunk. Early decided to feel around.

"Spare," he said and pounded his fist on the tire. "Well aired-up . . . tire tools, a jack. That's it." Early backed his way out of the car.

"Nuthin', huh?" the stationmaster asked.

"Just a minute here." Early got down on his knees. He leaned inside the driver's side of the car and, with his hat brim and his ear pressed against the grit on the floor, peered under the front seat. "Of course."

He reached under and drew out an empty whiskey fifth—Wild Turkey—and a booklet. Early opened the latter. He scanned the first page, recognized the writing. He had one of Judith Smitts's diaries in his hand. Early pushed himself up, slapping the dust from the knees of his tans. "Constable," he said to the stationmaster, "I want you to do two things for me."

He held up an index finger. "Give an affidavit to your judge telling him what you know about this car, how long you believe it's been here, and what you saw me do today."

Then Early raised a second finger. "Next flatcar you get in

243

here, put this car on it, and rail it to me in Manhattan. Put the affidavit in the glove box."

The train slowed as it approached Wakeeney.

Early stood in the doorway of the passenger car, his hat on and his valise in hand, watching the depot grow in the distance.

"You're gonna have to jump," the conductor said. "You got the engineer mad at you, and he's not gonna stop."

"And if I break my leg?"

"I'll make Henry send you a get-well card."

"Thanks."

Early aimed himself forward. He pushed off and out, and when his boots hit the gravel ballast, he ran, ran hard and ran out his momentum, the train picking up speed, the last car passing him and leaving him in silence, the only sound the crunch of stones beneath his boots as he strolled on to the depot's platform, a cricket sawing away in the dry twitch grass that bordered the ballast.

A woman in denims and a straw cowboy hat came out onto the platform. She called to Early, "Wouldn't happen to be the Riley County sheriff, would you?"

Early touched the brim of his hat in response.

"They throw you off?" she asked.

"Something like that." When he came close, he saw the badge pinned to the woman's shirt. "I was expecting an Adam Clark."

"I'm Evelyn Clark—Eve—Adam's wife and this term his deputy." She laughed. "Last term, I was sheriff and Adam was my deputy. Understand you need a lift down to Howdy's place."

"That's right."

"I'll take that," Eve Clark said, and she relieved Early of his valise as he stepped up onto the platform. "My pickup's out front. Adam and I both got one. Cars aren't too practical out here when the bottoms go out of the roads in the spring."

"We drive Jeeps," Early said as he humped along to keep up with Clark, she sweeping like a dust devil through the depot and outside.

"They'll getcha anywhere," she said as she flung a hand out toward a flame-red Studebaker. "Whaddaya think of her?"

"You ever go to Topeka, you'll never lose it in a parking lot."

"I like it." Clark opened the door. She threw Early's valise in and followed it, settling behind the steering wheel.

Early eased onto the passenger seat. The back of his hat bumped against a gun rack, and he twisted around and took note of a Savage Thirty-ought-Six with a mammoth scope on it, twenty power, he guessed. Below the rifle a pump shotgun, a Remington.

"Ever have need for those?" he asked.

Clark started her truck.

"They're for show," she said, a smile crinkling at the corners of her eyes as she backed the rig around. She aimed it for a dirt street. " 'Course our Legion post has a turkey shoot each fall to raise a little money. I've won it the last three years, so the word gets around, you don't mess with little Evie."

Clark bucked her pickup across the railroad tracks and onto US Two-Eighty-Three, a wide graveled road. Dust billowed out behind her truck as it picked up speed, the speedometer coming to peg on sixty.

"Adam tells me," Clark said, "you think Howdy's son killed his wife."

"Got a letter from him. Says Bill told him."

"Lordy, these family things get messy, don't they?"

"You know Bill?"

Clark peered ahead at a ranch truck loaded with baled hay trundling along on her side of the road. She swung out to pass. "Not really," she said. "I grew up in the next county over. Didn't marry Adam until Bill was off in college."

"Kids?"

"Pardon?" Clark asked as she swung her truck back to the right side of the road.

"You and your husband?"

"Two from my first marriage. Both in grade school now. My first husband was killed in the war."

"Had to be hard."

"He was a deputy. When he joined the Army, I wangled the job for myself. Couldn't have made it if I didn't have my mother to look after the children. Then when Albert was killed—he didn't even get out of the States, mind you, killed in a training accident they told me—I couldn't have made it if I didn't have the job to go to every day."

"And Sheriff Clark?"

"Met him a couple years later. We took a liking to one another and everything since, as they say, is beautiful history."

"After the rain," Early said.

"The sun does shine," Clark answered.

"So what can you tell me about Bill's parents?"

She glanced at Early. "Solid citizens. Good people. Howdy's been a deacon in his little Baptist church forever, Adam says, and he and his wife have taught Sunday school for all of that long. If Howdy tells you something, you can count on it being the Lord's honest truth."

"And Bill?"

"As I said, I only kinda knew of him. Went to college late, I'm told, and spent most of the war there. Why he didn't join the Army or wasn't drafted has been a wonder to Adam, and to me now that I think about it."

"May have had a friend on the draft board."

"That's possible."

Early itched at his mustache. "Bill ever known to be violent?"

"I asked Adam. He says no, that he only remembers him as being unremarkable."

A quarter of an hour after Clark and Early left Wakeeney, Clark moved her foot from the gas pedal to the brake. She wheeled her truck off onto a dirt track that wandered west along the meandering Smoky Hill River. Several miles on, Clark guided her truck off onto another track, less distinct, that led into the hills north of the river. The truck rumbled over a cattle guard in a break in a line fence.

"We're on Howdy's ranch now," Clark said. She nodded toward where the track angled off into a shallow canyon. "Buildings and corral are up there 'bout half a mile, tucked back in where the winter winds can't get."

A jackrabbit came out of a thatch of grass and sat, watching the red pickup pass by.

The track made a bend. Beyond it laid a cluster of buildings hugging the west wall of the canyon, a corral further out and, to the east side of it, a windmill, the fan facing the southwest and turning at a lazy rate, the air here cracking clear, the sky overhead the color of a blue-white diamond, the sun baking.

"My field glasses are under the seat," Clark said. "Get them out for me, would you?"

Early grubbed around until his fingers felt a leather case. He drew it out and took the glasses from it. Early saw Clark hunched forward against the steering wheel, peering at the near horizon.

"I see someone up on the windmill," she said. "Put the glasses on him and tell me who he is."

"How am I going to know?" Early asked as he raised the binoculars to his eyes. He fiddled with the focus wheel.

"You can describe him, can't you?"

"Sure. Nothing unusual about the fella. Wait a minute. The

hair coming down from under his hat at the back is longish, kind of like Buffalo Bill."

"White?"

He squinted at the image in the glasses. "Hat shades it. Could be."

"That's Howdy. His wife chops his hair back to collar-length when it gets below his shoulders." Clark turned her truck off the track and held tight to the steering wheel as the pickup rocked over rougher ground. After some moments, the truck rolled out onto dirt well churned by the hooves of cows crowding in to get to the concrete water tank at the base of the windmill. But no cattle were in sight.

Clark stopped her truck. She stepped out and looked up at the man on the high scaffold of the windmill. She shaded her eyes from the sun that seemed, to Early, to burn brighter in the west than it did at home.

"Howdy," Clark called out, "brought somebody who needs to talk to you."

"You all keep your britches on," came a voice from above. "I'll be down in a minute."

Clark and Early leaned against the fender of her truck. They watched Howdy Smitts step over the side of the windmill's scaffold and onto a ladder and back his way down, a dented bucket in one hand. When Smitts stepped from the ladder onto the dirt, he set his bucket on the water tank's ledge.

"Gotta take care of the machinery," he said. Smitts pulled a rag from the bucket and scrubbed at the grease on his hands. "You don't and your machinery quits takin' care of you."

"Howdy, this is the sheriff from Riley County."

"Figured that. Don't get many strangers coming this far out unless they got purpose."

"Says you wrote him a letter."

"Yup." Smitts threw the rag back in the bucket. He took out

a bar of soap and soaped his hands in the stock tank. "Grease out of place can be miserable stuff. . . . Sheriff, Jen and I liked Judith. Thought she was about the best thing that ever happened for our son."

Early held out the letter. "You wrote this then?"

After Smitts shook the water from his hands, he took a pair of steel-rimmed glasses from his shirt pocket and put them on. He tipped his head back, peering through the bifocal at the paper. "I did. You had some doubt?"

"My county attorney said I had to confirm it."

"Now you got the thing confirmed." Smitts took a bandana from his back pocket. He wiped his hands dry.

"When was Bill here?"

"Wednesday last."

"He have the child with him?"

"No, and that really bothered me. I asked, and he said Isaac—don't know where they got that name, sure wasn't in our family—said he'd left Isaac with a friend. Bill looked a wreck. Second time he was here since spring."

"Really?" Early said. "When was the first?"

"Night of the day Judith was killed, only we didn't know Judith was dead, not until a day later and Bill got back to Manhattan and sent us a telegram. You remember that, Evie."

Clark turned to Early. "I brought it out."

"I have to ask, Mister Smitts," Early said. "You didn't come to the funeral."

"Well, something just didn't feel right. I kept replaying the conversation we had had that night—just the most disjointed stuff. It was like Bill couldn't focus on anything for more than a minute. I could tell something wasn't right, but I couldn't get Bill to tell me what it was. Come time to get on the train, I couldn't do it. Jen and I came home."

"So you thought your son killed Judith."

"No, not at the time. But there was just something telling me, 'Howdy, you and Jen don't belong at that funeral.' "

Early took out his notebook and pencil. He jotted a couple words. "Tell me about Wednesday last."

A blue fly buzzed past Smitts's battered Windcutter hat. He snatched the fly from the air, popped it between his hands, and let the insect's broken body fall to the dust. "I spray and spray, but never get them all. . . . Bill drove in about this time—we talked right where we are now—looked like he'd been pulled through a knothole, big circles under his eyes—puffy like he'd been crying—and he hadn't shaved that day. He rambled for awhile about nothing. Then he did start to cry, and that's when he told me."

"Told you what?"

"What I put in the letter, that he'd killed Judith. . . . I asked him why he was telling me and telling me now, and he said he needed someone to forgive him."

"Did you?"

"You a Christian?"

"I understand you're a Baptist, Mister Smitts. Me too."

"Sheriff, murder is a violation of God's law. I can't forgive that. Maybe God can, but not me."

"Your wife?"

"Jen wasn't here. She was over at the Thomasons'—the next ranch yon way—" Smitts waved over his shoulder "—helping Missus Thomason put up squash. I wanted Bill to stay, to talk to his mother. But when I told him I couldn't forgive him, he just bolted. Jumped in that new car he's got and scratched dirt."

"Know where he went?"

"I assume to get Isaac. From there, I don't know."

"Help me understand one thing. I've seen killing but nothing even remotely as violent as this, not even in war, and war's awful. Where's this come from?"

"Can't be sure," Smitts said. "I got my suspicions, and, if you tell my wife, I'll deny it because she doesn't know. I've kept it from her."

"What's that?"

"There's a streak in Bill. It's surfaced a couple times that I know of, first when he was, oh, fifteen or so. I sent him out to bring in some of the young stock. He came back on foot, said his horse got away and he couldn't catch her. I found the horse some weeks later, in a ravine, dead—shot."

"Bill carrying a rifle?"

"Out here, we all carry a pistol or a rifle when we're riding. Snakes, you know. . . . Bill said it wasn't him, and I didn't find his rifle, either."

"You said a couple times?"

"Yeah." Smitts took off his Windcutter. He combed his fingers through his mane of white hair—a gesture of hesitation. Early recognized it, had used it himself when he needed to think twice about what he wanted to say. Smitts resettled his hat. "Five, maybe six years later when Bill was in college over at Fort Hays, he hit a girl, beat her pretty bad over what I don't know. I had to buy him out of trouble to keep the big who-daddy from kicking him out of school, and I bought him out of trouble with the girl too. Did it all without Bill's mother knowing."

"But why not tell her?"

"She always thought her boy was near perfect, and he was for the most part . . . for the most part."

Early closed his notebook. He slipped it back in his pocket. "If we catch your son, you testify at his trial?"

Smitts leaned against the concrete water tank. He pushed his heel at the dirt. "If it comes to that I guess."

"You don't think we'll catch him."

"Sheriff, this is open country out here. Man puts his mind to it, he can just evaporate, never leave a trace."

CHAPTER 23

Good News

Early, the only one to board the Union-Pacific's Number Seventy at Wakeeney, pushed back through the first two passenger cars to the dining car, lights coming on in response to the sun slipping below the horizon behind the train, the train pounding away toward the night that had already come to the east. He found he had the dining car to himself except for a lone couple at a distant table. Early dropped his valise and hat on a chair at a table set for two, and took the chair on the opposite side for himself.

A menu lay there on the linen tablecloth, and to the side, by the window, a small crystal vase with a rose. Early couldn't help himself. A sucker for roses, he sniffed it before he opened the menu and commenced reading the evening's selections.

An ebony hand placed a goblet of water to his right.

"Sheriff Early, what will you have tonight?"

Early twisted around. He stared up. "Tony?"

"The same."

"I didn't know you worked this train."

"Luck of the draw. What may I get for you?"

"What do you recommend?"

"Well, Eddie's cooking up some lamb chops and shrimp scampi for him and me. What say I have him make an extra portion?"

Early laid the menu aside. "Excellent, but only if you'll eat with me."

" 'Fraid that's against the railroad's rules, but since I'm quitting the railroad—"

"The heck you say."

Tony Haskins grinned, his broad smile adding new light to the dining car. "I'll tell you about it just as soon as I bring you your scampi," he said and left for the galley.

Early rescued his valise and hat. He set them under the table. Caught with a moment of time and little to see outside the dining car's windows, Early instead took notice of a painting that hung on the wall at the end of the car. Was it a painting or a print? Print likely. And he recognized the style without even needing to see the signature—a Remington—a cavalry unit riding hard, right out of the frame toward the painter and all who looked at the picture.

Tony slid a dish of shrimp scampi sizzling in lemon butter in front of Early and set a second dish across from him. "Like that painting, do you?" he asked as he slipped into the chair opposite Early.

"Yes. That Frederick Remington, he just had a feel for what the Old West was. What I really like is the way he painted his cowboys."

"How so?"

"There wasn't a handsome kid among them. All his cowboys were scruffy and beat up, but never beat down, even when they were carrying a motherless calf on their saddle in a blizzard."

Early forked up a hot, peppered shrimp. He ate it while Tony ate one of his.

"So you're quitting the railroad," Early said as he reached to sip his water.

Again Tony grinned. "Yessir. The Seventy gets into Chicago in the morning. I spend a day with my family, then catch the

Cardinal the next morning for Washington. I'm going to be President Truman's steward."

CHAPTER 24

September 24—Saturday Afternoon
Manhunt

Early and his horse cut a beefy Hereford calf away from a small herd. When the calf ran, Early swung his lariat once and let the loop fly out low, under the calf's rear hooves. In the instant the horse set her own hooves, Early yanked up the rope, spilling the whiteface onto the dirt of the corral.

"Jimmy," Walter Estes called out from the gate of Osage orange poles he held open, "you sure can throw a rope."

"I'm gettin' better. Been out of practice so darn long." Early walked his horse toward the gate, dragging the bawling calf behind. A cow bellowed. She bolted out from the others and stampeded toward her calf. Early spurred his horse. She kicked into a gallop and raced out the gate with the calf still on the end of the line. "Cut 'er off, Walter!" Early hollered.

Estes slammed the gate, and the cow veered away, bellowing, spit frothing from her mouth.

Early reined his horse in near the branding fire. And four cowboys—three of them neighbors—ran out, all in chaps like Early, one—Hutch Tolliver—with horn loppers, a second with a syringe, and a third with a hot iron. The fourth, fat Roger Arnold, squatted on the calf's shoulders while Early's horse leaned into the lariat rope, keeping the calf stretched out.

Less than a minute and they had the work done. Tolliver pitched the loppers aside and loosened the rope that bound the calf's hocks. He whipped the loop away. "Let 'er go, Rog," he called to his partner.

Arnold came up, the calf almost as fast. She stagger-trotted away, bruised, burned, and bloody, to join a bunch of calves beyond the corral, all dehorned, vaccinated for brucellosis, branded and, the bull calves, cut—deprived of their bullhood.

Thelma, in a loose dress that hid her expansive middle, came up with Nadine Estes, the two visiting and laughing, carrying a tray of glasses and a pitcher of iced lemonade.

"Jimmy, take a break," Thelma said, her smile large. She held up the pitcher.

"Don't have to tell me twice." Early waved the other men over as he walked his horse toward where the women stood with Estes, Estes sweeping a dripping cold glass across his forehead.

"Jimmy," he said, "you spittin' dust like me?"

"Dust and cow hair."

Thelma filled a glass, and Missus Estes handed it up to Early.

Arnold helped himself to a full glass before he leaned an elbow against Early's saddle. "How many we got left, Cactus?" he asked.

Early studied the cattle in the corral. He moved an index finger across them, counting. "Looks to be maybe ten or a dozen." Early downed half his lemonade, only to choke. He puckered his lips and spit an errant seed to the side.

Estes checked the back of an envelope. "Unless I failed to mark a couple down, I'd say a baker's dozen, Jimmy."

"Half an hour then?" Arnold asked. He pushed his Small Alpine Stetson onto the back of his head.

Early laughed. "That sweet young thing you married keeping you on a short rein?"

"Well, she does miss me if I don't get home for supper."

Tolliver, gangly, tall—taller still in his Big-brim Alpine—came up. He dodged in and patted Arnold's girth. "You sure haven't missed many suppers, have you, Rog?"

Arnold twisted away, snickering.

Tolliver grabbed at Arnold's ribs, and the fat cowboy went up in hoots of laughter, sloshing lemonade onto Early and his sweaty horse. The horse jumped to the side, and Arnold went down, Tolliver on top of him, working at Arnold's ribs.

"Children, children, children," Early said as he reined in his horse, "we got company."

Everyone looked up to see dust rising on the lane leading to the Estes ranchstead, a red bubble light revolving. A state police cruiser came off the lane and into a slide that threw up more dust and scattered the calves the ranch crew had worked on.

Early's horse, shy from the lemonade spill, shied even more. She trampled and danced as Early, hauling on her reins, worked for control.

Dan Plemmons stepped out of the cruiser. He waved his way through the dust cloud. "Cactus," he said on spying Early, "sorry to interrupt your party, but he's been spotted."

"Bill?"

"Yup."

"Where?"

"Concordia. A railroad dick saw him driving through. He had his office relay a call to me, then followed Bill to the Washington County line."

"The fella gave up?"

"No. Had his office call ahead for a Washington deputy. Got one to shadow Bill to Clay County. Looks like he's coming home."

"The boy?"

"He's with him."

Early swung down from his horse. He handed the reins to Estes. "Walter, this is important. The others will help you with the last calves. It'll take you a little longer, but you'll get it done."

Thelma grabbed hold of Early's arm, all the joy of the day gone, fear etching into her face. "Don't go," she said.

"Thel, I'm sorry. It's my job." He turned away and motioned for Tolliver to follow. The two trotted off, their chaps swishing and slapping, toward their Jeeps parked by the barn. Both shucked their chaps and strapped on gun belts. While Early got out a denim jacket and pulled his Winchester from its scabbard on the hood of his Jeep, Tolliver rummaged in the back of his, coming up with a jacket of his own and a sack.

Plemmons, back in his cruiser, drove up to the cowboy lawmen. "No need to take three vehicles unless you want to, Cactus," he said, his elbow out his window.

Early pointed to Tolliver and the backseat, then made his way around to the front passenger door. He got in next to Plemmons. "You're solid on this?" Early asked as he laid his rifle against the center of the seat.

Plemmons stepped down on the accelerator. "It's the car, the license plate, the man looks right, and he's got a boy with him."

"Anyone try to stop Bill?"

"I put the word out. Everybody was to lay back."

"So the fool's coming home."

Plemmons picked up his radio microphone. He pressed the transmit button. "Any Clay County officer on this frequency, come in."

Static crackled, then, "Deputy Conroy here."

"Conroy, Trooper Plemmons. You tailing that Ford Woody?"

"Yessir. I'm 'bout a quarter mile back on Twenty-Four, coming out of Clay Center. This old boy's sure not in any hurry."

"Call me if he turns south on Eighty-Two."

"You want me to follow him into the next county?"

"The guy lives outside of Leonardville. I want you to follow him all the way home."

"I don't know about this."

Early took the microphone from Plemmons. He squeezed the transmit button as the cruiser bounced through a dry wash on the way to the county road. "Deputy Conroy, this is Riley County Sheriff James Early. I'm making you a deputy in my county for the next twenty-four hours. You oughtta be home long before the end of the day."

"I better call my sheriff."

"Don't bother. . . . Clay County dispatcher, you on the frequency?"

A woman's voice came back. "This is the Clay dispatcher."

"Ma'am, Riley County Sheriff James Early here. Rustle up Sheriff Smith wherever he is and tell him I'm borrowing his Deputy Conroy, would you?"

"Sheriff's right here."

"Cactus?"

"Art."

"So this is the guy that killed that teacher down your way?"

"Her husband."

"My Lord. . . . Sam?"

"Conroy here."

"You stay with him. If you keep your eyes open, you could learn a thing or two from Sheriff Early."

"If you say so."

"Cactus?"

"Go ahead, Art."

"You want me to come down?"

"We got three of us now. If we pick up our local constable, that's four, and your deputy makes five. That's enough. I don't like posses."

"Good luck then."

"Thank you, Art."

Plemmons ran his cruiser out onto the county highway. He turned west toward Leonardville and a bank of low, scuddy clouds the color of dry dirt. Plemmons flipped on his bubble light. "So your constable is around?"

"Somewhere," Early said. He glanced back at Tolliver, bareheaded in the backseat. "How many walkies you got in your sack?"

"Four."

Early smiled. "Makes one for each of us and one for Mose. Hutch, when we get there, we'll scatter out around the perimeter of Bill's property, hunker down. I don't want him to see us when he drives in."

"We could do a roadblock," Plemmons said as he steered his cruiser on.

"Dan'l, a man's dangerous in a car. He could run one of us over, and I don't cotton to that."

"It's your arrest. You call how we do it."

The trooper negotiated his cruiser around a rutted curve. Ahead and on a rise stood the Smitts house—lonely, looking abandoned, the parched yard ragged from lack of care. Early motioned toward the windshield. "There's Mose at the mailbox, making like a letter carrier."

Plemmons let off the accelerator. He flipped the bubble light off, slowed his cruiser, and stopped beside Mose Dickerson's Chevrolet coupe.

"With all of ya here, Bill must be on his way, huh?" Dickerson asked through the side window of his car.

Early leaned toward the constable. "He's in Clay County now."

"What do ya want to do, Jimmy?"

"Catch the bastard."

Plemmons's radio came to life. "He's turning onto Eighty-Two. Trees along here. I'm gonna lose sight of him for a bit."

"Roger your call," Plemmons said into his mic.

Dickerson scratched at his sideburn. "Eighty-Two . . . that makes him about ten miles out."

Early bailed from the cruiser and waved for Tolliver to do the same. Early came around between the two cars. He stopped at the driver's window of Dickerson's and leaned down. "Got your shotgun, Mose?"

"In the trunk."

"Hutch's got a walkie for you. Hide your car in those scrubby trees over yonder, then hustle behind Bill's barn. You cover the back of the house."

Dickerson took a war-surplus walkie-talkie from Tolliver and drove away.

Early pointed Tolliver to the west side of the property. "There's a ravine over there where you can keep out of sight."

"You?" Tolliver asked as he took a walkie from the bag. He handed the bag and its remaining radios to Early.

"East side. Dan'l and I'll tuck his cruiser in by Mose's car. We'll watch from there."

"Leaves the front door open for Bill. I like that," Tolliver said. He hustled off.

Early got back in the cruiser. Plemmons whipped the car around and drove down the road, beyond the yard. The sun, growing pale in the last minutes, disappeared as the scud advanced overhead.

Plemmons glanced up at the clouds. "We're in for rain," he said as he herded the cruiser off into an open field.

Early also studied the clouds. "Friendly Neighbor called it this morning. Said there was real moisture behind the front for once, and I tell you I can feel it."

Plemmons drove on to the stand of scrub oak and sumac. He went well into the stand before he killed the motor. The lawmen abandoned the car, but not before Plemmons gathered up his field glasses from beneath the seat and got a rain slicker from the trunk. Early and he then worked their way forward, to the edge of the stand, to where they could squat down, their backs against tree trunks and tall weeds in front of them.

Plemmons raised the binoculars to his eyes. "There goes Hutch down," he said. Next he swung the glasses toward the barn. "If your constable is back there, I sure can't see him."

Early brought up his walkie. He squeezed the transmit button. "Mose, you in place?"

"I'm here, Jimmy."

"Hutch?"

"Down in a deer bed. Real soft grass here."

"Don't you go to sleep on me."

"Right."

A chill wind rustled up out of the northwest, rattling the fall-dried leaves in the oaks. Early set his walkie aside. He pulled on his jacket and turned its collar up. "Frontal passage. Damn, wish I'd brought my gloves."

Plemmons handed Early a pair.

"You wouldn't happen to have some coffee, too, would you?" Early asked as he worked his fingers into the tan, fleece-lined gloves.

Plemmons settled back against the rough bark of a tree trunk. "Got a pot and a can of grounds in the trunk. I could drain some water out of the radiator."

"Did that more'n once in the war. You could get some real strange tastes if the Jeep's radiator hadn't been flushed for awhile, but the coffee was always hot."

"You like your time in the Army?"

"You like your time in the Marines?"

"Up until they kicked us out of a landing craft, onto a beach in the Mariannas. They taught killing in boot camp. Now we had to do it."

Early snapped off a bluestem leaf. He chewed on it, the taste flat. "Bad, huh?"

"Like you, I know what hell is. Only three in my platoon got off the beach."

"Yeah. Can't help but wonder if luck didn't have a lot to do with those things."

Plemmons cast a sideward glance at Early, Early gazing at the horizon, as if he were gazing into the face of a memory. "How's that?" Plemmons asked.

"My squad, we once went three months without losing a man, other than a wound or two, but nothing to take anyone out of the field. Morning of the first day of the fourth month—I know because the sergeant appointed me to keep count—when we came out of our holes . . . damn . . ."

"What happened?"

"An Eighty-Eight opened up on us." Early's eyes changed. They came into a sharp focus, and he peered up the road. "Where the heck is Bill?"

Plemmons glanced at his wristwatch. "He should have been here, even poking along. Want me to go to the car and call Conroy?"

"Maybe you better."

Plemmons laid his field glasses aside. He got up and meandered back toward his cruiser.

Early picked up the glasses. He put them to his eyes and scanned the front and side yards of the Smitts place, then the horizon to the west. "Dan'l," he called out, "car coming."

Plemmons came crashing back through the sumac and ragweed. He went down on one knee, grabbing the binoculars Early held out. Plemmons peered through them, starting at the mailbox and panning west. "Got him . . . whoops, it's a little rolly out there. He just went down in a dip. Ahh, there he comes, up over . . . It isn't a Ford."

Early came up. "What is it?"

"Chev . . . 'Forty-Six, maybe . . . slowing, turning in . . ."

Early pointed at the car as it came broadside. "Sumbitch. That's a Clay County sheriff's car. What the hell's going on? Can you see who's driving?"

"Not for sure," Plemmons said, the field glasses to his eyes. He followed the cruiser up the driveway until the car stopped in front of the house. A man got out.

"It's Bill," Plemmons said, "and he's got his kid with him."

Smitts, in a suit with his necktie pulled loose and his hair disheveled, lifted a boy from the car. He carried the child up the steps to the front door and inside.

"I don't like this," Plemmons said.

"Can't say I do either." The first spits of rain flicked across Early's face. He brought up his walkie and spoke into the mouthpiece. "Mose? Hutch? Bill's in the house with the boy."

"Heard the car."

"It's not Bill's. He's got a Clay sheriff's car."

"Jesus . . ."

"Mose, work around until you got a clear shot at the back door. Hutch, you cover the west windows. Dan's gonna do the same on the east side of the house."

"You?"

"I'm going out front. See if I can talk Bill out. But if he comes out your way, put enough buckshot and bullets around him to drive him back inside. Don't kill him, and don't hit the boy." Early picked up his rifle. He motioned for Plemmons to move to the side and scooted out low, running hard toward the Chevrolet. Early's foot went in a chuckhole and he sprawled forward. Holding tight to his rifle, he rolled and came up—grass stubble and dirt on his face—and ran on. He stopped only when he had the Clay patrol car between himself and the house. He glanced inside the car, saw nothing of interest and slid down,

265

his back against the cold metal of the door.

Early, breathing hard, turned the volume down on his walkie. He whispered into the mouthpiece, "Hutch?"

"I'm ready."

"Mose?"

"Got me a good place."

"Dan?"

"Let's get this thing done."

"Bill's got to have a gun, so don't you boys go nuts on me." Early set his walkie on the ground. With his sleeve he rubbed the dirt from his face, the dirt smearing, wet from the rain spits. Early hollered, "Bill!"

No response.

The spits became a mist. Early twisted around. He came up, leveled his Winchester across the hood of the car and squeezed off one round, blasting out chunks of glass from the house's front window.

Early cupped a hand beside his mouth. "Bill? Have I got your attention? Come on out. You're going to jail!"

The front door opened a crack. Out came a gun barrel. Early dropped, and a pistol shot shattered much of the windshield, glass bits going down Early's collar. He brushed away what he could, came up, and pumped four bullets into the door. Early dropped back down. "Bill, you're getting me a mite upset. I got more firepower than you. Talk to me!"

"Sheriff? What about my boy?"

"Your parents want him. So do Judith's parents. They're all good people, Bill. You can't beat that."

"Give me a minute."

Early edged toward the headlight. He peered around the fender. "Minute so you can blow your brains out? Not gonna happen. Pitch your pistol out the door. Let this be done now."

Something moved the front door of the house open a bit

further. A hand and pistol came into sight.

"Come on, Bill, throw the gun away."

Once more, no response. An eternity seemed to pass before the hand flipped the pistol into the yard.

Early reached back for his walkie. He pressed the ON switch and spoke into the mouthpiece. "He's thrown his gun out. This is too easy. I don't like it."

Tolliver came back. "Mose and I could go in through the kitchen door."

"You ever get that tingly feeling you're not alone? Check your backs."

"Right."

Early again set his walkie aside. He peered around the fender. Again he cupped a hand to the side of his mouth. "Bill? Come on outside where I can see you!"

The door swung full wide, and Bill Smitts edged out with his hands up, at shoulder level. A second man came out as well, behind Smitts. He held the boy in one arm, a claw hand showing.

"Sheriff Early?" the man called out.

"Steph?"

"Mister Smitts is mine. And I have Isaac. The boy's got my name. He's my son."

Early sat back against the front tire, the first of the heavy raindrops splatting around him. "Steph, how long you been in that house?"

"Three days. I had a feeling Mister Smitts was coming in."

"And my constable didn't see you?"

"Nobody sees me when I don't want to be seen."

"Except me."

"Except you. But you didn't come around."

"What do you want, Steph?"

"To leave here without anyone getting hurt. Sheriff, I will

dispose of Mister Smitts for you, let you know where you can find the body when Isaac and I are out of your country."

"Doesn't work that way." Early pushed himself up. He stepped away from the cruiser. As he did, he brought his Winchester to his shoulder and moved forward at a measured pace.

"Sheriff," Isaac Daniel Stephanowitz said, "stop there or I will kill him now and you."

"You could, but you'd be dead before either of us hits the ground. I got a trooper on your right and a deputy on your left. Fifty-yard kill shots are nothing new to them."

Stephanowitz glanced to the side.

Smitts's hand twitched. "He means it, sheriff. He's gonna kill me."

"Aww, Bill, you're a dead man anyway. You murdered your wife, for chrissake. Riley County juries don't take kindly to that."

"But I was in Abilene. You know I was."

"Bill, your alibi's gone to hell."

Stephanowitz interrupted. "Excuse me, can we negotiate?"

"You got nothing to negotiate with." Early straightened. He stood as tall as his frame would allow, the rain splatter increasing. He squinted along his rifle's sights, zeroing on the Israeli's forehead. From the corner of his eye, Early glimpsed a movement through the front window, inside the house. A gimpy man in a duster and a sweat-stained Stetson, water dripping from the brim, eased out the door, the stock of a shotgun at his shoulder. He put the ends of the barrels against the back of Stephanowitz's head, the Israeli flinching at the touch.

"Think this is where ya give it up, fella," Mose Dickerson said, his voice as flat as a prairie.

Early motioned to the side with his rifle. "Move away, Bill."

As Smitts did, Plemmons ran in through the rain. He grabbed

Smitts and hauled him farther to the side.

Tolliver trotted in. He reached for the child who in turn reached out to him. "Friendly little guy, aren'tcha?" Tolliver said as he took the boy from Stephanowitz.

"Steph," Early said, "that's a mighty nice Beretta you got there. Mose is going to take it from you, then you're going to come out to me."

Dickerson inched to the side. He held his double-barrel firm in his trigger hand, while with the other he took the pistol from the Israeli.

Stephanowitz stared at Dickerson, his eyes empty of emotion. Then he turned away, to Early, and walked down the steps and into the rain.

"The boy really your son?" Early asked as he lowered his rifle.

"I saw myself in his face, in his eyes," Stephanowitz said.

"He's not his son. He's mine," Smitts bellowed from the side.

Early swung around. "Bill, that's enough from you. . . . Dan'l, throw him in the back of your cruiser and haul him to jail. Hutch and I, we'll come along with Mose."

"What about the Clay deputy?"

"I expect we're gonna find him in a ditch somewhere." Early put his arm around Stephanowitz's shoulders. "How do you like our Kansas rain?"

"It's cold."

"Not to us. We've been waiting months for this one. . . . Where's your car?"

"In Mister Smitts's barn."

"Should have guessed. . . . Steph, I'm feeling generous because you didn't ventilate old Bill and me. I'm going to let you get in your car and drive away on your promise that you'll catch a couple flights to Tel-Aviv or Haifa or wherever home is for you, and you never come back here."

"Go without my son?"

"You got that right. From what I read in the papers, it's a dangerous life in your country right now, still a lot of shooting. He'll do better here. And he's got two sets of grandparents who want him."

CHAPTER 25

September 26—Monday Morning
The Chase

Early sat rubbing his face at the trestle table in Walter and Nadine Estes's kitchen, exhaustion showing in the gray skin beneath his eyes, the kitchen flush with the aromas of a breakfast in the making.

Walter, across from Early, slurped his coffee, his white hair uncombed. Nadine, in well-worn bib overalls and an apron, stood at the stove, stirring crumbled bacon and chopped onions into scrambled eggs crackling in a skillet.

Thelma came in, a cotton bathrobe over her nightgown. She leaned on Early and wrapped her arms around his shoulders.

"You all right?" she asked. "You didn't sleep well. Kicked off the covers more than once last night, rouncing around."

"God awful memories. . . . Thel, Bill killed a Clay deputy yesterday."

"You can't blame yourself for that."

"I told his sheriff he'd be working for me. I was responsible for him."

"You couldn't know it was going to happen."

"That doesn't make it any easier."

Nadine Estes placed a plate of eggs and biscuits in front of Early. "Jimmy, you gotta let it go. It'll eat you alive if you don't."

"Yeah, maybe." Early patted Thel's hand. He drew her around, and she sat beside him on the bench seat. Early pushed

271

his plate to her. " 'Fraid I don't have much of an appetite."

"Me neither," Thelma said. "Maybe if it dries some, I'll go for a walk. Friendly Neighbor said it's going to be a good day. I need to be outside."

"And I need to be in the office. Paperwork on this one's going to be horrendous."

"Then you better eat something, Jimmy."

"A bite maybe." Early poked his fork at the scrambled eggs.

"Dammit, Cactus, he murdered my deputy. I want him prosecuted for that." Spade-bearded Clay County Sheriff Art Smith banged around Early's office while Early, leaning forward, worked the blade of his pocketknife across a whetstone. He turned the blade with each stroke, honing its edge to a scalpel-like sharpness. Hutch Tolliver lounged in the corner, and County Attorney Carl Wieland fanned himself with a folder of papers.

"Not going to happen, sheriff," Wieland said, aiming his folder at Smith, "not just yet. We're going to take the cases in the order the crimes were committed."

"But if you get a conviction on that teacher's murder—"

"And we will."

"—Smitts is going to be executed before you get him to court for my deputy's murder."

Early raised a finger.

"Cactus?" Wieland asked.

"How about this? Ask the judge to delay sentencing until after the second trial. You can run the trial in on the next week or even the next day. We're all set to go."

"Except for the murder weapon. You don't have a murder weapon for either case, and old Bill isn't going to tell us where they are."

Smith whipped around to Early. "Is that right?"

Early studied the edge on his blade. With it, he shaved a few hairs from the back of his hand. "Now, boys, this is one sharp knife," he said and folded the blade into its handle. "Art, the gun Bill had didn't kill your deputy. Wrong caliber."

Smith swept off his hat and knuckle rubbed his scalp. "Jimmy, I thought you were better than this."

"The gun's got to be out there somewhere. I've got a constable and three deputies out searching the ditches and the ravines. Hutch and I are going out, and you're welcome to come along."

"Damn right I'm coming."

Mose Dickerson pulled against sumac bushes as he worked his way up the side of a steep ravine toward where Early and Sheriff Smith stood, Smith chewing snuff with the ferocity of an angered bull, Early with his hands thrust in his back pockets.

"That's his car," Dickerson said. "Rain washed out his track 'cept where the car went over. If I hadn't come on that, I'da never gone down there. He threw brush over the car so you couldn't see it from up here."

"A gun?" Early asked.

Dickerson shook his head. "Foller me," he said and hop-stepped out into the pasture.

Fifty yards on, the three stopped at the edge of a pond, the bank around it well churned by the hooves of cows rambling down into the water to drink.

"This is on a straight line from the ravine to the road," Dickerson said, first pointing in one direction, then the other. "If I'm Bill and I'm wantin' to get rid of a gun, I'd throw it in that pond. Muddy bottom like it's got to have, nobody's ever going to find it."

Early pulled off his cattleman's hat. He raked his fingers back through his hair before he resettled his hat. He glanced at Smith.

"Art, he's right."

"Look," Smith said, "I could get a pump out here tomorrow morning with a gas engine. We could pump that sucker dry."

"Except for the mud."

"Still and all, there's a chance we might see the gun with the water out of there."

"Always a chance."

"Eight o'clock then?"

"You want to do it," Early said, "we'll be here."

Early had had enough. He sent his deputies and Dickerson home, called dispatch with the message that he was going out of service, and drove away for the Rocking Horse E.

Rotten day.

Just one damn, awful rotten day.

The only thing that saved it, and Early was certain of it, was the rain that had come the day before. The rain slaked the thirst of the bluestem pastures and brought a hint of green, the beginnings of new growth. The ranchers in the area might go into the winter with enough grass to help carry their cattle through. And if winter brought enough snow and spring enough rain, next year might be decent. Herds moved to Nebraska would come home to the Flint Hills. Walter Estes hadn't had to ship his. He had a creek pasture and hay that he scrounged from neighbors who'd shipped their cattle north. He hadn't had to draw on his winter feed, and Early felt relief for that.

He rambled his way along the lane toward the ranchstead, his mind on ranching, a far more pleasurable subject than the murders of a schoolteacher and a deputy—one killer for both and he was in jail, but convictions in doubt because, well, the damn weapons. Where were they?

Early made the turn around the barn, toward the grove of cottonwoods and the house. Before he stopped, Nadine Estes, in her bib overalls, came running.

"Jimmy, Thelma's gone!"

Early bailed from the Jeep. "When?"

"An hour ago maybe. I was working in the kitchen, not even thinking about her."

Early glanced around. "Any of the horses gone?"

"No."

"Walter?"

"He took his truck. He's out on the road, thinks she may have walked to Leonardville."

"Archie?"

"The dog? I've not seen him."

"He with Walter?"

"No."

"Then he's with Thel. They've gotten to be best buddies, so she's all right."

"But where is she, Jimmy?"

"She goes for walks when I'm not here. Where does she like to walk best?"

"Of course, the creek pasture."

"Damn, that's a mile. Into the Jeep."

Nadine Estes hurried as fast as her elderly legs would carry her to the passenger side of Early's Jeep and horsed herself into the seat. Early popped the clutch when he hit the driver's seat. He spun the steering wheel, whipping his vehicle into a turn that aimed it north, away from the buildings and out through a pasture, the grass stubby, the land flat. He stepped the accelerator to the floor, and the war machine responded.

Nadine Estes, one hand gripped tight to the seat frame, the other braced against the dash, yelled over the whine of the motor and the wind, "Walter never drives this fast."

"This too much for you?"

"No, kind of a thrill."

Early held the speed until a fence line appeared on the horizon. He aimed the Jeep for a gate that hung open, shot through, and slowed as the ground beyond fell away toward Worrisome Creek ambling through the pasture on its way to the Big Blue River to the east.

"There." Early pointed to the side, toward a lone cottonwood, a giant growing in the bottomland, a gaggle of cattle lounging in the tree's shade. He wrenched the Jeep in the new direction, toward someone and a smaller black form meandering through grass long enough to brush the underside of the Jeep.

Nadine Estes took her hand from the seat. She poked Early. "That's Thelma all right, and Archie. You're not gonna run them over, are you?"

At that, he swung the Jeep wide, took his foot off the accelerator. He veered to the side of Thelma and the dog, neither of whom appeared to be aware that they had company, then wheeled across in front of them.

The dog let out one loud bark. He twisted back to Thelma who stood mute, shading her eyes with her forearm. When no response came from her, the dog raced off toward the Jeep.

Early idled in closer to Thelma. "Hi-dee," he said.

"Hi-dee."

"You all right?"

"Just walking with Archie. Soppy, my shoes are wet as wool in rain. Why are you here?"

"Nadine didn't know where you were, so we came looking."

"Oh."

"You want to go with us to the house?"

"If I can drive, Jimmy. You never let me drive anymore."

Early glanced at Nadine Estes who mouthed the words "Why not?"

He stepped out of the Jeep. "Sure, there's nothing for you to run into out here."

A smile, so welcome to Early, came to Thelma's face. She ensconced herself in the driver's seat while he stepped up on a rear tire and into the back. He slapped the seat beside him, motioning for the dog to jump in, and slapped the seat again when the dog didn't.

Archie, a Newfoundland the size of a small horse, gave Early a perplexed look.

"He's not a jumper, Jimmy," Nadine Estes said.

"You mean I have to—"

"Yes."

Early grimaced. He hopped over the side, his gaze locked on the dog. Early patted his leg. "Come on, Arch."

That brought a ruckus of tail wagging as Archie wandered in. Early scooped him up. He staggered under the dog's weight as he made his way to the side of the Jeep. Just as Early hefted the dog up—higher—to go over the side, he stepped in a pile of cow manure. Early's boot slid out from under him. A yelp, followed by a wild dance, and Early came down on his back, Archie across his chest, unconcerned. He licked Early's face.

Nadine Estes and Thelma bolted out of the Jeep. They came hustling to Early, Thelma going down on her knees. "You all right?" she asked.

"Me or Arch?"

"I can see he's all right. Are you?"

"Aside from what I fell in and dog spit on my face?" Early gazed at a cloud drifting overhead, a meager thing and the first to have appeared since the storms of yesterday. "You know, the sky's kinda nice, looking up at it like this."

"Jimmy—"

Nadine Estes grabbed the dog's collar. She hauled him off Early and to her side of the Jeep. There she gestured for Archie to hop in, and the dog clambered up. He squeezed between the

277

front seats to the backseat and settled himself, ears up, looking eager for the ride ahead.

Thelma helped Early to his feet. She glanced at his backside as he came up. "Jimmy, you're going to need some clean clothes."

"I guessed that."

"And you smell, too."

"You make me feel so good." Early shooed the dog to one side of the backseat. Again he stepped up on a rear tire and inside. After Early sat, he put his arm around the dog. "Pooch, you are a trial."

The dog swiveled his head, bathing the side of Early's face with his wet, raspy tongue, Early scrunching up.

Thelma, in the driver's seat, pulled hard on the floor shifter.

That set off a clashing of gears. And Early's face twisted into the sourest of expressions, as if he had sucked on a lime. "No no, you gotta step the clutch all the way to the floor," he said, pressing a hand against his ear, to block out the racket.

"The seat's too far back."

"Well, slide it forward."

"I can do that?"

"Yes. Pull up on the lever under your left leg."

Thelma glanced down. She felt for the flap-shaped piece of metal, found it, and pulled up, and Early pushed the seat forward.

"Oh, that's so much better," Thelma said as the seat locked into its new place. She stepped on the clutch, and the gears meshed. Thelma let out the clutch and at the same instant stepped down on the gas. The Jeep bolted off, startling the dog, Early, and Nadine Estes, Early grabbing for his hat.

Thelma let off on the gas pedal, pitching everyone forward. Then she disengaged the clutch, slammed the shifter into second, and tromped hard on the accelerator, snapping everyone back.

"Thelma!"

"Something wrong?" she asked as she jerked the vehicle into third.

"It's not a bucking horse."

"What?"

"The fence, THE FENCE—"

Thelma's mouth gaped open. She whipped the Jeep to the side, shot it through the open gate, the motor howling, the Jeep's speed increasing.

Early sucked wind at the sight of a dip ahead. But before he could form a word of protest, the Jeep whammed into the dip and out, the machine going airborne. It slammed down hard and raced on, devouring the distance between it and the ranch buildings.

"Thel, slow up!"

"Am I going too fast?"

"Dammit, yes!"

She did a dance with her feet, coming off the gas, stepping on the brake and the clutch at the same time, flinging everyone forward. Her shifting hand whipped the transmission into second gear, and the Jeep racked down more, to a saunter. Thelma steered past the corral and toward a wash line in the yard by the house, the wash line where half a dozen pairs of Levis and an equal number of blue work shirts hung slack in the still afternoon air.

"Wasn't that fun?" she asked as she stopped the Jeep.

Thelma didn't have to turn around. Early heard the absolute joy in her voice and knew the warmth of the smile that would be on her face. Could he be truthful and say that was damned awful?

"Fun?" Early asked. "I guess."

He clambered over the side. The dog hopped over the other side of the Jeep, and Nadine Estes came away from the passenger seat. "Fresh clothes there on the line," she said. "I'll get a bucket of water so you can wash out the backseat."

Early stopped. "Me?"

"You were the one who sat back there, Jimmy. If it had been me, I woulda walked home."

Early burst out laughing.

"What's so funny?"

"If it had been you and Walter out there, you would have walked home to keep the seat in Walter's truck clean?"

"Absolutely I would have done that."

"Yeah, sure," Early said.

Nadine Estes went on to the house and Early to the wash line, still sniggering over the thought as he shucked his shirt. Behind him the radio came on in his Jeep. "It's four thirty-five in the PM on your Friendly Neighbor," a voice said. "And now I'll play a Red Foley record for you, 'The Grass Green Hills of Home.' "

That was a new one to Early. He didn't recognize the melody. He pitched aside his shirt, pulled off one boot, then the other, and stripped himself out of his stinking, manure-greased pants. Early took a fresh pair down from the line. He stepped into them, glancing as he did at Thelma still in the Jeep. He buttoned the fly. "You gonna shut it down and get out?"

"Just want to listen to this. . . . It was fun driving, wasn't it?"

Early transferred his stuff from the pockets of his filthy jeans to the pockets of the clean ones. He leaned against the wash-line post and, when he reached down for one of his boots, saw from the corner of his eye Walter Estes's International rambling along the lane coming from the county highway. Early pulled on one boot and then the other as the truck came around the barn, Estes waving his hat out the side window. Early took down a

280

clean shirt. He thrust an arm into a sleeve and went toward the Jeep and Estes's truck.

The Jeep rolled. It rambled, then shot away, Estes swerving to the side as Thelma and the Jeep passed by within a hand's distance, Early running, his shirt and its empty sleeve streaming behind him. He bellowed, "Walter, I want your truck."

Estes stepped hard on the brake, and the truck swung catawampus in the yard. He hurried himself off the high seat, and Early hauled himself up and inside the cab. He slammed the door.

"What's going on, Jimmy?"

"If I knew, I wouldn't need your truck." Early stabbed the transmission into reverse. He backed the truck around and, in an effort to find first gear, jammed the transmission into second. That killed the engine, and Early ground away at the starter.

Estes came running, waving his arms. "Sometimes it's—"

The engine roared.

Early diddled with the gear shifter and caught first. He rolled the truck out of the yard and into the lane headed for the county road. Early saw the Jeep dip through the wash a quarter-mile on, and he double-clutched, slipping the transmission into second. To Early, accustomed to driving a lightweight Jeep with a V-Eight engine, Walter Estes's tandem handled like a lumber wagon. But it came with an advantage, a two-speed rear axle that on a long, flat, straight road might allow Early more speed than his Jeep possessed. He rolled through the wash and through the ranch gate that Estes had left open, downshifting, horsing the heavy truck up onto the county road. The truck swayed and rocked, and Early set to the business of double-clutching up through eight gears. The International shook through sixty-five, then seventy, and smoothed out as its speedometer needle rose through eighty to peg at ninety-two.

Early clung to the steering wheel, watching the truck eat

away at the distance that separated it from the Jeep.

The Jeep's taillights flashed on. Curve ahead, Early could see it. And the intersection with State Twenty-Four that ran south to Manhattan, and north a way and then west to Clay Center.

Early brought his foot off the gas pedal and onto the brake. He stepped down, playing off speed, swaying the truck around the curve, downshifting, setting up for a square ninety to the right. But the Jeep went straight, across the highway and on east toward the Big Blue Valley, the Jeep's taillights masked by dust roiling up where the county road went from pavement to gravel.

A school bus lumbered up from Manhattan, and a freight truck came over a rise from the north. Early saw them both and slowed. He timed the other vehicles and shot the International across the highway behind the passing school bus, the freight driver hauling on his air horn, mouthing words Early didn't want to know.

The flat, paved road fell away behind, the gravel road twisting, rising, and falling as it snaked out ahead through the Flint Hills. Early pushed his speed up to fifty-three and dropped it back for the turns. He topped a hill and spotted the rear of his Jeep disappearing half a mile ahead over a rise he knew fell away on the far side into the deep valley of the Blue River. Early downshifted for the rise and the fall away and the first of the near switchback turns. The Jeep ran out of sight beneath cottonwoods far below.

Shift up, shift down, crank the steering wheel into a turn, twist it in the opposite direction to bring the truck straight. A woodchuck, humping alongside the roadway, scrambled off into the brambles as Early in Walter Estes's truck rumbled by.

The International rolled out of the last turn and onto the flat of the valley floor. Early stepped down on the accelerator. Where was Thelma and the Jeep? The cottonwoods, two turns that Early could remember—or was it three?—and the viaduct of the

Kansas & Nebraska Railroad . . . he wouldn't see the Jeep until he got to the other side. He pushed the truck for all the speed the road would allow him, steering under the cottonwoods and through the first turn. The air rolling in through the window smelled different here, not of grass on the high ground, but of drying cornfields and pumpkins.

Early downshifted again, and then he saw it, under the viaduct, his Jeep—on its side, the wheels spinning.

CHAPTER 26

September 26—Monday Afternoon
New Life

He sat in the gravel, cradling Thelma's head and shoulders, stroking her hair, weeping—wishing it were he who was dead—the tips of his fingers wet, the color of Indian paintbrush. Sorrow and the smells of gasoline and an overheated engine swirled with the scents of sun-dried cornfields in the early evening air of the valley of the Big Blue River.

"Sheriff."

A voice, but Early couldn't make it register.

"Can I help, sheriff?"

He twisted around, toward where he thought the voice had come from, peered up over his shoulder, his vision blurred by tears. The sun slapped into Early's eyes, and he squinted. A shape there silhouetted, someone . . . a flat-brimmed Stetson, the front pulled low, the face lost to shadows.

"Sheriff?"

That voice again. So whispery.

"Sonny?"

"Yeah. Got a camp in the brush beyond the viaduct. Heard this and came. This not your wife, is it?"

Early raked a sleeve beneath his soppy eyes.

"She dead?"

"Yes."

"What's she doing, driving down here?"

"Running from demons."

"How's that?"

"You wouldn't understand."

Sonny Estes knelt. He lifted Thelma's lifeless hand and laid it across her stomach. "She pregnant?"

"Our first."

Sonny touched Thelma's rounded midsection. "Sheriff?"

"Huh?"

"I feel movement. Think yer baby's alive."

"Oh God."

"What do you want to do?"

Early hauled his hand down his face, twisting his cheeks and jaw, stretching them, elongating them. "The hospital," he said.

"Your baby won't make it, be dead before you get there. Sheriff?"

"Uh-huh?" Early brushed at a curl at Thelma's temple, worked the curl behind her ear.

"Ever cut into a cow to take her calf when you knew the cow was going to die anyway?"

"Couple times."

"I've helped my dad do it, too."

"Cut into my wife?" Early's hand stopped. He forced himself to look at Thelma's face, forced himself to consider what she might want done.

"Sheriff," Sonny said, "you got a couple minutes at most, no time to argue this. Your wife's dead. She's still holding your baby. Don't you think we ought to save it?"

"Oh damn . . . oh damn."

"Better try, shouldn't we? Can't help but think she'd want you to have this baby."

"She would." The words came as a ragged whisper.

"We better get on with it. We can work right here."

"Yeah, that's . . . that's fair."

Sonny wriggled his fingers, for Early to lean Thelma forward, into his hands. "That's the way," he said as he took hold of her shoulders, her head lolling to the side. "You get up now."

Early worked himself onto his knees.

"Dad always kept a blanket behind the seat. You get it."

Early stumbled away to the International, to the cab. He fumbled a patterned red blanket out and, when he returned, he saw that Sonny had laid Thelma out on the gravel, had ripped her dress open.

Sonny knelt there, next to Thelma, pulled a filleting knife from a sheath on his belt.

Horror flashed across Early's face. "What you doing?"

"Cutting into her."

"Not with that gawddamn sword." Early pitched the blanket aside. He dug his pocketknife out as he went down on his knees, opened the blade. He flexed his fingers, to chase the tension from his hand before he put the point at the far side and below Thelma's navel.

"You gonna cut there?"

"It's the best way."

"No time, man. Split her down the middle like a watermelon. Lift the baby out."

"Butcher my wife?"

"Dammit, sheriff, pretty work don't count here." Sonny grabbed Early's hand. He hauled it and the blade it clutched to the top of the bulge. "Cut from here down."

Early hesitated.

"Gawdammit, man, do it."

Early bit at his lip. With reluctance, he forced the point into the skin. He drew the knife up and over the bulge and down toward the crotch, the skin cleaving away from the steel, separating—bloodless—exposing the outside of the uterus wall.

"Cut that wall now," Sonny said.

"I know what I'm doing."

"Gawd, yer slower than Methuselah."

"Shut the hell up." Early again positioned his blade, this time at the top of the uterus. He pressed down, sliced, and again drew the blade down. "There's the sac. See it? I got to cut it."

"You just talk, talk, talk, don't you?"

"I'm getting the job done."

A blue fly buzzed in close, then another, drawn by the scent. "Gawddamn, get those flies away," Early bellowed.

Sonny swung at the first and missed. He clapped the second between his hands, and, with a fuss of waving, scared the other off.

Early, focusing, pierced the amniotic sac, the thinnest of walls. He cut it away and fluid spilled out, filling the cavity. There open to the world laid the baby—slick, wet, and blue. Early reached in with both hands. He scooped up the child.

"You a daddy now," Sonny said.

"Yeah. How're you at tying knots?"

"What?"

Early nodded at the umbilical cord splayed out, leading back into the uterus. "You gotta cut it and tie it off."

"That cord's too stiff. What if I used a string?"

"You got string?"

Sonny pulled a hank from his back pocket.

"Do it then."

"About here?" he asked, holding the cord a short ways from the child's body.

"Good by me."

Sonny whipped the string around the cord once and a second time, then tied it off. He pulled the knot tight, doubled it and pulled it tight again. With the blade of his filleting knife glinting in the evening sun, Sonny sliced through the cord above the knot.

"Wish I had iodine to splash on that cut," Early said. "Your dad wouldn't happen—"

"Yeah, in his jumble box in the cab." Sonny scrambled up. "I'll get it, and you get that blue baby to breathing."

He disappeared. Early heard him rummaging in the cab as he lifted the child by its—no, by her—heels. Head down, he milked the mucus from the baby's throat and mouth, and, as a last gesture, smacked the child on her bottom.

The baby, flaccid as a washrag, did not respond.

Early smacked the child's bottom again.

Still no response.

Desperate, he cradled her in the crook of his arm, covered her mouth and nose with his own mouth, and puffed a breath into the baby's lungs.

Then another.

"Come on, baby, breathe," he said and puffed another breath into her lungs.

And a fourth breath. Early rocked back on his haunches. He watched, and the child's chest tremored up with no help from him. It held a moment and fell, then tremored up again.

"She's alive, isn't she," Sonny said. He gazed down from where he stood next to Early, a work-stained box under his arm.

"Yeah, I need that blanket to dry her off. Cut it in half, huh?"

Sonny laid the box aside. He snatched up the blanket, folded it and razored it along the fold, handing half to Early who wiped the child clean with it. When satisfied, Early laid the baby on the dry half.

Sonny hunkered down. He got a small bottle from the box, screwed the cap off and daubed a finger in. He spread the iodine over the cut end and around the child's umbilical cord, drops falling onto the baby's stomach. The child yeowled at the burn of the disinfecting fluid.

"Got lungs on her, don't she?" Sonny said through a snicker as he brought out a gauze pad. He tore off the paper wrapping and placed the pad over the knotted end, snugged it tight with a strip of adhesive tape. "Think we got it, Poppy."

Early lifted Thelma's hand. He pressed it against the child's face. "Thel," he said, "we got us the baby you wanted."

"Girl, huh?" Sonny asked.

"Appears so." Early released Thelma's hand, and Sonny busied himself covering her with the soiled half-blanket while Early folded the sides of the dry half-blanket over the child.

"Got all her fingers and toes, Poppy?"

Early cradled the baby as he had Thelma. He gazed into the child's face. "Got all her fingers and toes."

CHAPTER 27

September 26—Monday Evening
One Loss Forever

Early and Doc Grafton stood together in a room, the room white, smelling of antiseptic, Early with his hands in his back pockets, Grafton his arms folded across his chest. They gazed down at the child asleep in the bassinet.

"Our baby things are a helluva lot better than that horse blanket you brought her wrapped in," Grafton said. He leaned against Early. "You were one damn fool to take her, you know that? But I'm sure glad you did."

"She's so small."

"She's the better part of a month and a half shy of full term. She'll grow. They all do. . . . I'm sorry about Thelma."

"Yeah. Her world had changed. She wasn't comfortable in it."

"I guess."

"It's a hard way to get peace."

"You think she crashed the Jeep?"

"I don't know. I'd like to think not, but I don't know."

Grafton rocked back. He rubbed a hand over his hair. "Cactus, I made some calls for you . . . to Sherm over at the funeral home and to Gladys."

Hard lines formed around Early's eyes.

"Now don't you go getting upset on me," Grafton said. "You're in no shape to arrange a funeral, and Gladys will work with Sherm. She'll do it all. You got to let your friends carry you for awhile now, you hear me?"

The Esteses hustled into the nursery from the hallway, followed by Mose Dickerson, Nadine Estes bee-lining it for Early. She hugged him hard. "Jimmy, I'm so sorry."

Early allowed himself to return the hug. It all welled up, and he snuffled, words failing to form, failing to come out.

"You let it go, Jimmy," Nadine said as she squeezed him about the ribs. "You let it go. Mose said you got the baby. This her?"

"Yes. Sonny helped."

Nadine Estes leaned back, her eyes wide. "Is he here?"

"Didn't want to come in. Stayed with the truck."

"There's nobody with the truck, Jimmy. Mose parked right next to it."

Dickerson pulled his hat off. "He get away again, Jimmy?"

"He wasn't exactly caught."

"What would you call it?"

"He just came out of the brush and helped. We were a little too busy to think about much else."

Estes put his gnarled hand on Early's shoulder. "I'm glad you let my boy go."

"I didn't have him to let him go."

"Jimmy," Dickerson said, "if that's the way you want to think about it, that's all right. . . . So this is the little girl, huh?"

James Early, in the only suit he owned, a black band around his right sleeve, sat on a dirt pile next to an open grave, his cattleman's hat beside him, a breeze stirring at his hair. He sifted soil from one hand to the other and back again, the soil cool to the touch, not yet dry enough that it had given up its earthy smells.

Mose Dickerson stepped away from the funeral party moving

out toward their cars and pickups parked at the side of the Worrisome Creek Baptist Church's iron-fenced cemetery. He gathered up a handful of golden leaves that had dropped from a maple and limped his way back toward Early. "Mind if I sit with you a spell?" he asked.

Early didn't say a thing, just continued sifting soil.

Dickerson settled next to him. He set the leaves aside and pulled a handkerchief from a side pocket. Dickerson rubbed the handkerchief at the tip of his nose as he gazed around. After a bit, he looked up at a red-tailed hawk riding the currents, the sky above the bird a milky blue. "Guess if you got to be buried, this is a pretty good place."

"It's all right."

"You got some trees, and you're not far from the pastures, and the little church here where your friends come, you're not forgotten. . . . I'm thinking when I die, I might have it written out that they bury me in my car."

Early glanced at Dickerson, puzzlement twisting an eyebrow.

"Well, I drive it all the time on my mail route. It's kind of a part of me." Dickerson picked up a leaf. He studied its veining. "You put something special of Thelma's in her casket?"

"Yes."

"Uh-huh."

"In the evenings when she didn't have schoolwork to do, sometimes she'd read a Shakespeare sonnet. I never understood them—some of the words and what they call meter—but Thelma said those sonnets were the best poetry. I put the book in her casket."

"Anything else?"

"Uh-huh."

"What?"

"Had the newspaper editor take a picture of our little girl. Nice picture. I put that in there too."

"That's really good, Jimmy. She had to like that." Dickerson laid the leaves out in a line. "What you gonna do now?"

"Take some time away, I guess—get my head clear. Ranch work will do that. Walter says he's got a lot of work to do to get his place ready for winter, so I told the county commissioners Hutch can be sheriff for awhile."

"He won't catch Sonny."

"Never tell. He might."

"Naw, Hutch don't know where he is."

"And I suppose you do?"

"Yessir." Dickerson pulled from his inside coat pocket an envelope. He held it out. " 'Twas in the morning mail for you at the post office."

Early took the envelope. He turned it over and read a Fort Leonard Wood, Missouri, return address but no name.

"He's in the Army," Dickerson said.

"How do you know that?"

"Held the envelope up to the light. I could read a few words through it and Sonny's signature."

CHAPTER 28

October 14—Friday Afternoon
The Last Search
Early, in work jeans, a denim jacket, and leather gloves stained with creosote, wrestled a railroad tie to the edge of a hole. He dropped an end in and held the tie upright—straight, a new corner post for the fence that fronted on the county road—while Walter Estes shoveled dirt in around the tie. They changed places, and Early grabbed up a spud bar. With the round, hammerlike end, he tamped the dirt tight, ramming and slamming the spud bar down until the dirt around the tie became as hard as the flinty limestone that lay none too deep beneath the soil.

Early tossed the spud aside. He went after another tie—for a bracing post—but before he got it up on its end, a Jeep pulled off into the ditch, Hutch Tolliver in his Big-brim Alpine Stetson behind the steering wheel and the county attorney—Carl Wieland—in the passenger seat.

"Hutch, Carl," Early said. He touched the brim of his cattleman's hat in a light salute.

Tolliver leaned on the steering wheel. "Chief, we got us a damn mess of trouble."

"How's that?" Early asked as he stripped off his gloves and ambled over.

"We're gonna lose the trial against Bill Smitts."

Wieland entered the conversation, working his lone hand like a boxer jabbing at an opponent. "The jury's not buying our case. I can see it in their eyes. We got no witnesses. We got no confession. We got no weapon."

"Bill's dad?" Early asked.

"I think some would like to believe him, but that woman says Bill was with her all night and the next morning."

"Anyone see Bill there?"

"No."

"His car?"

"No."

"Anyone see her out in the morning with or without Bill?"

"Not that Hutch could find."

"It's a standoff, isn't it?"

"We need that goddamn weapon, Cactus."

"Appears so. Well, I've had a thought or two about that. . . . Walter," Early said, turning to Estes, "hate to leave you on your own, but I'm going to have to go for a ride with these fellas."

"I can manage the bracing. You go on."

Early moved alongside the Jeep. He stepped up on a rear tire and on over, into the backseat. After he settled himself, he slapped Tolliver's shoulder and waved ahead.

"Where to?" Tolliver asked as he rolled the Jeep up onto the county road.

"Bill's place. I've been thinking that maybe we didn't look everywhere we were supposed to."

Tolliver shifted into second. "Where could we have missed?"

"Did we look up top in Bill's shop or for any loose floorboards?"

"We stamped all around that floor."

"But up top?"

"I don't know. I didn't go up there."

"I didn't either."

"I thought you had."

Wieland twisted around to Early. "What the hell kind of

searchers are you men, anyway?"

"Apparently, not too good."

A black Chevy coupe came over a rise in the approaching lane. Tolliver tapped his horn and, as the two vehicles passed, Early waved for the driver—Mose Dickerson—to turn around and follow.

"You want me to radio for some more help out here?" Tolliver asked.

Early squeezed the county attorney's shoulder. "We got Carl to supervise. We won't miss anything this time."

"Oh, yeah," Wieland said, "you don't find that damn axe, now you're going to blame it on me, right?"

"Aww, you fret too much."

"Cactus?"

"Yeah?"

"How you getting along without Thelma? I'm not being nosey, but people around the courthouse ask and they really care."

"It's not too bad as long as I keep busy, and I got our little girl, fussy little one. But I tell you, when I go to bed at night and there's no one lying next to me, it's hard."

"I'm sorry."

Early wiped at the corner of his eye.

Tolliver guided his Jeep around the ruts where the road curved away toward high ground and the Smitts's residence, the place on the horizon appearing more lonely and abandoned since Early had been there last, almost a month ago, the front window, partially shot out, fully gone now. Kids probably or hoboes, Early guessed.

Tolliver turned off onto the driveway, Dickerson behind him, the vehicles parading up and around to the barn behind.

"What are we doin'?" Dickerson asked as he hop-stepped away from his car.

Early, out of the Jeep, put an arm around the constable's shoulders, and they walked on together. "Look a few places for that axe we didn't look before."

"Like where?"

Tolliver rolled the door open, and all went on inside, the shop building musty from having been closed too long.

Early gestured toward a ladder that led up to a loft. "Like up there."

Tolliver scurried up the ladder.

"And if it isn't up there?" Dickerson asked.

"Did you look in the stove?"

"Sure."

"Did you look up the stovepipe?"

"Now who's gonna put an axe up a stovepipe?"

"Did you look?"

"Chief," Tolliver called from the loft.

"Yeah?"

"He's got some lumber stacked up here, darn little of it, and that's all."

"Nothing more?"

"Spider webs count for anything? . . . Yeesh."

"What?"

"Snake shed its skin up here, and here's another one."

"Stovepipe next?" Dickerson asked.

"Yup."

The two lawmen went over to the wood stove in the center of the shop. Early wrapped his arms around the pipe. He lifted and brought the pipe up off the stove and back.

"And you want me to look up there, don'tcha?" Dickerson said.

"Well, I can't."

"This is some kinda Laurel and Hardy thing, idn't it? I look up there and all the soot falls down in my face." Dickerson slapped the pipe. Soot swooshed down, hit the floor, and billowed back into the air, setting off a racket of hacking and coughing from Early and the others, Wieland scuttling for the door.

"Least ways," Dickerson said, spitting to the side, "now we know nothing but soot was up there."

Early eased the pipe back onto the stove. He stepped back, waving soot from the air. From the corner of the shop, he helped himself to a long measuring stick. Early leaned on it, one hand over the other, thinking.

"You know, this is nuts," he said. "I have this habit, when I'm sitting in the outhouse, of writing notes to myself about whatever's on my mind. This morning, doggone it, I dropped my pencil down through one of the holes. You don't suppose Bill could have dropped that axe down the septic tank?"

Tolliver, down from the shop's attic, nudged Early. "Chief, you don't by accident drop something in a septic tank. You'd throw it in there. It'd be awful deliberate."

"That's what I mean. And of all the places to hide something, that's the one we'd never think to look."

"You saying we got to?"

"Yup. Hey, if I'm wrong, I'll buy you supper." Early thumbed at a spud bar in a corner and fishing waders hanging from a nail. "Grab them and bring them along."

Soot covered, he shambled off, out of the shop and on toward the house, Tolliver a couple paces behind, and Dickerson limping after them. Wieland, brushing soot from his suit, joined the line of march.

Fifteen feet short of the kitchen, Early stopped. He pointed down at a square of concrete set in the sod and motioned for Tolliver to slip the spud bar through the iron handle sticking up from the concrete. Early grabbed one end of the bar and Tolliver the other, and together they horsed the concrete aside.

Fumes roiled out of the hole, wrinkling Wieland's nose. "Smells like—"

"Don't say it," Early said. "That's what it is. You city types with your sewers, you don't know the joys of bucketing out one of these things."

He dropped the end of the measuring stick in, the stick sliding through his hand until it struck bottom. "These suckers are about what, eight-feet deep? Let's see how much muck we got in here." Early pulled the stick up hand-over-hand until the wet showed—two and a half feet by the marks on the stick.

He dropped it back down and probed with it, Dickerson on one knee, peering in, Tolliver standing, watching over Early's shoulder, and Wieland by himself, a ways off, kicking at the sod.

"Got something here," Early said, "a couple, maybe three inches thick."

He probed to one side of his strike, then the other. "Whatever it is, it's not very wide . . . Oops, here's something, got some give to it . . . and it's wide, really wide."

"It's shit, that's what it is," Wieland said.

"Carl!" Early rolled back on his haunches. He gestured at the hole. "If that's the axe down there, you want it, don't you?"

"Of course."

"Then you pull on those waders, and we'll lower you down in, and you can get it."

"Hey hey hey, you're the one who said I was here to supervise."

"You don't make life easy for us, Carl." Early reached down. He snapped off three stems of grass and placed them in his fist, an end of each out. He held his fist over to Dickerson. "Short straw goes in."

Dickerson drew out a grass, then Tolliver. Early opened his fist, revealing his, and each looked from one stem of grass to the other.

Tolliver pitched his into the hole and went for the waders. "Sure hope I get a raise for this," he said.

Early winked at Dickerson. "Maybe we can get it out of Carl's budget."

Tolliver kicked off his boots. He stepped, a leg at a time, into the waders and pulled the straps up over his shoulders. He fiddled with the adjustment buckles until he had the straps long enough that he could stand straight. Tolliver then sat on the edge of the hole, his feet inside. He hauled off his big-brimmed hat and made a business of presenting it to Early. "I'm not wearing this down there."

"I wouldn't either, Hutchy."

Tolliver lowered himself down, down until he hung by his fingers, his legs to his knees in the liquid muck. And he let go, dropping the last inches.

Early leaned out over the hole. "How is it down there?"

"Not where I'd want to spend a vacation."

"You got a vacation coming?"

"Vacation, Thanksgiving, Christmas, New Year's," Tolliver said as he worked the toe of his wader around the bottom, feeling, feeling. "Got something."

He glanced up to Early.

"Well, you're gonna have to stick your hand down there to get it."

"Aww, cripes." Tolliver unbuttoned the cuff of his sleeve. He pushed it to his shoulder and plunged his hand into the sludge. When Tolliver's hand came up, it clutched what appeared, in the gloom inside the septic tank, to be a sack, water spilling from it. Tolliver held the sack up to Early who hauled it out.

He dropped the soppy, stinking mass in the grass and, with his pocketknife, cut through the sacking. Early laid it open. "Here's your axe, Carl."

He held the filthy weapon up.

"Cactus, his lawyer's going to say anybody could have thrown it in there. Any chance for fingerprints?"

"In all this? We're not miracle workers."

A larger object—flat—came up through the hole. "Got it, Chief?" Tolliver asked.

Early swiveled back. He grasped the object and brought it out, the thing longer by a foot than it was wide, the thickness about three inches. He raked a hand down the face of it, swiping off the muck as Tolliver hefted himself up and out of the septic tank, his arms and hands and waders wet with filth.

"Bet I know what we got here," Early said. "Wrapped in rubber sheeting and sealed with that good old black electrical tape. He wanted to keep what's inside clean and dry. Intended to get it back."

Early sliced through the sheeting. Next he made a crosscut and laid the flaps back.

"The wedding picture," Dickerson said, gazing at it.

"Going to be fingerprints on this, but then you'd expect Bill's prints to be on it."

Wieland, clutching a handkerchief to his nose and mouth, squatted down. He studied the portrait of a younger Bill Smitts and Judith Silverberg Smitts, he in a cravat and a Prince Albert coat, she in a dark blue suitdress and a pearl necklace. "So we still have no proof. Why would he wrap the picture like that anyway? Why would he want to keep it? I wouldn't."

"Maybe it's not the picture," Early said.

"Well, it's sure not the frame."

Early scratched the point of his blade at a portion of the frame. "Gold-painted wood. . . . Just a minute." He stood the picture on end, turned it, and ran his hand down and across the back.

"Now this is interesting," Early said and laid the picture face down on a clean area of grass. Working with the deft touch of a surgeon, he drew his knife along the inside edge of the frame. Early cut through the fabric backing—one side, top, bottom, and the other side—and lifted the fabric away.

Wieland brought his handkerchief down from his face.

"Railroad bonds," Early said. He picked them up and riffled through them, counting. "Bearer bonds, sixty-three thousand dollars worth, and you and I know where these came from."

"But in a shit hole?" Wieland asked.

"Safer than a bank vault. Bill figured nobody'd ever look here, and he was right . . . 'til now."

ABOUT THE AUTHOR

Jerry Peterson taught speech, English, and theater in Wisconsin high schools, then worked for a decade in communications in Wisconsin, Michigan, Kansas, and Colorado. He followed that with a decade as a reporter, photographer, and editor for newspapers in Colorado, West Virginia, Virginia, and Tennessee.

Peterson left daily journalism to become a graduate student at the University of Tennessee/Knoxville. There he began collecting stories that he has incorporated in short stories and novels he sets in eastern Tennessee's Great Smoky Mountains and the Flint Hills of Kansas. Several of his shorter works have been published in literary journals and anthologies, including the Great Manhattan Mystery Conclave's *Manhattan Mysteries.*

Peterson is a member of the writers' group *Tuesdays with Story* and the Mystery Writers of America.